Davis nodded as he pressed his lips gently to hers.

The kiss was tender, until it wasn't, every ounce of emotion the two were feeling for each other exploding between them. Falling back against the cushions, he pulled Neema down with him. As she fell against the expanse of his chest, his hands danced down the length of her arms and across her back. The tips of his fingers rested against the curve of her buttocks, heat burning beneath the tips. Her arms snaked around his shoulders and back, her hands clinging to him hungrily as her mouth twisted and turned with his. The kiss had become frenetic, both anxious for each other's touch.

When he shifted his body beneath hers, Neema straddling his legs, there was no hiding the rise of nature that pressed against the front of his slacks for attention. His excitement was on full display as he pressed himself against her.

Neema suddenly sat upright, pulling a closed fist to her mouth. "I'm sorry. There's something we need to talk about first," she started. "There's something important I need to tell you."

* * *

Don't miss future installments in the To Serve and Seduce miniseries, coming soon...

* * *

If you're on `Twitter`
think of Harle
#harle

D1005577

Dear Reader,

Let me start by first saying thank you. Thank you for being so supportive of me and my writing. Thank you for waiting so patiently for this installment of the Black family series. I can't begin to tell you how much that means to me.

Stalked by Secrets is the story of Neema Kamau and Davis Black. Davis is the youngest son in my fictional family, and although he doesn't wear a badge, as the city alderman, he is very much dedicated to his Chicago constituents.

I loved breathing life into Davis and the enigmatic Neema. The two challenged me during a time when I didn't appreciate having one more thing added to my list of must-do's. But they were exactly what I needed, and I hope they do for you what they did for me. I hope you will enjoy them together as much as I enjoyed writing them!

Thank you again for your support. I am humbled by all the love you show me, my characters and our stories. I know that none of this would be possible without you.

Until the next time, please take care and may God's blessings be with you always.

With much love,

Deborah Fletcher Mello

STALKED BY SECRETS

Deborah Fletcher Mello

HARLEQUIN

ROMANTIC
SUSPENSE

Recycling programs
for this product may
not exist in your area.

ISBN-13: 978-1-335-62888-6

Stalked by Secrets

Copyright © 2021 by Deborah Fletcher Mello

This edition published by arrangement with Harlequin Books S.A.

For questions and comments about the quality of this book,
please contact us at CustomerService@Harlequin.com.

Harlequin Enterprises ULC
22 Adelaide St. West, 40th Floor
Toronto, Ontario M5H 4E3, Canada
www.Harlequin.com

Printed in U.S.A.

A true Renaissance woman, **Deborah Fletcher Mello** finds joy in crafting unique story lines and memorable characters. She's received accolades from several publications, including *Publishers Weekly*, *Library Journal* and *RT Book Reviews*. Born and raised in Connecticut, Deborah now considers home to be wherever the moment moves her.

Books by Deborah Fletcher Mello

Harlequin Romantic Suspense

To Serve and Seduce

Seduced by the Badge
Tempted by the Badge
Reunited by the Badge
Stalked by Secrets

Colton 911: Grand Rapids

Colton 911: Agent By Her Side

Harlequin Kimani Romance

Truly Yours
Hearts Afire
Twelve Days of Pleasure
My Stallion Heart
Stallion Magic
Tuscan Heat
A Stallion's Touch
A Pleasing Temptation
Sweet Stallion
To Tempt a Stallion
A Stallion Dream

Visit the Author Profile page at Harlequin.com for more titles.

To Bubba, Biscuit, Gravy and Titus.

Woof, woof, boys! Woof, woof!

Chapter 1

Davis Black stormed into the kitchen of his parents' home. He slammed the stack of dirty dishes he carried into the sink, pausing as they crashed harshly against the bottom of the metal pan. He was super pissed, rage rushing through his system with a vengeance he hadn't known possible. It was emotion he was struggling to contain least he lash out and hurt someone. He clenched his hands into tight fists, his fingernails digging into the palms of his hands. His jaw was tight, the muscles in his face beginning to throb. To release the wealth of tension, he screamed at the top of his lungs, his rage spewing in a deep guttural roar that had him sounding like a wounded animal ready to attack. The family members in the other room went quiet and Davis shrieked again.

He was furious but didn't know who he wanted to be mad at more. His mother, who had just announced he and his siblings had a long-lost brother that no one knew about. His older brother, Mingus, who'd just called him out in front of the whole family, threatening to expose a secret he had no interest in sharing. Or the rest of the Black family brood, all acting as if nothing in the world was wrong with any of them. Toss in the fact that someone was trying to blackmail his parents, putting the entire family at risk, and he was ready to spit nails.

Davis was thoroughly irritated that he hadn't been able to respond to his mother's news or his brother's pronouncement; instead, made to bite his tongue and check his attitude. His father and his other siblings had been quick to chastise him, putting him on blast for his insolence. Now, what he wanted most was to punch something. Or someone. Hard.

The family's Sunday dinner to celebrate Simone's release from the hospital had not been without the usual dramatics that seemed to follow the Blacks. Six weeks earlier his youngest sister, an attorney, had been shot in a drive-by, the bullet intended for the father of her unborn child. The two had been preparing to announce a major lawsuit against a drug company they claimed was poisoning its patients with contaminated product. Simone's boyfriend, Dr. Paul Reilly, had discovered the crime and now the two were local heroes in the medical community.

Sitting around the table breaking bread was supposed to be so much about normalizing their lives yet, more times than not, it was everything but normal. With his parents and his brothers all working for the Chicago judicial system, they spent most of their time on edge, chasing demons that threatened the peace and quiet throughout the city. These mandatory family gatherings inevitably left one or more of them deep in their feelings and tonight was no exception. Davis hadn't thought it possible, but his family had finally taken dysfunction to a whole other level.

Now, every one of them, his brothers Mingus, Parker, Ellington and Armstrong, and his sister Vaughan were headed to their respective homes feeling like they'd been slapped with a sledgehammer. Davis didn't include Simone because with her, he was never sure what he might get. Things that rattled the rest of them sometimes barely registered on his sister's emotional radar.

Davis heaved a soft sigh as he leaned against the counter. He was emotionally exhausted, and seriously considering taking a break from his family. Between his parents' expectations, the sibling rivalry that really wasn't supposed to be a competition and trying to figure out what he needed for his own life, he was simply tired. He took a deep breath, held it deep in his lungs before blowing it back out. He was just about to head back into the dining room when Armstrong and Parker came through the door.

"I just wanted to check on you before Danni and I take off," Armstrong said. "It sounded like you were having a hard time in here."

"I'm good," Davis muttered. He and his brother exchanged a look before Davis dropped his eyes to the tiled floor.

A moment passed before Armstrong nodded. "I also wanted to apologize. I didn't mean to snap at you the way I did."

Davis shrugged. "I shouldn't have spoken to Mom like that." He thought about the tone he'd taken with their mother after her announcement and contrition furrowed his brow.

"No, you shouldn't have," Parker agreed. "But we understand. It was a shock and we all have questions."

"And Mom will answer them as soon as she's able. She's always been honest with us about everything," Armstrong added.

"Obviously not about this," Davis snapped, his arms folded tightly across his chest. "If she had been, there would be no way anyone would think they could blackmail her with the information."

The brothers all exchanged anxious glances, everything about the situation unsettling.

"No," Judith Harmon Black said as she suddenly entered the room. "I wasn't up-front about this because I had no intention of ever telling any of you. This was not something I ever thought I'd have to deal with again. It's a moment in my life that I'm not proud of. And it's a moment in my life that I had put behind me."

An awkward silence descended over the room. Judith moved to Davis's side and pressed her palm to his cheek, the gesture meant to be comforting. Davis was her baby boy, the youngest of her brood. He was also the most sensitive, taking every one of their issues to heart even when it had nothing at all to do with him. His mother understood his frustrations better than anyone, and he knew that it hurt her heart to see him struggle. She leaned to kiss his cheek.

"I'm sorry," Davis apologized. "What I said to you before was rude and disrespectful."

His mother nodded. "Apology accepted! None of this is going to be easy, but each of you needs to understand that nothing that happened in my past, and nothing that will happen going forward, will change how much I love you all."

"We love you, too, Mom," Armstrong said. He

reached to give her a hug, and then he hugged Davis. "I need to run, or my wife is going to be late for work!"

Chicago police captain Parker Black, head of the district Armstrong's wife, Danni, reported to, laughed cheerily. "You better hurry then. I hear her boss is a monster!"

They all laughed with him, his jest lightening the mood.

"We good?" Armstrong asked, his question directed at Davis.

"We're fine," Davis said. "We can talk more later."

They all watched the man make his exit then Davis shifted his attention to Judith. "Was Ellington able to help? I mean…well, did you make a decision about contacting your…your…" Davis hesitated, swallowing his emotion before finishing his question. "Your son?" The word seemed to suddenly catch in his throat as he thought about the child his mother had never acknowledged until forced to do so.

Judith took a deep breath. "No, I haven't made any decisions. Your father and I want to discuss it more before I do anything. I'll want all your input, as well. This impacts our entire family, so it's only right that you all have some say in what we do."

Davis wrapped his arms around his mother's shoulders and hugged her warmly. His earlier anger had been assuaged, the wealth of it lifting like morning mist lost to a rising sun. Despite the uncertainty, his family always came together for each other. He knew they would weather whatever storm blew in their direction. It was the one certainty in his life that he trusted without reservation.

His father, Chicago Police Superintendent Jerome

Black, suddenly barreled through the door. "Who wants to go to Vegas?"

They all turned to look at the man, confusion washing over their expressions. In the other room, Vaughan, the eldest daughter, cried out with glee as she and Ellington celebrated loudly.

"What's going on?" Judith questioned, eyeing her husband curiously.

"Simone and Paul are eloping to Vegas. They just sent a text asking if we all want to fly out to join them."

Davis rolled his eyes skyward, not at all surprised by anything his sister did. Only Simone would want to get married just hours after their mother's bombshell announcement. "Why is she rushing?" he asked. "Especially now, after what happened at dinner this evening?"

"It's Simone," Parker responded. "Why does she do half the things she does?"

"She's pregnant," their mother interjected. "I'm sure her hormones have a lot to do with it, but she's happy and Paul loves her. We should all go to support them."

"I have to be here tomorrow afternoon, so we'll need to fly right back after the ceremony," Jerome said. "And I know Armstrong and Danni won't be able to make it. Danni's working undercover on a case and Armstrong's not going to stray but so far from her."

"Mingus and Joanna are going," Davis said, reading a text message on his cell phone screen. "And Paul's paying for the airline tickets for any of us that want to go."

"I have a few days of vacation," Parker said. "We should go and hang out for a day or two. Do a little brotherly bonding. What's your schedule look like?"

"There's nothing on my calendar that I can't move," Davis said with a nod. "And, I could use a break."

He paused for a moment. He did need some rest and time away with his brothers, who were his best friends in the world, sounded exactly like the answer to a multitude of his problems. Because his stress levels were at an all-time high, his emotions often getting the better of him on his best days. Only Mingus knew just how much it had become a challenge for him to get through each day, and his brother had almost spilled those beans earlier that evening.

You need to tell them, Mingus had admonished; loudly, so that the whole family could hear. Then the questions had come and Davis had stormed out of the room and into the kitchen to avoid answering.

He was still nodding. "I say we should do it!"

"Then let's go to Vegas!" Parker exclaimed.

Judith clapped her hands excitedly. "Let's just get your sister married before you boys go off looking for trouble, please!"

Davis smiled. "Trouble? Not us!"

Davis exited the family home, still in his feelings but not as raging mad as he'd been earlier. His mother had hugged him tightly, holding him longer than usual. Yet, despite his best efforts, he'd found himself unable to ease fully into the comfort she usually brought to their interactions.

"You good, son?" Jerome Black questioned as he walked him to his car.

Davis shrugged. "I'll be fine."

Jerome nodded his head slowly. "If you need to talk…"

"I don't," Davis snapped. He felt his father bristle slightly.

The patriarch coughed, drawing his closed hand to

cover his mouth. An awkward moment of silence rose swiftly between them. It hung heavily in the evening air and then it didn't, a cool breeze carrying it away.

"It's cold out here," Davis said. "You should go inside."

"I need a favor from you," Jerome said. He shot a look over his shoulder toward the stately home, down one side of the street and then the other.

Davis blew a soft sigh. "Yes, sir?"

"I need you to take a meeting with Alexander Balducci."

Davis turned to stare at his father. His eyes were wide, his brow furrowed. "You need me to take a meeting with Alexander Balducci? Are you crazy?"

The Balducci name was synonymous with every criminal element in the city. One of the oldest crime families in Chicago history, the Balduccis were notorious. His father and the Balducci patriarch, Alexander, had a long-time friendship that many didn't understand. For years, the two had walked on opposite sides of the law. Their children also had a lengthy toe-to-toe history with fatal outcomes. His brother Armstrong, a distinguished police detective, had gone up against Alexander's two sons and both Balduccis had lost. One his freedom and the other his life. But through it all, Jerome had maintained a relationship with the man others publicly distanced. Their long-standing friendship was why many questioned the police superintendent's credibility, assuming he had to be a dirty cop.

"No," Davis said, shaking his head vehemently. "Why would you ask me to—"

"I'm not asking," Jerome said sternly. "He needs your assistance with something, and I told him you would help.

I'll call and let you know when and where." He turned abruptly and headed for the front door of his home.

Still shaking his head, Davis didn't bother to respond, knowing he'd been dismissed. He slid into the front seat of his car and as he pulled out of the parking space, he bellowed, a litany of profanity spewing past his full lips.

Days later, Davis sat with Mingus, Parker and Ellington, the brothers all gathered around the bar at The Orleans Hotel & Casino in Las Vegas, Nevada. They had already downed a round of shots and were ready for the next as they debated where to grab dinner.

Their sister's wedding had gone off nicely. With Simone and Paul exchanging vows to seal the deal on their relationship, their baby sister's well-being was one less thing for them all to be concerned about.

Davis exhaled loudly before guzzling another ounce and a half of black rum.

"Maybe you should slow down there," Parker admonished, eyeing him with a raised brow.

Davis shrugged his broad shoulders. "It's Vegas. It's what we do in Vegas."

Ellington laughed. "Some of us. Not all of us."

"What's with you lately?" Parker asked. He leaned forward in his seat, eyeballing Davis from three barstools away. "You've been in a mood."

"He's been a pain in the ass!" Mingus muttered under his breath. He turned to Davis. "Tell them already!"

Davis gave him a dirty look, his irritation clearly evident. He gestured at the bartender, tapping at his empty glass.

His brothers all sat, breaths bated, curiosity rising full and thick between them.

"Either you tell them or I will," Mingus persisted. He swallowed his own drink and gestured for another.

"I'm going to therapy," Davis said, the words spewing past his lips like rapid fire from a pistol. "I've been having a hard time lately and Mom suggested I go speak to someone." Embarrassment suddenly colored his cheeks a deep shade of apple red.

Ellington and Parker exchanged a quick look. "That's it?"

Davis shrugged. "We don't do therapy unless it's around the dining room table with Mom and Dad telling us there's nothing wrong with us. It's embarrassing. People will think I'm weak if anyone finds out."

"That's not true," Parker stated. "I've gone to therapy off and on for years. My job isn't easy and, every so often, I need an impartial person to vent to."

Davis's eyes widened. "You?"

Parker nodded. "Mom suggested it when I was struggling after my last promotion."

"Why haven't you ever said anything?"

Mingus grunted. "For the same reason you didn't."

Ellington laughed. "That male pride will get you every time. There's no shame in a Black man going to therapy if he needs it."

"Maybe not, but we sure as hell don't talk about it. It's like some dirty little secret we think will make us look weak if our boys find out about it," Davis said.

"Weakness is not admitting you have a problem when you do and then not doing something about it when you can," Parker said firmly.

"I know that's right," Ellington echoed. He and Parker high-fived each other.

"Do the girls know?" Davis questioned.

"Oh, hell no!" Parker exclaimed, a low chuckle escaping past his lips. "And you better not tell them, either."

"Definitely don't tell Simone," Mingus added.

"Says the guy who ratted me out," Davis quipped sarcastically.

Mingus shrugged and the brothers all laughed.

"So, has therapy helped you at all?" Ellington asked.

Davis shrugged. "Too soon to tell. I know I just need to get out of my own way and allow the process to do what it's going to do."

"It's hard work," Parker said. "Just be open to the possibility."

A wave of relief seemed to wash warmly over Davis, comfort coming from the solidarity they shared. He allowed himself to settle into the wealth of camaraderie, taking from it what he needed most in that moment. Laughter was abundant as they continued to banter back and forth.

"I bet Dad doesn't know anything about any of us going to therapy," Davis said after a few minutes. Concern peppered his next comment. "I'm sure he'd have something to say about it if he did."

Mingus shrugged. "Dad knows what he needs to know. Stop worrying about Dad and take care of yourself however you need to."

"He wants me to take a meeting with Balducci," Davis suddenly blurted out. "Do you know anything about that?"

The brothers shot each other a look.

Ellington shook his head. "Did he say why?"

"It doesn't matter why," Mingus interjected. "Dad wouldn't ask if it wasn't important."

Davis threw up his hands in frustration. "I'm a city alderman, for Christ's sake! An elected official who's supposed to stand up against men like Balducci! How is that going to look?"

Parker nodded. "Mingus is right. Dad would never have you do anything that would jeopardize your position or impede your responsibilities as a city official."

"My being an alderman is why I don't need to take a meeting with Alexander Balducci. I can't risk how that may look to my constituents. I have to consider what they may think."

Mingus laughed. "Saying no to Dad is much riskier than taking that meeting. Just take the meeting."

"Take the meeting," Parker and Ellington echoed in unison.

Davis shook his head and threw back a shot of rum.

"Until then—" Mingus tossed back his own shot "—someone figure out what we're eating. I'm starved."

"I say we just hit the prime rib joint upstairs," Davis concluded. "The food is good, and we won't have far to fall when the night is done and finished."

The brothers all nodded. "Sounds like you're feeling better," Mingus said with a chuckle.

Davis tossed back another shot and laughed.

"Neema! Neema!"

Neema Kamau found her father's voice especially irritating as he called out from behind her. She stole a quick glance at her wristwatch. She was already late for her job at the *Chicago Tribune* and she didn't need a lengthy lecture about something that really wasn't important to her. She thought about ignoring him but knew that would only make the lecture that came later even more unbearable.

She turned slowly, meeting the look he was giving

her head-on. He stood there, hands locked tight against his waist, his expression stern. "Yes, Baba?"

"Are you coming to the restaurant tonight?" Adamu Kamau queried. "We could use the help."

The restaurant he referred to—the Awaze Grill—was the family business, and it was his pride and joy. Born and raised in Kenya, her father had immigrated to the United States when he'd been in his early twenties. A naturalized citizen with a doctorate in mathematics, he had been one of the most prolific analytical minds to ever work for the Pentagon. But a massive heart attack ten years ago had shifted his priorities and redirected the lives of his wife and children.

The move to Chicago had been the first big change, the whole family leaving DC to follow him to Illinois. It was only recently that Neema had realized her parents opening their family restaurant was truly a dream come true for the two of them.

The building on West Reynolds Street had been purchased outright, the couple dipping into their life savings to make it their own. After renovations, Awaze Grill was born, featuring the best recipes of their east African culture. For her family, it was a second home of sorts. For her parents, the restaurant quelled any feelings of emptiness they had for their African culture in America. Being able to share that culture with others made everyone feel like family to them. For Neema, working when she was needed rewarded the gratitude she often felt for all her parents had done for her.

Raised according to her parents' Kenyan culture, Neema knew that family was central to everything. Children were expected to honor their parents and fulfill any obligations asked of them. Saying no to her father was not an option, nor would she have even considered it.

"Yes, Baba." Neema nodded. "If you need me to work, I'll be there."

He nodded his balding head. "Also, I need you to stop by that alderman's office. You know the one."

"Alderman Black?"

"Yes, him. He needs to do something about the drug activity on the corner. It isn't good for the neighborhood, and the police aren't doing anything to help with the situation."

"I sent him a letter last week, Baba. We should probably give him a little time to respond."

Her father shook his head. "No. You need to follow up in person. To be sure he understands how big the problem is. These young boys are getting out of hand. One of them cursed me yesterday. Outside of my own front door! No respect! No respect at all!" The old man threw his hands up in frustration.

Neema shuttered a soft sigh. "Yes, Baba. I'll try to run by his office on my lunch hour."

Her father gave her a nod then stepped forward to give her a kiss on the cheek. "You're a good daughter, Neema. You have a good day."

Neema smiled. "You too, Baba!"

Once she was out the door, Neema sighed with audible relief. It hadn't been nearly as painful as she had anticipated. In fact, she was feeling slightly guilty for imagining a doomsday lecture from her father. She'd been certain her late-night hours the previous evening would have had her father on a rampage. It wasn't often that she agreed to dinner and drinks with her coworkers, specifically because of how her parents reacted when she did. It was one thing when her shift at the newsroom required her to be out all night. It was something wholeheartedly different when she was out all night socializing. She was surprised her father hadn't mentioned it at all.

Much like her father, Neema had moments when she herself overreacted, having to bite her tongue to keep from being snarky. The morning had begun to feel like one of those days, other things on her mind. Like her stagnant career and the fact that she saw no hope of things improving.

Admittedly, she had promised her father to use her lunch hour to reach out to their district alderman. But, truth be told, Neema had no interest in trying too hard. She knew who Davis Black was. Everyone knew the city alderman and his family. The Black name was synonymous with most everything that happened in the Chicago judicial system. His father was the police superintendent. His mother was a federal court judge, and all his siblings were gainfully employed cops, attorneys or civic leaders. They didn't just make or enforce the law. Most of the Chicago community considered them *to be* the law.

For months, Neema had been angling for a story on the Black family. Something that would carry her byline and merit national attention. She dreamed of a Pulitzer Prize and the accolades of a breaking news story. It would validate her decision to forgo a career in medicine, like her parents had wanted, for the degree in investigative journalism that she had achieved. It would show that she'd made the right decision following the one and only time she'd defied them.

Her love for journalism had started in high school after working on the school newspaper. What was meant to pass some time and be an easy grade had changed

the entire trajectory of her life. Now she just needed it
to pay off and become the career she wanted it to be.

In college, she'd worked on the school's newspaper,
Central Michigan Life. She'd been the news editor, a
senior reporter and a copy editor. Her senior year, she'd
interned at the *Flint Journal*, covering city government
and breaking news. After graduation, she'd gotten her
first official job with the *Morning Sun*. As a staff reporter, she'd embraced local city township and public
education beats, gaining valuable experience in both
hard news and feature writing. That position had lasted
three years when she'd been offered a position with the
Chicago Daily Herald writing lifestyle articles about
foodstuffs at the Long Grove Apple Fest, algal bloom
in Herrick Lake and the nice women who volunteered
at the community gardens. It had paid well but lacked
the substantive bite of the stories she wanted to write.

By happenstance, a friend whose husband was a pro-
ducer for the *Chicago Tribune* had given her a heads up
that they were looking for a news reporter. Neema had
jumped at the opportunity. The *Tribune* was the most-
read daily newspaper of the Chicago metropolitan area
and the Great Lakes region. With the sixth highest cir-
culation for American newspapers, and unlike many of
its competitors, its numbers were growing.

Although Neema still occasionally got the usual
fluff story about school spelling bees, she'd been able
to write more serious pieces about Chicago's political
scene, corporate corruption, and the challenges facing
the education system.

Social media had significantly changed how news
made it to people's front doors. The political outcry
from a presidential administration about newspapers
and reporters being the delegates of fake news had not

served the industry well. It also hadn't helped that some news organizations had gone the way of tabloid sensationalism over quality reporting. But the *Tribune* had stayed true to its roots, maintaining its print presence and expanding its digital footprint.

Most newsrooms were still the stomping grounds for white males, their boys' club mentality not at all inclusive of women in general. Women of color, far and few between, were an anomaly. For Neema, every day in the office was an uphill battle trying to prove her worth in a world that saw little value in her humanity let alone her ability. But it was a fight Neema welcomed, even when the struggle sometimes felt unsurmountable. So, one lead, just a hint of impropriety somewhere in the city, or with one of its stellar citizens, could once again change her life. But everything about Davis Black and his picture-perfect family felt too elusive to ever amount to anything that Neema could use and she didn't have the time to waste chasing dead ends.

Minutes later she sauntered into the *Tribune*'s new offices at Prudential Plaza. It was a stark contrast to the original offices at Tribune Tower on North Michigan Avenue. Neema had started in the newsroom while they'd still been in the landmark building that had housed them for almost an entire century. It was one of the most recognized newsrooms in the world with its neo-Gothic beauty that rose some thirty-six floors into Chicago's skyline. Inside, it had been a roach-infested dump with large cubicles from the 1970s, built-in file cabinets, antiquated television sets that sat on desktop corners and ceiling tiles that routinely leaked and crumbled. It was currently undergoing a renovation, having been sold to a Los Angeles-based developer who was turning the space into luxury condos.

Neema remembered well the first time she'd walked into the building's lobby for her interview. She'd been instantly smitten with the space, the walls engraved with quotes about the media industry. Her journalistic spirit had been instantly inspired. The new office space was ultramodern and much nicer, yet lacked a certain *je ne sais quoi* possessed by the old building.

Taking the elevator to the offices on the twenty-seventh floor, Neema shot a quick glance to her watch. The noise level when she stepped into the newsroom was just a semblance of what it could be, voices raised as reporters shouted over each other. The open-concept space was set up with honeycomb-like pods comprised of desks that shifted from sitting to standing at the push of a button. Floor-to-ceiling windows gave them all spectacular views of Millennium Park.

The digital team and breaking news team both sat room-center under a massive TV mount hanging from the ceiling. The other departments—lifestyles, food and dining, and sports—clustered around them. The open floor plan had taken some getting used to, but it fostered a wealth of organic conversation that most of the staff found engaging. This morning was no exception.

"What's going on?" Neema questioned as she hurried to her desk, noting the burst of activity in the room.

Rose Edmonds, the digital news editor for the investigative team, greeted her warmly then shrugged her narrow shoulders. "They're debating the merits of gun control and active shooter drills in the public school system. Brooke scored a sweet interview with the chief executive of the NRA."

"Lucky Brooke," Neema stated as she cut her eyes in Brooke Donovan's direction. She gave the woman a nod and a bright smile, Brook returning the morning greeting with a wink of her eye.

The statuesque, blue-eyed blonde was an on-air personality who'd fallen into journalism by chance. She had dated an NBC newscaster in her late teens, the man having groomed her for the spotlight. He'd been her first husband and the father of her two oldest children. After their divorce, Brooke had struck out on her own, landing the job with the *Tribune*. She was passionate about news and had been a star in the newsroom ever since.

Despite them being polar opposites of each other, Brooke had proved herself to be a good friend. She'd gone to bat for Neema a few times, helping her to fight for stories the managing editor would have passed on her for without a second thought. Neema was genuinely happy for Brooke, but it also struck a nerve, reminding her that she needed to step up her game.

It took most of the morning for Neema to wade through the multitude of emails in her inbox and then clear away the mess on her desk. She had just completed a half dozen follow-up calls on a story she was working on about the new school superintendent when the managing editor for investigations called her into his office.

George Pappariella had been with the newspaper since forever. He was old enough to be her father and wore his age like a badge of honor. He was also set in his ways, and considered women in the newsroom an affront to the American spirit. It wasn't often that he addressed Neema, or any of the other women directly, usually preferring to delegate through third parties.

"How's it going, Nina?" he asked.

Her eyes narrowed ever so slightly. "It's *Neema*," she said, repeating her name slowly. "Nee…ma."

He nodded. "Neema, yes. Okay. Well, how are things?"

"Things are well, sir," she answered, attitude cling-ing to each word. "Thank you for asking," she quipped politely.

"Good to hear." He quickly dismissed with the small talk. "We're going to have to ask you to do some night shifts for the next few weeks. Fuller needs some time off to help with his kids, so he's taking a short leave of absence. We need you to start tonight."

Her eyes widened slightly. Jason Fuller had been hired to do the late-night news beat about six months ago. His very pregnant wife had recently given birth to twins, boys named Wayne and Garth, after the char-acters from that 1990s movie *Wayne's World.* "I can't start tonight. I have a prior commitment."

Pappariella looked up from the papers he'd been shifting from side to side atop his desk. "Excuse me?"

"I'll be delighted to help out, but starting tonight's not possible. I have a prior commitment that I cannot cancel. And the union requires employees be given suf-ficient notice of any schedule changes."

Pappariella bristled slightly. "I was under the impres-sion you were a team player, Nina."

"I am. I can't however speak for *Nina,* since I don't know anyone by that name. My name, sir, is Neema. *N-e-e-m-a.* Neema."

The man's face skewed, his mouth puckering as if he'd tasted something sour. Heat flooded his cheeks with color, his olive complexion suddenly turning a deep shade of Christmas red. He bit down against his bottom lip before finally responding. "Can you start tomorrow? Is that sufficient enough notice?"

Neema gave him a smug smile. "It is. Thank you."

He waved her away, the gesture dismissive.

Neema turned on her chunky heel.

As she closed the office door behind her, the smirk that blessed her expression was telling. It wasn't necessarily a win, she thought to herself, but felt immensely rewarding to have stood up for herself.

Chapter 2

The three-day getaway had Davis feeling like a new man. Excluding his sister's wedding, the trip to Las Vegas had been uneventful. He and his brothers drank much, ate well and gambled a lot. There had been laughter from the time they woke in the morning until they dropped into their beds at night. During their waking hours, there'd been an abundance of attention from some very beautiful women. Over that last dinner together, they had vowed to take more time cultivating their sibling bonds, to focus more on self-care and to learn to let go of those things they couldn't control. It had been cathartic and everything Davis thought he needed.

He moved through the entrance of his office, flipping on the lights and dropping his briefcase onto the desktop. He'd had an assistant. Rebecca, or Becky for short. Becky had been a super-focused computer geek studying at the University of Chicago. Two weeks before his Vegas trip she had handed in her resignation, leaving the country to study overseas. Now he had to start the interview process over again, and until he found someone new, prepare his own coffee.

He'd just inserted a compact K-Cup into the Keurig coffee maker when the front door swung open and Mingus sauntered inside. Davis instinctively knew his brother's visit wasn't a casual call to see how he was doing. His brother's expression was dour and Davis felt his good mood drop into the pit of his stomach.

"Hey, what's up?" he said, the two men slapping palms and bumping shoulders in a one-armed hug.

As was his way, Mingus got right to the point. "That meeting Dad wanted needs to happen tonight. Seven o'clock. At that African restaurant on West Randolph Street."

"Awaze Grill?"

Mingus shrugged. "He said you'd know the place. Something about goat and chapati."

Davis gave him a slight smile. "Best curry and fried flat bread in town."

His brother nodded. "He said don't be late."

"Will Dad be there?"

Mingus shrugged. "Just make sure you are," he said as he headed out the door.

When Mingus turned the corner out of sight, Davis grabbed his coffee and headed to his desk to get what was already proving to be a very long day started.

The telephone began ringing but Davis let it go to voice mail. A familiar voice suddenly sounded from the device and he felt himself smile. Mrs. Anne Boyd, a resident in the twenty-fourth district, was calling to complain about stray cats passing through her front yard.

Last week it had been about a tree limb hanging hap-
hazardly over the sidewalk. Before that, it had been the
mailpersons and their willful disregard for her hedges.
He and Becky had found her amusing, even when she
was most annoying. It hadn't taken Davis long to figure
out Mrs. Boyd was simply lonely, needing her weekly
phone call so that there was someone she could talk to.
Davis made a mental note to stop by her home to sit
and chat, if only for a few minutes.

Davis considered it an honor to represent the constituents in his district. Technically, he was just a sitting member of the city council with a fancy-sounding
title. The West Side of Chicago embraced a large community of working-class, low-income, poverty-stricken
minorities, its residents mostly Black, Puerto Rican and
Mexican. There were also some smaller communities of
blue-collar, lower middle-class and middle-class white
residents of historically Polish, Italian, Czech and Greek
descent. Most recently, newer communities of middle-
class and upper middle-class white residents created by
rapid gentrification, selective corporate investments and
unequal distribution of city resources had taken root.
The diversity of his district gave Davis hope about the
future of Chicago and what it might mean for the generations that came after him.

The West Side was home to the University of Illinois at Chicago, and the United Center, home base for
the Chicago Bulls and Chicago Blackhawks. It boasted
three of Chicago's largest parks: Humboldt Park, Gar-
field Park and Douglas Park. Additionally, Cook County
Jail, the United States' largest single-site jail, and a se-
cretive interrogation facility maintained by the Chicago
Police Department, were both on the West Side of Chicago and in his district.

Policing the district and staying on top of the community's needs had proved to be two full-time jobs in a twenty-four-hour day. Wielding a surprising amount of power, Davis was responsible for most things that happened in his district. He was the first point of contact when something went wrong on someone's block or if something needed to happen that required city approval. He'd become a master negotiator and was responsible for a budget in excess of one million dollars for capital improvement projects like repaving roads, replacing traffic signals or upgrading street and alley lighting.

He was two years into a four-year term and clearly earning his six-figure salary to do right by the people who'd voted him into office. Even if it meant sitting with an old woman to talk about cats. He wasn't, however, sure he could sit across the table from one of the city's most notorious crime lords for casual conversation. Most especially knowing the man wanted something from him. A favor that he imagined could easily cripple his political career.

The decadent aroma from the restaurant's kitchen greeted Davis at the front door. He took a deep inhale, hoping to still the nerves that rippled in the pit of his stomach. There was a nice crowd enjoying their evening meal and he suddenly found himself feeling self-conscious, hoping he wouldn't be recognized.

As if reading his mind, Mingus tossed him a look over his shoulder. "They have a private meeting room upstairs. Balducci has rented it for the evening."

Davis nodded as his brother led the way, guiding him toward the back of the building and up a short flight of steps to an area used for events. Two men in dark suits stood guard outside the door, eyeing Davis and his brother coolly. Mingus gave them both a nod and they stepped aside, allowing them to pass. Davis suddenly had questions. Clearly, Mingus found nothing wrong with the predicament they were standing knee-deep in the midst of. Everything about this meeting had Davis on edge. He thought his brother's level of comfort with the situation was deeply disturbing.

Alexander Balducci sat in the center of the room, occupying a table set to seat four. He was a big man, tall and wide, with a solid beer gut. His complexion was a strange shade of yellow-brown, highlighting the slight white rings around his eyes from too much time in a tanning bed. His eyes were a bright blue, crystal pools of water that made you feel like you might drown in them if he stared too hard. Women found him attractive, the man always nicely polished in his expensive wool and silk suits and Italian-leather shoes. He carried himself with an air of authority that many found intimidating. Davis, acutely aware his own anxiety level had risen tenfold, squared his shoulders as they moved forward.

A young woman sat at Balducci's side. She was strikingly beautiful, with a porcelain complexion and raging red hair pulled into a messy ponytail high atop her head. She held an Apple iPhone in the palm of her hand, her attention on the screen. As Davis and his brother approached the table, she never bothered to look up from whatever it was that was keeping her occupied.

Mingus greeted the man politely and made the introductions. "This is my brother, Alderman Black. Davis, this is Mr. Balducci," he said.

Alexander stood and extended his hand. "Alderman, it's a pleasure. Your father speaks quite highly of you."

Davis returned the handshake. "Mr. Balducci."

Alexander gestured toward an empty seat. "I appreciate you taking time out of your schedule to speak with me."

"My father didn't really give me much choice," Davis said sternly.

He suddenly felt Mingus's hand on his shoulder. "I'll be outside," his brother said as he excused himself from the room. Neither man spoke as they watched until Mingus had exited the space.

Davis took a seat in the chair the other man had pointed him to. He tossed a quick glance at the woman, who was still focused on her phone, dismissive of them all.

"Well, I'm glad your father could be persuasive," Balducci said, a slight smile pulling at his thin lips.

"Well, I'm not sure why..." Davis started.

A commotion at the door stalled his comment and had their attention. An elderly man carrying a tray of lidded serving dishes came through the entrance. He was followed by a woman who eyed them all curiously. Davis recognized the restaurant's owner. The man was chattering eagerly, seemingly excited to be serving their meals. The waitress didn't seem as enthusiastic.

"I took the liberty of ordering for the table," Balducci said as he grasped the corner of a cloth napkin, shook it open and dropped it into his lap.

"I won't be staying," Davis quipped.

The redhead lifted her eyes for the first time, tossing Davis a look. Curiosity washed over her expression before she shifted her gaze to Balducci. He gave her a slight nod of his head and she turned back to her cell phone. She never spoke and her companion didn't seem interested in introducing them.

"These dishes are the very best cuisine of my home,"

the proprietor was saying, a wide grin spread full across his face. "My wife and I prepare it all ourselves, the recipes passed down through generations of our people."

Balducci nodded. He gestured toward Davis. "The alderman's father, our illustrious police superintendent, speaks quite highly of your menu. I look forward to the meal."

"Alderman Black!" the man said, his eyes widening as recognition swept over him. "I did not realize you would be here this evening. Welcome, sir! I am Adamu Kamau."

Davis forced a smile to his face. "It's very nice to meet you, Mr. Kamau, and I'm honored to be here." He extended his hand in greeting.

"My daughter was supposed to stop by your office this afternoon to speak with you about the drug traffic in the community. My neighborhood is overrun with criminal activity. We need places and activities for our young men. You need to do something about that, sir. I would like to talk to you and maybe give you some suggestions on how to help these young people."

Davis nodded. "I appreciate that, Mr. Kamau. It's not a good time right now, but I'd love to sit down with you to have a conversation. Perhaps you can call my office later this week to schedule an appointment?"

Mr. Kamau turned to the young woman standing in the shadows behind him. As he stepped aside, Davis got his first good look at the beauty who'd been standing politely in wait. There was no denying the family resemblance. The young woman had her father's expressive eyes. Her features were chiseled, high cheekbones, lush lips, and the coloration of her skin deep and rich like black marble with the faintest hint of a mahogany undertone. Davis's jaw dropped slightly, his eyes widening with a shimmer of intrigue. Because the woman was beautiful!

She wore all black. Tailored slacks, a buttoned shirt, and an apron tied around her waist, fit her neatly. She was lean and petite in height with modest curves and the tiniest waist. Her shoes were sturdy, Dr. Martens' Mary Janes in polished black leather. Her hair was cropped close, the sides shaved in a faint fade. Gold hoop earrings and a hint of lip gloss finalized her look, complementing her lush lips and chiseled cheekbones.

Shifting forward in his seat Davis struggled not to stare. His temperature had risen, and his heart was suddenly beating faster than normal. He took a deep breath and held it, hoping to calm the nerves that had surfaced with a vengeance. For a brief second, their eyes locked. She stared intently, and then her father spoke her name, pulling her gaze from his.

"This is my daughter, Neema. Neema will call your office and arrange time for you to speak with us."

Davis practically jumped from his seat to extend his hand toward the exquisite beauty. "It's a pleasure to meet you, Neema. I'm Davis. Davis Black."

Neema gave him the slightest smile. "It's very nice to meet you, too, Alderman," she said softly.

"Please, call me Davis."

She gave him another smile but didn't bother to respond.

Neema's father was grinning from ear to ear. "She will call," he said as he gestured for her to place the food on the table. As she lifted the last silver lid with a well-practiced flourish, her father watched approvingly, his hands folded behind his back as he rocked from side to side. "Is there anything else I can get either of you?" he inquired after he'd explained each dish.

Balducci shook his head. "No, thank you. It all looks delicious."

Mr. Kamau nodded. "Enjoy your meal, gentlemen." He waved Neema out the door, throwing one last glance over his shoulder.

Watching her leave, Davis had been hopeful for one last shared look between them. He found the emotion surprising. As Balducci cleared his throat, he realized the man, and the woman with him, were both staring in his direction. Balducci's companion was smiling at him, a smug look across her face.

Davis felt a rush of heat color his cheeks. "I'm sorry," he said, hoping to shift the attention to something else. "But we haven't been introduced. I'm Davis Black."

She flipped the length of her red hair over her shoulder as she reached to shake his hand. Her hand was cool, her fingers almost icy. "My name's Ginger."

Balducci interjected. "Ginger is my personal assistant, but she won't be staying," he said as he stole a quick glance at his wrist. "She has someplace to be."

Ginger rose from her seat, grabbed a wedge of flat bread from the basket in the center of the table and swallowed a quick bite. "Business calls," she said. "It was nice to meet you, Davis Black. Please tell Danni I said hello when you see her."

"Danni?" he questioned, referring to his brother Armstrong's wife. "You know my sister-in-law?"

"We're old friends," she said. Ginger smiled and winked at him. The gesture felt slightly salacious and Davis felt a rise of perspiration bead across his brow.

Ginger lifted her designer purse from the table, steadied herself on her very high heels and then moved swiftly out the door.

An awkward silence swept through the space. Davis

watched as Balducci filled his plate with a generous serving of curry goat, pilau rice and fried plantains. The man began to eat as if he were famished, filling the quiet with small talk about the weather, the Chicago Bears and the rate of growth in the city. He gestured at the food, encouraging Davis to eat, but Davis would not budge. He sat with a slight pout tugging at his full lips and his hands folded together in his lap. He was ready to be done with their conversation and as far from Balducci as he could get. Balducci didn't seem to take the hint.

His father's history with Alexander Balducci was far from wine and roses. Davis knew that it went back to well before he'd been born.

Alexander's eldest son, Leonard, had been a career criminal, one who had made Jerome Black work hard for his money. Years ago, Leonard had worked to put the family business on the map. He and his crew had hijacked trailer shipments and sent the cargo overseas. It was Armstrong, Davis's brother, who had caught them after they'd taken down a truck full of TVs and electronics. The security guard had barely been able to signal the alarm before he'd been killed. There'd been a shootout at the docks, and Balducci's son had taken a bullet. It had been one of Armstrong's first cases, the first time he'd had to discharge his weapon, and it had happened mere weeks after their father had been promoted to superintendent. Leonard Balducci had died days later and when most had anticipated the two fathers would have parted ways, it seemed to solidify their strange relationship instead.

Most recently, Armstrong had arrested Alexander's other son, the man charged with trafficking children and teens and the promotion of prostitution. Again, the

two fathers had moved past that bump in the road with
their friendship still solidified.

As Davis sat there lost in thought, he found himself
thinking about the beautiful woman named Neema.
Curiosity was thick, its viselike grip tenacious. He had
questions. Something about her had piqued his interest and he was suddenly determined to discover all he
could. He looked forward to her reaching out on her
father's behalf to talk about the crime in their neighborhood. He found himself plotting when and how to
call her if he didn't hear from her in the next day or so.

Davis would have preferred to be talking with her
than with Balducci. Even continuing the conversation
with her father would have been a better time as far as
he was concerned. But despite his best efforts to engage
the man, Balducci wasn't ready for serious discussion.
As he noshed on his meal, he said very little that had to
do with why Davis was there, preferring to keep up the
casual chat. He gestured a second time toward the table
of food, his insistence evident in his stern tone. "Eat,"
Balducci admonished. "Please, don't waste the food.
It's very good. Your father made an excellent choice."

Realizing it wasn't worth the argument, Davis
reached for the bowl of curry and scooped a serving
onto his plate. It didn't hurt that he was also hungry,
having missed his midday meal. He ate as Balducci
asked questions about his family and his efforts in the
community. Only once did he mention his own family,
noting that his youngest son was a Dallas Cowboys fan.

Davis had just swallowed his last forkful of rice and
meat when the man finally got to the point of their
meeting.

Balducci rocked back and forth in his seat, the front

chair legs lifting slightly from the floor each time. His eyes locked on Davis's face.

Davis pulled his napkin to his lips and wiped his mouth. He took a sip of the chilled water in his glass, resting it gently back against the table. He turned slightly in his seat and gave Balducci his full attention.

"Why am I here, sir?"

"There's something I need done and I need to trust that it will be done discreetly. I also need to trust you'll keep it confidential. Your father volunteered your services. He assured me that you could be trusted to do what I need and to keep it to yourself."

"My father shouldn't have made you any promises, especially since he didn't discuss it with me first."

Balducci hesitated for a moment before he nodded. "At least hear me out before you decline."

Davis gave him a slight shrug. "Okay," he said, folding his arms across his chest. "I'm listening."

Balducci pushed his plate to the middle of the table.

"I know that you are acquainted with Gaia Russo. Is that correct?"

Davis hesitated before answering. Gaia Russo was renowned in the community for her activism in the city. If there needed to be a fight for political or social change, Gaia Russo was usually at the forefront of the public protest, never hesitating to take her activism to the streets. The two had worked on many committees together and Gaia had helped with his campaign, instrumental in convincing young voters that he had their best interests at heart. A talented artist, Gaia often hawked her paintings and sculptures at local events, but had yet to garner the national recognition her talent deserved. She was also a mother, her eight-year-old son the light of her life. They had history and he considered the young woman a good friend.

Davis took a deep breath before nodding his head. "That's correct."

The man smiled ever so slightly. "Gaia is my daughter," he said matter-of-factly, making the pronouncement as though he were only stating the time of day. "But she doesn't know that I'm her father, and I need to keep it that way."

Davis's eyes widened in surprise, his expression questioning. "Why are you telling me this?"

"Because it's come to my attention that my daughter and grandson are going through a difficult time. I'd like to help, but for reasons that I can't explain, I need to remain anonymous."

The man had been holding Davis's gaze and then abruptly shifted his eyes away. A muscle in his face twitched, the anxious tick pulling at the corner of his right eye.

"So, what is it that you want me to do?" Davis asked.

Balducci reached into the breast pocket of his suit jacket and extracted a manila envelope. He set the envelope on the table, a stack of one-hundred-dollar bills peeking past the flap. The envelope bulged, looking as if it might burst at the seams. Davis's brow furled as the two men locked gazes a second time.

"Buy a painting or two. Invest in her art with my money. She trusts you."

Davis sat back in his chair. He had questions and wasn't even sure where to begin. Why didn't Balducci just buy her artwork himself? Why was her parentage a secret? Why Davis and not one of the man's other employees? Even the redhead could buy artwork for him, right? Why the cloak and dagger of secrecy? What was Alexander Balducci really up to?

Balducci seemed to read his mind. "I would prefer not to enlist anyone in my employ to do this for me. Not everyone needs to know my business. And my daughter and her son are safer if no one knows our connection to each other. Unfortunately, in my business, I've made many enemies. I can't trust that Gaia will allow me to protect her if she's told, and I might not be able to keep her safe if someone goes for her to get to me."

"She deserves to know the truth," Davis stated, judgment like barbed wire around each word.

"I promised her mother I would never reveal myself. I'm honoring that promise. I'm only trusting you because your father trusts you to keep my secret. And I trust your father."

"So, you want me to just randomly throw money at her under the guise of collecting her art."

"I want you to help me invest in my daughter's career and allow her to support herself and her son without her feeling like she's being given a handout."

"Why don't you just mail her a money order anonymously?"

"Because she will only donate it to one of those charities she's always raising money for. She won't consider it income for her and her alone."

"You don't know that."

"Yes. I do. I tried that a year ago. She gave every dime of it away to some shelter for battered women." Balducci spat the statement out like he couldn't comprehend his daughter's generosity.

"And what makes you think if I gave her money, she wouldn't do the same thing with it?"

"She has a child to feed. She will know it's earned

income for her services. She will use it to take care of herself. I think when I sent it anonymously that she may not have trusted the intentions for it."

Davis mulled the request over in his head. It all felt slightly crazy to him and, even though he thought Balducci was being extra for no sane reason whatsoever, he found himself considering the request.

"There's ten thousand dollars in that envelope. I'll give you another ten thousand to spend on her next month."

Davis's expression was incredulous. "You don't think your daughter won't have questions if I suddenly start throwing ten grand in her direction every month. Hell, even I'd have questions."

"Make something up, son. I hear you're quite creative when it comes to problem solving. But if it helps, she has a gallery showing that opens this week. The owner is a friend of mine."

"I don't know about this…" Davis started.

For a good ten minutes, Balducci pled his case, defended his position.

Davis asked questions and voiced his concerns, not at all on board with being Balducci's errand boy but not declining, either. Because he did know Gaia was going through a difficult time. He knew his friend struggled with having to work two full-time jobs to support herself and her son. He knew that, like most single mothers, Gaia balancing needs over wants came with its own set of challenges because someone else's young life was in her hands. Doing what Balducci asked might ease that burden briefly, but then what? What challenges would Davis be throwing on his friend's already full plate? What disappointments would he be responsible for igniting if the truth ever came out? And, just as important, could he live with himself when this all felt like he was making a deal with the devil?

"And if I say yes, what then?" Davis finally asked.

"Then nothing. I'm asking for a favor, and if honored, I'll owe you my gratitude."

"I don't want anything from you."

"I'll still owe you should the day ever arise that I can repay this favor."

"And how long do you expect me to do this?"

The man shrugged. "Just a few months. I'll figure something else out after that. As you said, it's not a charade that can be never-ending without questions being asked."

Balducci pushed the envelope toward him. Davis's hand rested on the table and the edge of it brushed against his fingertips. The door to the room suddenly opened and Neema stepped inside. Both men bristled as if caught with their hands in the cookie jar.

Without giving it a thought, Davis palmed the mailer filled with cash, slid it off the table and into the pocket of his jacket. Admittedly, even under the best circumstances, the overt gesture seemed cagey and Davis hoped Neema hadn't been paying attention to either of them as she'd stepped into the room.

Balducci stood abruptly, leaving Davis no chance to change his mind. "Thank you," the man said as he extended his arm for a quick handshake. "I'll be in touch." As he moved past Neema, he gave the young woman a nod of gratitude. He paused, stopping to pull cash out of his wallet to give her a tip for her service. "Thank you," he said again as he moved past her. "I'll settle the bill with your father. I'd like to thank him personally for his hospitality."

"Thank you," Neema said politely. She slid the one-hundred-dollar bill into the pocket of her apron. As Balducci exited the room, she turned to stare at Davis, who was eyeing her intently. The moment was suddenly awkward as she moved nervously toward the table to gather the dirty dishes.

"Is there anything else I can get for you, Alderman?" she asked.

Davis smiled and shook his head. "No. Thank you," he said. "But please, call me Davis."

Neema smiled, her thick lashes fluttering ever so slightly. She eyed him curiously. Davis Black was almost too pretty for words. Having only seen him from a distance and in photos alongside his very attractive family, she'd not realized just how good-looking he was. He was jaw-droppingly handsome with picture-perfect features, the hint of a keenly edged beard and mustache, and hazel eyes flecked with gold. She didn't want to fetishize his warm complexion but standing there, eyeing him keenly, all she could think about was butter pecan ice cream, imagining what that might taste like against her tongue. He wore an expensive navy wool blazer, plaid shirt, denim jeans and retro Air Jordan sneakers.

His stare was intense, something in the look he was giving her that made her want to search out a mirror to see what it was that he saw. His gaze was heated, a hint of fire shimmering beneath the narrowed lids. She felt herself gasp, her breath catching deep in her chest. The moment was suddenly intimidating and usually there was very little that overwhelmed Neema.

"Please, do call me," Davis was saying. "I'd really like to speak with you, and your father, about your concerns. In fact…" He pulled a business card from his pocket and picked up a pen that had been left on the table. He jotted down his phone number and held the card out to her. "Here's my private cell phone number. Call me at any time. My schedule is very flexible this week."

"We will," Neema answered as she looked at the small card resting in the palm of her hand.

Her father suddenly moved through the door, calling her name softly. "Neema! Do not bother the alderman. He's an important man." He smiled at Davis. "I hope that you and Mr. Balducci enjoyed your meal, sir."

Davis nodded. "Yes, sir. We did. Thank you kindly."

"We appreciate your business. It helps to have such important men like yourself supporting the small businesses in the community. Your father was here just last week. He's an admirable man, your father."

"Thank you, sir. My father says the same thing about you."

Mr. Kamau grinned broadly at the complement. "Please, if you need to use the room a little longer, do not let us rush you. Mr. Balducci has paid for the entire evening. Perhaps you'd like coffee and dessert?"

"No, sir. But thank you for offering. I was just heading out, but I wanted to make sure I gave your daughter my direct number. I look forward to speaking with you about your concerns."

Mr. Kamau clapped his hands together excitedly. "Thank you! Thank you so much for everything you do." He tossed his daughter a look. "He's a good man, our alderman. A good man!"

Neema's eyes widened, slightly embarrassed by her father's enthusiasm for the young politician. The old man was gushing with praise and she could only imagine what Davis Black had to be thinking about the two of them. She felt Davis eyeing her and color flushed her cheeks. She moved to clear the dishes away, fighting to ignore the lingering look he was giving her.

With a nod of his head and one last glance toward Neema, Davis said his goodbyes and exited the building. Outside, he suddenly remembered the cache of money secreted away in his jacket pocket. Balducci was long gone, but something about their encounter left Davis with a bad taste in his mouth. He couldn't put his finger on it, but he sensed that favor, and Alexander Balducci asking for his help, wasn't going to end well.

The thought of everything that could possibly go wrong weighed heavy on his spirit like toxic waste flooding the late-night air.

Chapter 3

It was nights like this one that made Neema regret she still lived with her parents. Her mind was racing, and her father's continuous warbling was beginning to wear on her nerves. It had been a good night for the business, the rental of the event space exceeding a normal night of income. He was still riding an emotional high about the guests he'd been able to serve and rub elbows with. Despite his enthusiasm, Neema understood that her father had no idea the significance of what they'd just witnessed.

Davis Black and Alexander Balducci huddled in private conversation was huge! And what about the money she'd seen change hands? Because Neema was certain she'd witnessed Davis Black pocket an envelope of cash as the two had sat together at that table. Neema instinctively knew there was a story there and that it had dropped into her lap for a reason. Was the handsome alderman taking a bribe? In exchange for what? What could Balducci, a renowned criminal, be wanting from the city official? Was Davis Black corrupt? What degree of criminality had she stumbled upon?

Neema needed to process what she knew with what she'd seen. She needed to do a little investigating to try to determine the connection between the two men. She had to figure out what they were up to. But in that moment, her father was making it hard for her to think with his humming and singing like it was midafternoon and not midnight.

Neema groaned softly to herself. Her parents had been ecstatic when they'd purchased the Jackson Boulevard home. The nineteen-hundred square foot Georgian-style property boasted four generous bedrooms and three baths. The polished hardwood floors and renovated kitchen had sold it for her mother. Her father had lauded the garage bays and the oversize lot with its great curb appeal. But despite all its pluses, the walls were far too thin for Neema's liking.

She had followed them to Chicago because that's what a good daughter did. When her mother had insisted she take the bedroom on the top floor with the faded floral wallpaper and shag carpet, Neema hadn't argued because making the case for her own apartment would have caused a rift between them.

Instead, she had paid for the renovations to make the space hers. Renovations that had included new plumbing, not only for her bathroom but the whole upper level. Now, the shag carpet was gone, replaced with a Persian rug that evoked Old World style with its rich colors and brilliant pattern. The walls were painted a soft gray and built-in bookcases flanked a restored fireplace. The decorative touches reflected her eclectic style and her parents had obliged her choices with nominal interference. Being a good daughter was an art form and between the move to Chicago and acquiescing to their demands, Neema had taken her craft to a whole other level.

Neema paid her parents rent each month for the privilege of locking her room door without them taking issue with her needing her own space. But there was nothing she'd been able to do about the home's sparse insulation that allowed sound to vibrate from room to room. So, her father singing slightly off key, his deep baritone voice echoing off the walls, was an annoyance she had to occasionally bear.

After firing up her computer, Neema slid on her Bose wireless headset, canceling out every ounce of noise that wasn't coming directly from of her speakers connected to a small sound system in the corner of the room. She pushed the play button on a reggae playlist and settled herself comfortably in the leather executive's chair at her desk. Buju Banton was first in rotation and the rhythmic beat of the song "Destiny," along with his deep, raspy voice wrapped around the lyrics, soon had her tapping her toe and bobbing her head in time to the music.

She typed Balducci's name into the Google search bar first, pulling up every public article she could find about the man. His philanthropic endeavors were numerous, his efforts lauded by many. One or two articles questioned his connection to his son's arrest the previous year, but nothing pointed at any illegal ties. The most recent articles lauded his accomplishments on the city's energy board as well as his stake in rebuilding Chicago's west side.

Neema shook her head as she noted the many com-

mittees and corporate boardrooms he'd been welcomed
to sit on. Despite the rumors of his not so legal enterprises, it seemed he was well respected. He had also
profited nicely in some of Chicago's biggest real estate
deals, responsible for most of the gentrification in the
inner city. And in at least ninety percent of those news
articles, police superintendent Jerome Black was like-
wise named, his actions mirroring those of Balducci's.

Neema googled Davis Black next. There weren't
nearly as many articles about the man and most had
been written when he'd announced his candidacy for
office. Fluff pieces about his likes and dislikes, him at
ribbon cuttings, giving speeches at local high schools
and pinning citizenship awards on senior citizens.
There were numerous photos of him standing with family members as one or the other accepted an award, and
a few pieces about his activism in the neighborhood.

Nothing she read raised any red flags, the man's actions not nearly as public as that of others in his circle
of family and friends. But then, she thought, maybe that
was the red flag she was looking for. Why *wasn't* Davis
Black doing as much as it seemed his siblings were?
Was he being purposely low-key in his public dealings
to not draw attention to himself or his actions? Neema
realized she needed answers to questions that she hadn't
even begun to ask, and she wasn't going to get them
reading through old news articles. She set a reminder
on her cell phone to call Davis Black in the morning.

Shutting down her computer, Neema moved to the
queen-size bed, the headphones still engaged.

Slipping between freshly laundered sheets, she
flicked off the light on the nightstand and settled back
against the rise of pillows behind her head. Closing her
eyes, Neema allowed herself to settle into the rise of

darkness. She breathed in and out slowly, every muscle in her body beginning to melt like warm butter. Her countenance was languid, and she could feel sleep starting to call her name. Yuna was in her ear singing "Crush" and when Usher joined in with a sultry falsetto in the upper range of his vocal registrar, Neema palmed her cell phone and pulled up the last image of Davis Black she'd saved on her phone.

She drew her hand across the cell phone screen, the pad of her index finger slowly outlining his features. There was no denying that he'd been blessed with good looks. But pretty on the outside didn't necessarily make him pretty on the inside and she didn't have a clue what kind of person Davis Black was. If she went digging, what secrets would she discover about the man? Neema mused. Was it possible that she might unearth a dark secret he didn't want exposed and, if so, what would she do then? She continued staring while Coldplay, Colby Caillat and James Morrison played sweetly in her ear.

As she thought about the handsome man and her next steps, Neema let Boney James lull her to sleep. Hours later Davis Black was skipping naked through her dreams.

When Davis sauntered into his brother's office the next day, Mingus Black was staring at his computer. The expression across his face was affable, something humorous playing on the screen. Still in his feelings, Davis wasn't interested in knowing what his brother found so amusing. He tossed the envelope of cash onto the desktop, the mailer landing with a resounding thud. Mingus lifted one brow as he tossed Davis a look.

"What's that?"

"Ten grand that Alexander Balducci wants me to

use to buy artwork. And he plans to give me another ten thousand next month and maybe the month after that." Davis dropped into the upholstered chair in front of the desk, sinking into the cushions as if the weight of the world was holding him hostage.

Mingus leaned back in his own seat. "And your problem with that?"

"Where do I start? We both know this money is dirty!"

"Do we?"

Davis rolled his eyes skyward. "If it was legit, he'd go buy his own damn paintings and write a check."

Mingus laughed, shaking his head slowly. He pulled open the top drawer of the desk and lifted his business checkbook from inside. With the pass of an ink pen, he filled in the blanks, signed his name across the bottom, and tore the voucher from the book. As he slid the document across the desk toward Davis, he dropped the envelope of cash into a bank deposit bag and secured the zipper. With a flip of his wrist, it disappeared into the desk drawer. The transaction was as simple as the two trading a stick of mint-flavored gum for a handful of Tic Tac candy.

Davis blinked, his eyes wide as he eyed the check made payable to him for the total sum of five thousand dollars and some change. On the comment line, his brother had neatly printed the words 'Consulting Fee Deposit.' He lifted his eyes back to Mingus, questions piercing his expression.

"Homeland Security requires the bank to start asking questions if you deposit ten grand in cash at one time, or any amount the teller might deem suspicious. Since you don't regularly deposit that kind of money, and you just look like you're committing a crime, I suggest you not do that. This should make things a little easier for you. They will barely blink at a check written on a business account they know. In a day or two, I'll write you a check for the other half. Feel free to send me an invoice, or not. That's your choice. I'm good either way."

"And what are you going to do with the cash?" Davis finally asked.

"Most of my business is in cash," Mingus answered. "My clients aren't interested in leaving a paper trail. I have a few accounts in multiple banks around town. I'll spread it around and deposit most of it. Some of it I'll use for incidentals."

Davis shook his head. "We're both going to jail."

Mingus laughed again. "I'm sure I'll see the gates of hell well before I ever see the inside of a jail cell."

"Well, I don't have your confidence."

"Look, you worry too much."

"And you don't worry enough."

Mingus chuckled again, the wealth of it gut deep. He spoke after composing himself. "Look, the old man just needs you to help with a family problem. No one gets hurt and you'll actually be helping his daughter."

"You know?"

Mingus shrugged. "I know enough."

"Then why didn't he ask you to do it?"

"You're friends with Gaia. It wouldn't draw any unnecessary attention. I tend to run in circles that might not be in her best interest. Besides, I have no doubt she likes you. Didn't you two date or something?"

"Or something. It wasn't like that, though," Davis said as he thought about his friend Gaia Russo. The two did have history, their connection going back to high school. But dating hadn't been an option for them. Gaia had been head-over-heels in love with Carl King, her son's father and one of Davis's best friends. Carl had been an aspiring basketball player who could barely string a full sentence together. He'd been everything Davis hadn't been; flashy, arrogant and the love of Gaia's life.

Davis had been what he was with most women: a supportive friend and sounding board when things went wrong with their love lives. He'd been there when Carl hadn't been selected in the NBA Draft Lottery and taken his frustrations out on Gaia. He'd been there when Carl had been recruited to play in Barcelona, promising a very pregnant Gaia that he would be there to support her and their son. And he'd been there when, leaving his life and family in the United States behind, Carl had married a Spanish barista named Lola. Davis had been a good friend and nothing more, Gaia wanting nothing from him and him having little else to give.

What they had found in common was their commitment to the community. Their shared activism for the pursuit of change and their desire to be a part of that change for the betterment of others. Being of service to those in need had kept them tied to each other. They were friends, the simplicity of the relationship working for them even when it shouldn't have. When Davis gave unsolicited advice that Gaia had no interest in hearing… When she hadn't wanted a friend and he had still insinuated himself into her life… One more reason why Balducci's request had him on edge. He never wanted to do anything to jeopardize the tenuous friendship he and Gaia shared.

He changed the subject. "What do you know about Adamu Kamau?"

"Who?"

"The man who owns the African restaurant."

Mingus's gaze narrowed ever so slightly, his broad shoulders reaching for the ceiling. "Nothing. Should I?"

"I met his daughter last night. Her name's Neema. She waitressed our table."

The slightest grin pulled full and wide across Mingus's face. "So, do you want to know about the father or his daughter?"

"I just…w-well…" Davis stammered, his face turning a brilliant shade of deep red. He realized he'd clearly opened the door for a wealth of teasing and suddenly wished for a deep hole to drop into and disappear. He shook his head, the two men locking gazes.

Mingus laughed and Davis laughed with him.

"She was gorgeous!" Davis gushed, meeting his brother's stare.

"So, call her. Get to know her. Unless you want me to do a background check on her and her family? I can do that for you."

"That's definitely not why I was asking. I was just curious."

"Just curious?"

Davis met his brother's smug expression. "Don't start, Mingus. It was just a question."

Mingus held his hands up as if he were surrendering. "Well, I look forward to hearing more about this Neema when you learn more."

"Yeah. Sure," Davis said as he moved to his feet. He had turned toward the door when Mingus called his name. "Yes?"

"Don't forget your check. And cash it quick. I'm good for it today. No telling what might happen tomorrow," he said with a soft smirk.

Moving back to his brother's desk, Davis picked up the check, folded it in two and placed it into the breast pocket of his jacket. "Thanks," he said, giving his brother a nod of his head.

"Whatever you need, little brother! Whatever you need."

Minutes later, Davis was maneuvering back to his own office when his cell phone rang. The device connected with the Bluetooth in the vehicle, the call ringing loudly through the automobile. He didn't immediately recognize the number that flashed across the dashboard, but that wasn't unusual. For the briefest moment, he considered letting it go directly to voice mail and then changed his mind, engaging the call instead.

"Hello?"

A woman's voice echoed out of the speakers. "Yes, hello. I was hoping to speak with Alderman Black. This is Neema Kamau calling."

There was a moment of hesitation, Davis suddenly feeling like he had conjured her up by speaking her name. Her calling surprised him; it felt like a moment of disbelief, good fortune, and maybe a little celestial magic.

She spoke again. "Hello? Are you there?"

Davis suddenly slammed on brakes, narrowly missing the back of a Ford pickup stopped at the red light. He felt his breath catch deep in his chest and shook away the reverie he'd fallen into. He took a deep inhale of air and held it just briefly before gusting the breath past his full lips.

He stammered. "I-I'm sorry… Hello! Yes! This is Alderman Black… I mean Davis. Davis Black! Neema, hello! How are you?"

He could feel her smiling through the receiver, or at least he imagined she was smiling because he was, his grin pulling from ear to ear. Moving after the truck, through the green light, he pulled off into an empty parking spot and shut down his car. "I'm sorry. I'm just a little surprised to hear from you."

"You told me to call. To schedule a meeting with my father. Did you not mean it?"

"No! Yes! Of course! Yes, I did. I'm sorry!" He paused, taking a moment to stall the rise of nerves. "I don't know what I was thinking. I'm glad you called, though."

"My father is anxious to have that conversation with you."

Davis chuckled softly, remembering the other man's exuberance. "When is he available?"

"Are you able to meet with him tomorrow morning?"

"I can. Does ten o'clock work for him?"

"That would be perfect."

"Will you be joining us?" Davis asked, a hint of hope in his tone.

There was a moment of hesitation as Neema seemed to ponder the question. "I'm not sure," she finally answered. "I may have another commitment."

Davis nodded, his head bobbing slightly even though she couldn't see him through the phone line. "Maybe you'll consider having dinner with me tomorrow night?" he asked.

"Dinner?" There was a wide sliver of surprise in her tone and her response sounded almost as unexpected as his question. "You want to have dinner?"

Davis chuckled. "Why not?"

"Because we don't know each other like that."

"But that's how we get to know each other. Every great relationship starts with a first date!"

Neema laughed. "Who said anything about a date?"

Davis laughed with her. "We can call it a meeting if that will convince you to join me."

"You're rather brazen, aren't you?"

"Actually, I'm very much an introvert and quite shy. But I come out of my shell when I need to, and I imagine I need to if I'm going to convince you to let me wine and dine you."

"My father taught me to be wary of men with silk tongues."

"Your father is a very smart man. And I think he likes me. I'd venture to say that he would approve of me taking his beautiful daughter to dinner and a movie. I could always ask him for his permission, if you prefer."

Neema laughed again, heartily. "That won't be necessary," she gushed. "And who said anything about a movie, too?"

"Too soon?"

"You're a funny man, Davis Black."

"I have moments. And I really am a good guy, so give me an hour or two of your time and let me show you."

"I'll have to think about it," she finally said.

"Is this a good number to reach you on?" Davis asked, eyeing the ten digits highlighted on his phone screen.

"Now you plan to stalk me?"

"No, not at all! It's just in case I need to plead my case to convince you to say yes to dinner."

Neema giggled. "Good day, Mr. Black!"

"It was a pleasure speaking with you, Ms. Kamau. I look forward to seeing you again soon!"

Disconnecting the call, Davis pumped a fist in the air. His day had started shakily but was quickly looking up. Neema's melodic tone with the barest hint of an accent had been like the sweetest honey in his ears. And despite his initial fumbling, once he'd recovered from the surprise, the conversation had gone well.

As he started the engine, checking for traffic before pulling his car back onto the road, he didn't pay any attention to the silver Mercedes that pulled in behind him, the redhead named Ginger sitting in the driver's seat.

Neema couldn't help thinking that working the night shift was like the kiss of death for her career. Stepping out from behind her desk to ride shotgun for eleven hours with Nicholas Toppo, an overnight reporter, was painful at best. Everyone called the popular nighttime news jock Tiger for his obsession with the game of golf, but he was more slothlike than anything else. Everything about the man was slow. He rarely walked with any sense of urgency, took forever to get to a punchline in his many stories and by hour three had worked Neema's last good nerve because he talked nonstop. The police radio in the car chattered with static he often ignored for the Candy Crush game on his phone. For the life of her, Neema couldn't begin to understand how he still had a job. Were she to work in the same manner, she would have been escorted to the exit door without so much as a polite farewell.

Despite his questionable work ethic, he had taught her a lot. They'd been partnered together many times previously. She'd gotten to know him well and considered him a good friend. He'd welcomed her into his home, introduced her to his family. His wife was a delight to know and the two often went shopping together. Neema didn't have many female friends and enjoyed the camaraderie, the two women often laughing about Tiger and his antics. The couple had four children, three daughters and a son, who all called her "Auntie Neema." He treated her like a little sister, and she trusted him, even when he did get on her nerves.

Since their night shift had started, they had caught an exclusive: the story of a carjacking gone awry. When that was done, they followed two gunshot victims to the hospital, made late-night calls to public information officers, chatted with witnesses and drank coffee like they were guzzling water.

She was grateful for the moment of silence when Tiger pulled into the parking lot of a 7-Eleven on Dearborn Street for a restroom break, the abundance of caffeine sidelining his colon. Neema made her own beeline for the women's room. Once she and her bladder were well with each other, she purchased a large cup of coffee and a bag of Ruffles cheddar and sour cream potato chips. Returning to the car, she settled back in her seat for what would prove to be a lengthy wait.

Checking her phone, Neema saw that she had a multitude of incoming messages. A smile lifted her lips ever so slightly. Davis Black had left her one voice message and had sent her two text messages. He was persistent, she thought, amused by his jovial plea for her to say yes to having dinner with him.

Under different circumstances, she wondered if she would be as hesitant to reply. When she considered the news story she hoped to write, an exposé that might tarnish his good name and cast a light on his wrong-doings, she had to give serious thought to how that would play out if she started dating him. Not that she believed dinner would be a prelude to anything romantic between them. Because Neema wasn't looking for romantic. "Not at all," she said out loud as if she needed to convince herself. "This is all about me getting a story and making a mark in my career. Nothing more," she stated as she looked around to see if anyone was watching her talk to herself.

She reached for the foam cup that rested in the cup holder and took a sip of coffee. The beverage was freshly brewed and hot. *Besides*, she thought, *why would a man like Davis Black be interested in dating me?* Neema shook her head. She laughed heartily. "'Cause I'm all that and a bag of chips!" she said aloud. "Dammit, that's why!"

By the time Tiger returned to the car, his expression smug, Neema had started to doze. Startled from the trance she'd slowly slipped into, she gave him a wry stare, annoyance furrowing her brow.

"Did you have you a good nap, darling?" he said teasingly.

"I'm not your darling," Neema snapped, noting the time. "What happened? I was starting to think you fell in."

Tiger laughed. "Sometimes a man just needs a little quiet time with a magazine and the palm of his hand."

Neema grimaced. "That's just nasty!"

He pointed an index finger at her. "Because you have a dirty mind. I was talking about turning the pages."

She rolled her eyes skyward.

"Oh, what? I bet now you want to go run and file a harassment complaint against me. I made a joke. I can't help how you took it."

"I took it how you intended it. Why are you men such pigs?"

He shrugged. "Not all of us. Just an occasional one or two, and usually it's because we're trying to hide our own inadequacies."

"You're lucky we're friends or I would file a complaint."

He shrugged. "I don't know why you don't find me funny. Most people think I'm hilarious!"

"Most people don't know you like I know you. So, don't make jokes like that. Your locker room humor is best left in the locker room."

He laughed. "So, what's new with you? You've been oddly quiet tonight."

"Like anyone can get a word in with you," Neema quipped.

"Nah! I'm not going to take ownership of that. You have never had a problem having your say. That's how I know something's up with you. So, what is it?"

Neema shrugged. "Nothing's changed. My life is as boring as ever."

"You dating anyone?"

She shot him a chilly look.

Tiger laughed. "I only ask because Heather will ask me. Personally, I don't much care if you're making some poor guy's life miserable. But that wife of mine will give me grief if I don't ask and give her something when I get home."

"I hate you!"

He blew her a kiss. "Right back atcha, my friend."

"No, I'm not dating anyone," she said.

She suddenly thought about Davis Black and his request to have dinner with her. She gasped. Loudly. Her cheeks flushed with heat and she could feel Tiger eyeing her intently.

His smile widened. "You don't lie well. Who is he?"

"It's no one. And I try not to lie at all, thank you very much."

"There's something you're not telling," he said, his tone ringing with amusement.

Neema changed the subject. "What do you know about Alexander Balducci?"

"Please, tell me you are not dating that criminal!"

"He was having dinner last night at my father's restaurant. I was thinking there might be a story there."

"Be careful, please. Balducci is notorious for his crimes, but he's never been caught because he works very hard not to get his own hands dirty. The man is deadly, but no one will turn on him."

"Why is that?"

"They're scared. Balducci doesn't play nice. I thought for sure he'd go down last year in that sex trafficking scandal. Everyone knew he had something to do with it, but one of his kids took all the blame."

"I doubt his son *took* the blame. He could have just been guilty."

"Trust me, rubbing Balducci the wrong way could get you hurt. That's not a man you want to play games with. His kids won't even roll over on him! So, why are you asking about him?"

"Just curious," Neema answered. She thought briefly about sharing what she'd seen but decided against it. She didn't have enough information to give any credibility to her suspicions. She also didn't want to risk anyone trying to usurp her lead and steal her story, even if she did consider them a friend.

The police scanner suddenly crackled with a call coming in over the radio. Gunshots and a body near the downtown area required a heavy police presence. Neema tossed Tiger a quick look as he revved the car's engine, spinning the vehicle out of the parking space. As they slid into traffic, her friend called her name.

"Yes?"

Tiger gave her a bright smile. "So, who is he? You know you can tell me!"

Neema laughed heartily and ignored the question.

Chapter 4

Davis was pacing the floor, barely able to contain his excitement. He was a good hour from his morning appointment with Adamu Kamau and hopeful that the man's beautiful daughter would be joining them. She hadn't answered any of his messages and he couldn't help but think he had become a full-blown nuisance with his persistence.

It had been a good long while since any woman had captured his attention. Unlike his brothers, Davis was not as popular with the ladies as they were. Since high school, he'd bombed with the opposite sex more times than not. He was the brother who would get tongue-tied around women, even stumble over lines he'd practiced alone in front of the bathroom mirror.

His last relationship had survived all of six weeks. Fiona owned a chain of women's clothing stores that catered to females who weren't a size two. She'd been attractive, and bossy, and he'd been intrigued. Things had gone well between them right up until the moment he'd introduced her to Ellington.

They'd run into his family while dining out one evening and his brother had stopped by the table to say hello. Ellington had been ultra-charming, and it had taken all of ten minutes for Fiona to dismiss Davis from her life, hoping against all odds that his sibling would return her interest. She'd been obnoxious about it, flirting with his brother as if Davis weren't even there. She'd thrown herself at Ellington. Hard. Davis's only saving grace was the loyalty he and his siblings had for each other. Ellington had shut her down. Equally as hard. And that night had been the last time either of them had seen her.

Now, here he was, excited at the prospect of seeing Neema again. His excitement had manifested into nervous energy and he suddenly couldn't sit still. He moved to the window to look out on the street. The day was overcast and the temperatures had dropped substantially. Despite the weather forecast that predicted a twenty percent chance of light rain, it felt like snow was in the air. A gust of wind blew debris across the street, a candy wrapper landing on a small patch of grass at the edge of the sidewalk.

Davis returned to his oversize desk; he had a ton of work that he could be doing. Starting with figuring out his schedule for the month. He already had two interviews on his calendar, desperately needing a new assistant. Then there was the town hall meeting for an incumbent senator, a ribbon-cutting for a new business opening, and the kindergarten fun run at the neighborhood elementary school. He also couldn't forget his questionable art gallery jaunt to buy the requested artwork for Balducci. Between his responsibilities to the city and the hopes he had for his social agenda, his mother had called a family meeting. A gathering he had no intention of attending.

Davis loved his family and his mother was everything to him. But, admittedly, he was having a difficult time now that the dynamic of their family tree had shifted so drastically. He kept circling back to his mother having such a vicious secret that would never have come out had her back not been up against a wall. In Vegas, his brothers had joked that, despite them all being displaced in the family lineup, he was still the baby of the family. But now, being the eighth kid in line for the family inheritance instead of the seventh, his slice of the Black family pie had gotten a little slimmer.

He hadn't found their teasing amusing. Not that he was at all concerned that his mother's new son would somehow usurp his position in the family, but having held her in such high regard, everything about his mother's secret now tarnished the gold pedestal he'd placed her on. He had never before felt that his mother was imperfect. Now, suddenly, the matriarch was as flawed as anyone else. Davis heaved a heavy sigh, suddenly feeling bad about the thoughts that had sprung into his head.

He reached for a folder atop his desk and began to shift through the paperwork inside. There were at least a dozen proposals that needed his attention, so he figured he would read until the Kamau family arrived. Reading specs would keep him focused and out of his feelings.

It was a few minutes past the ten o'clock hour when Neema and her father stepped through the door to Davis's office. He stood abruptly, moving toward the entrance to greet them. Mr. Kamau was fussing, unhappy that they hadn't arrived fifteen minutes earlier. An apology streamed past his lips as he rushed to shake Davis's hand.

"No apology necessary, sir. I know that traffic can be a bear this time of the morning."

"You are too kind," Mr. Kamau stated. "My Neema said you would understand."

Davis turned, locking gazes with the young woman. Her dusky orbs shimmered, the light dancing across her dark complexion. She wore a simple white blouse beneath a tailored navy-blue jacket with denim jeans. A vibrant orange-and-white scarf was draped stylishly around her neck and gold hoop earrings complemented her closely cropped hair.

She is the most beautiful woman, he thought.

"Good morning, Neema," he said, his full lips lifted in a warm smile. He felt himself blush, suddenly embarrassed that he was feeling adolescent-giddy.

Neema smiled back. "Good morning." Her soft tone was like a gentle brush of air against his ear. "It's good to see you again."

There was a moment of pause as the two stood staring at each other. Davis didn't miss the look the patriarch was giving them as he glanced from one to the other, his eyebrows raised.

Davis cleared his throat. "Why don't we have a seat?" He gestured toward the two upholstered chairs in front of his desk. "Can I offer either of you a cup of coffee?"

"No, thank you." The two chimed in unison as they sat. Neema's father reached a large hand out and patted his daughter's shoulder.

Davis moved behind his desk. "So, Mr. Kamau, you said you were concerned about the drug activity on your street. Have you reported it to your local police precinct?"

"We have done that. Yes. And it has been much improved, although there are moments with these young boys who think that fast lifestyle is their only option. They are rude and disrespectful! They will sometimes cuss their own mothers. It is shameful! I believe that it is important we give them other options."

"I agree, sir. It's already been proved that positive social outlets allow young people to refocus their attention in a healthy manner. You may not be aware, but we have the Chicago Youth Centers here, which is dedicated to supporting at-risk youth in the city. There are currently six locations, one right here in Humboldt Park. They're doing some amazing things with our kids."

Mr. Kamau nodded. "I am sure some of these boys are approaching eighteen or older. Do they still qualify for those programs?"

Davis shook his head. "Unfortunately not. Once they turn eighteen, they're legally considered adults."

"Humph," the older man grunted softly.

"But there are other organizations working to help them with school or employment," Davis added. "So, there are other options available to them."

"So how do we move those young boys who aren't eighteen off the corner where they're being disruptive and into a center?" Neema asked, her gaze narrowed. Until her question, she'd been sitting quietly, eyeing Davis intently.

Davis shifted his gaze to stare back. "I can request increased police presence. I can also personally visit and talk with them. Sometimes all it takes is showing them that someone cares about what happens to them."

Mr. Kamau gave him a nod. "How can I and the other home and business owners help?"

Davis reached for a flyer atop his desk. He passed it to the man. "There will be a community town hall in the upcoming weeks. I hope you'll come and encourage others in your neighborhood to attend, as well. The more families there, voicing their concerns, the better."

"Yes! We will do that," Mr. Kamau said.

For the next few minutes Davis talked, the conversation between him and Mr. Kamau as easy as the flow of water. The topic shifted from community interests to the national political climate. They also talked food, television and pop culture. Before any of them realized it, a whole hour had passed them by.

During the chat, Neema had studied him keenly. Something like amusement painted her expression and, when Davis realized he was being scrutinized, he'd found himself feeling anxious again. He'd shot her an occasional glance but kept his focus on her father, even if it had been a struggle.

Mr. Kamau stood and extended his hand. "I appreciate you taking time out of your busy schedule to speak with us. We didn't mean to take up so much of your time."

Davis stood with him, the two men shaking hands. "It's been my pleasure, sir. I appreciate you voicing your concerns and, more importantly, wanting to be part of the solution."

He turned, his arm sliding out in Neema's direction. Their palms touched, skin gliding sweetly against skin, and a current of energy surged like a firestorm between them. Davis held on to her fingers a second longer than necessary, not wanting to let go.

* * *

Neema found herself holding her breath to stall the rise of heat that was suddenly consuming her. She gasped, her breath catching deep in her lungs. She snatched her hand from his, feeling out of sorts as she tried to play it off, pretending the simple gesture wasn't anything more.

"Is your invitation for dinner still open?" Neema questioned as they moved toward the exit. She'd folded her arms across her chest, her hands tucked beneath her armpits.

Davis smiled, his lips lifting to a full, deep grin. "It is. It definitely is!"

"Does seven o'clock work for you?"

"It does."

"I'll text you my address."

"So, you do text," Davis said, chuckling softly. "I was starting to wonder."

Neema smiled a little too sweetly. "I text when I have something to say."

"So, you were ignoring me."

She laughed. "I was."

Her father stood watching, his gaze shifting back and forth as if he were observing a tennis match. He seemed to find them entertaining, saying nothing as the two blatantly flirted with each other.

Neema was slightly self-conscious as the patriarch gave her a look. She shook her head. "I don't eat seafood," she concluded as she stepped through the door.

Mr. Kamau leaned closer to Davis, his voice dropping to a loud whisper. "My Neema is allergic to seafood. And to peanuts. Be mindful what you feed her. That one is my whole heart, and her mother and I would be devastated if anything happened to her."

"Yes, sir."

"And my Neema is a very good girl. Do nothing to tarnish her reputation or disgrace our family name."

"Yes, sir," Davis said.

"We hope to find her a good husband. Someone worthy who will treat her well. She will make a good wife. She's a very good cook, keeps a clean home and has promised her mother many grandchildren!"

In the doorway, Neema stood wide-eyed, her expression aghast. Her cheeks were a heated deep shade of embarrassed and she felt her heart palpitating like a high school drum line. "Baba!" Neema tossed her hands up in exasperation. "Unbelievable," she exclaimed.

The two men laughed, the wealth of the sound chasing after her as Neema spun on her orange-leather pumps and scurried back to her car.

Neema had a plan. Or at least the semblance of a plan, she thought as she stared at her reflection in the full-length mirror. Having a plan was the only reason she had agreed to dinner with the man. Dinner would open the door to that story she needed to boost her career. Dinner would be a game changer. At least, that's what Neema had been trying to convince herself of since she began getting dressed. Why else would she be excited about having dinner with Davis Black? And trying to convince herself that getting to know him was only a means to an end?

Granted, she'd been mesmerized at their meeting. The alderman had made quite an impression on her and her father. Not only was he intelligent, but it seemed that he also had a compassionate heart. He was likeable and she fully understood the campaign slogan that had described him as "good people." Their time together had made her want to know him better. Even if her agenda wasn't quite on the up-and-up.

So why was she feeling so out of sorts? Neema wondered. Why was she second-guessing herself? It wasn't like they were good friends or seriously dating. She just wanted to discover for herself whether Davis Black was as upstanding as he professed to be. Or if his campaign slogan was a lie. If there was a side to his persona that kept him tied to criminals like Alexander Balducci. A side secreted away from everyone else. It was her journalistic duty, she thought to herself.

The reflection staring back at her didn't look convinced. Neema slid her hands down the length of her silk dress, newly purchased for just this occasion. The price tag was still hanging from the sleeve. Searching the top drawer of her nightstand, she found a pair of craft scissors and used them to cut it free of the garment. She shook her head, unable to believe that she'd paid such an exorbitant price for the designer dress. But it was pretty, looked amazing on her slim frame, and she wanted to make a memorable impression at dinner.

"This is not a date!" Neema muttered under her breath as she headed out the door. "This is anything but a date!"

"I'm glad you agreed to this date," Davis said as he guided the way into Oriole. The two Michelin-starred restaurant was well hidden, the entrance off the back alley of a loading dock side street in Chicago's West Loop neighborhood. Its vibe was slightly unnerving and Neema couldn't help but wonder if they were in the right place. Only seating twenty-eight in an intimate dining room with its open kitchen made the restaurant a culinary favorite, the reservations list miles long.

"My parents love this place," he was saying as Neema eyed him with furrowed brow. "It's one of my mother's favorites, and the last time I was here, I had a spectacular meal."

He pressed a large hand to the small of her back as he maneuvered her into a freight elevator to reach the restaurant. The ride was dark and shaky at best, but Neema barely noticed, solely focused on the nearness of him. His touch was gentle, and brief, but left Neema nicely heated. She took a slight step from him, hoping the disconcertion didn't show on her face. She bit down against her bottom lip to stall the rise of anxiety that suddenly flooded her spirit.

As they stepped into the dining room, it was clear that Davis had chosen well. The ambience was warm and inviting, the lighting setting a whole mood against the wide-open kitchen at the far end of the room. With the brick walls, exposed timber ceiling, and banquette seating, it was intimate and comfortable.

"I've read the reviews," Neema said as her gaze skated around the room. "I never gave any thought to trying it, though."

"Really? Was there something about the menu that turned you off?"

"The price per plate, for starters!"

Davis laughed. "I admit, it's a bit pricey. But I'm showing off—you know that, right?"

"Burgers and fries would have done the job just as well."

He gave a slight shrug of his shoulders then shook his head. "No, that dress you're wearing required a five-star meal!" And it did, he thought, the formfitting red silk accentuating her slight curves. Its plunging neckline teased the round of her small breasts and the vibrant color against her dark complexion was jaw-dropping. She was stunning, and it took every ounce of his fortitude not to stare.

Neema smiled, holding her comment as the hostess, a tall blonde with ocean-blue eyes, greeted them warmly. The woman called him by name.

"Welcome, Alderman Black. Your table is ready, sir."

"Thank you, Lena. How are you this evening?"

"Well, thank you. And yourself?"

"I have no complaints."

The young woman named gave them both a bright smile as she led them to a corner table adorned with simple white linens.

"This is very nice," Neema said as Davis pulled out her chair.

"So, I've done good so far?"

"I'll reserve judgment, but it seems to be headed in the right direction."

"I can see you're not going to give me any slack, are you?"

"Should I?"

"I've never backed away from a challenge. I look forward to proving myself worthy," he answered, his expression smug.

Neema groaned, her eyes skyward as she took her seat.

Their server suddenly appeared as if by magic and welcomed them to what would prove to be an extraordinary eighteen-course meal. The first dish of paper-thin slices of seared scallops capped with dabs of caviar, a rye crisp and an egg yolk turned into gelato by a Pacojet set the stage for what would come. Eight courses in, they were swooning over the truffle-kissed fettuccine blanketed with hand-grated, toasted rye berries.

The tenth course was Davis's favorite. He had dipped grilled Icelandic steelhead trout topped with smoked roe into a rich artichoke-marjoram broth. They agreed the Thai-influenced chilled Alaska king crab dish with bursts of Cara Cara oranges in a milky Vidalia onion soup was a close second to being both their favorite.

"So, tell me…" Neema began. "You and Mr. Balducci…are you good friends?"

"We're definitely are not friends," Davis said sternly. "He and my father are friends. Why do you ask?"

She shrugged. "Just curious. He has quite the reputation. My father says he's done a lot of good in the community. And you two appeared close the other night."

Davis dropped into a moment of thought before he responded. "No, that was actually my first time being in his company since I was maybe ten or eleven. He had a business proposal he wanted to run by me. That's the only reason I was there. But he's not someone I have a whole lot of respect for."

"Why is that?"

Davis paused. "It's a long story for another time. It would kill our good mood, so let's talk about something else. Please."

"I'm sorry," Neema said softly. "I didn't mean to pry."

"No apology necessary," he said as he changed the subject.

Between the decadent dishes the conversation was easy. They asked each other questions, enjoying the opportunity to get to know one another. It was an engaging give-and-take where both felt heard and respected.

"I've never been to East Africa," Davis said, "but it's on my bucket list."

"I think you would like it. My parents and I go to Kenya every year to visit family."

"One of my college roommates was from Kenya. He said the same thing. We used to have some interesting conversations about the philosophical differences between Black Africans and Black Americans. And the disdain they sometimes have for each other."

Her brow lifted. "I imagine that was interesting."

"It was. It gave me a different perspective in how I saw things. When he and I first met, I didn't think we could ever be friends. He was standoffish and I thought he was looking down his nose at me. I later discovered he thought the same thing about me. We were the best of friends after that."

"Well, what I discovered in my travels is that people abroad have limited perceptions about Black Americans. And those perceptions are sometimes negative. In Africa, people are usually learning about Black Americans from missionaries who visit the country and most of them are white men. They're told that Black American women are loud, rude and incorrigible, and that as a people we are typically lazy, abusive and incapable of profound thinking. It was also disheartening to see their reactions when I told them that despite my Kenyan heritage, I was a Black American woman. I'm very proud to be a first-generation American, but for many in my family, I should only think of myself as Kenyan."

"It all plays into the negative stereotypes the media continues to perpetuate. People don't know what to expect when they never see us in a positive light in books and movies, which is a whole other conversation," Davis said, resignation fueling his words.

Neema continued. "What I discovered, though, is that Africans don't want to hear that their brothers in

America are failing. They don't want to believe the poison being spewed by the media and missionaries and even some tourists. They have grand expectations that we are doing well and being successful."

Davis nodded. "It's amazing what getting to know a person will do for you. We can erase so many stereotypes by simply talking to each other."

"So, why politics? I'm surprised that you didn't follow your father into law enforcement."

"I thought about it. But my mother encouraged me to get a law degree. Then I couldn't pass the Illinois state bar."

Neema laughed, pulling her hand to her mouth to muffle the sound. She had a beautiful laugh, joyful and slightly silly. The wealth of her mirth filled the room, drawing others to stare and smile in their direction. "I'm so sorry," she gasped. "You probably don't think that's funny."

Davis chuckled. "Quite the contrary. I think it's hilarious now! I've taken that exam three times. I finally just gave up. I've never tested well. It's truly a miracle that I made it out of high school and college. After my last failing, I took a short sabbatical and that's when I met Congressman Harris. I was one of his interns and realized I could make a bigger difference on the front lines, fighting for people's rights. He encouraged me to run for public office."

"And you enjoy being an alderman?"

"I do. Very much."

"So, what's next? Mayor? Governor? President?"

Davis laughed. "I need to get through my current term first. Then we'll see. Have you ever thought about being First Lady?"

"Aren't you funny!" Neema laughed.

Davis laughed with her. He reached for his wine-glass and took a sip of the beverage paired with the last course. It was a woody 2011 Cascina delle Rose Barbaresco served with paper-thin slivers of Mishima rib eye.

"But enough about me," Davis said as he rested his glass back against the tabletop. "I want to know more about you."

Neema shrugged. "There's really nothing to tell."

"Have you always wanted to be in the restaurant business? Or do you work with your parents by default?"

"Definitely default. Don't you know a good daughter honors her parents by giving up her life to live their dreams and wishes?"

"Do I hear a hint of resentment in your voice, Neema Kamau?"

"Not at all," she said facetiously.

Davis chuckled. "Have you ever done anything else? Or wanted to do anything else? What's Neema's dream?"

Neema hesitated for a split second, considering her answer before she spoke. She wanted to tell him about her journalism degree and her job at the paper. She didn't want to lie, but omitting a few key facts in her bio wouldn't be that bad. Telling him, she reasoned, might compromise her getting the story, if there was a story to be found. But why, she thought, did it feel so darn wrong?

She sighed softly and smiled. "I'm actually very happy with the choices I've made for my life. Don't let my snark give you the wrong impression."

Davis nodded. "So, do you waitress every night?"

She paused a second time, wanting to choose her

words carefully. "Not every night. I'm not waitressing tonight obviously."

"That's good," Davis said, his smile beaming. "Because I would really like to see you again. Maybe dinner tomorrow?"

Her laughter rang around the room once again. "We haven't even had dessert yet and you're already planning our next date," she said, the four-letter word slipping off her tongue before she could catch it.

Davis's wide grin filled his face. "I like dating."

Neema's eyes widened. "Do you date often?" she asked, curiosity filling the space between them.

"No. But I am hoping to date *you* often." His expression was smug as they locked gazes that held for a quick few minutes.

Neema blinked the moment away. "I'd be willing to bet you have many girlfriends, Alderman Black."

"You'd lose that bet. Badly. Women tend to throw me into the friend zone real quick."

"Is that a bad thing? To be a woman's friend?"

"No, not at all. But it would be nice to be more than a friend." His gaze dropped as he drifted into thought, memories of past relationships likely flashing through his mind like snapshots.

A moment of quiet bloomed full and thick between them. Neema stared, her eyes locked on his face as she studied the emotion that painted his expression. His brow was creased and there was the slightest twitch at the corner of his mouth. His mustache and the faintest hint of a beard had been meticulously edged. She suddenly wanted to reach out and trail her fingers along the line of his profile.

Their server saved her from embarrassing herself.

"Enjoy your dessert," the young man named Todd

said as he presented them with two plates that were visually spectacular.

The reputation of the restaurant's pastry chef and co-owner, Genie Kwon, had preceded her, every review written worshipping her confections. The night's dessert was an edible, crispy-wafer cylinder filled with a creamy sauce of white chocolate, milk chocolate and hazelnut, with caramelized banana chips and hits of lemon sauce and caramelized goat yogurt. The rich, decadent mixture melted against their tongues.

Neema heard herself moan. "This is divine!" she said, her voice a loud whisper. She leaned in close to him, the gesture feeling slightly conspiratorial.

Davis nodded in agreement, licking the last drop of chocolate from his spoon. "I think this dessert is officially my favorite course of the whole meal."

Neema held up her hand and gave him a high five. "I know it's mine," she responded.

Another hour passed as the two continued chatting. Neema discovered that Davis was far more conservative than she'd initially imagined. He believed in the concept of traditional roles for men and women, and he felt that chivalry was on a serious decline. He was very much a mama's boy, but in a good way. He held his parents in high regard and it was important to him that his actions always make them proud. He told her stories about his siblings, and it was clear they all shared a tightly knit bond. Being an only child, Neema was slightly jealous and said so.

"I wanted brothers and sisters. I used to pretend that my parents adopted all my dolls and they were my family. Then I'd boss them around."

Davis laughed. "Your parents didn't want more children?"

"My mother couldn't have any more. She developed preeclampsia with me, and the pregnancy was deemed high-risk. My father says he almost lost both of us and he would never put my mother through that again."

For a moment, Davis thought about his mother and the son she'd kept hidden. He considered telling Neema but didn't, despite the level of comfort he was feeling with her. Because he was comfortable, and he liked that he wanted to be open and transparent with her. To build a foundation of honesty and trust as they navigated the newness of their relationship. But that bit of family business wasn't public, and it would have breached his mother's privacy. Although he would have welcomed the opportunity to express what he was feeling, this was neither the time nor the place. He said instead, "My brothers are my best friends."

"And your sisters?"

"Bossy and Nosey are like two additional parents!"

Neema grinned. She suddenly looked around the room, realizing that they were the last two customers. Staff was clearing away the other tables and readying the space for the next day. "What time is it?" she questioned, her eyes wide as she reached for her cell phone."

Davis looked down at his own watch. "It's late. I hope I haven't kept you past your curfew?"

"Aren't you funny," Neema said, shooting him a smirk. "But I really do need to be going."

Davis waved his credit card in the air, gesturing for their server's attention. "I had a great time tonight. I meant it when I asked about dinner again."

Neema sat back in her seat, her hands clasped together in her lap. "I'd like that. I'd like that a lot."

"Tomorrow then?"

She laughed heartily. "I have to work tomorrow."

"What are you doing Friday evening? Would you be interested in going to an art show with me?"

"An art show?"

Davis nodded. "I have an old friend who has a show opening at the Taylor Gallery downtown. I was planning to go to show her my support. I'd love for you to go with me."

"An *old* friend?" Neema quizzed, silently noting that he wanted to show "her" some support. "Is this an old girlfriend?"

"More like a sister," Davis said with a soft chuckle.

She nodded, her expression smug as they stared at each other. A moment later, Neema said, "I look forward to meeting your friend."

Davis grinned. "Then it's a date!"

Chapter 5

Neema waved goodbye as Davis pulled his car from in front of her home and back onto the roadway. She had less than an hour to change her clothes and report to the office for her late-night shift. She'd already texted Tiger to let him know she was going to be late and she knew if she just headed to work in the dress she was wearing, he'd have questions she wasn't interested in answering.

As the car's taillights disappeared around the corner, she pushed open the front door and hurried inside. Bounding swiftly up the two flights of stairs, she was grateful her parents were still at the restaurant and not home to put her through an inquisition about her night out.

After kicking off her shoes, she pulled the dress up and over her head, dropping it to the floor. She snatched a pair of denim jeans and a knit tunic from a laundry basket of clean clothes and quickly dressed. Less than fifteen minutes after Davis had dropped her home, Neema was out the door again, headed to work.

Thinking about her evening had Neema knee-deep in her emotions. She was feeling out of sorts and trying to understand why was proving to be a challenge. She'd had a really great time. So much so, she completely forgot why she had agreed to the date in the first place. Hoping to get dirt on the man had taken a back seat to getting to know him. And in getting to know him, Neema had discovered that the more she learned, the more she wanted to know. Because she liked Davis Black. She liked him a lot. And liking Davis hadn't been in her plans.

She huffed softly to herself as she turned onto East Illinois Street toward North Michigan Avenue. She was only a few short minutes from work and all she could think about was the time she and Davis had shared. And how she'd wished they could have spent more time together. She'd had fun and it had been a long while since she'd had fun with any man. Ages since she'd allowed herself to relax and just enjoy the moment with a date.

Dating had never been a priority for Neema, despite her mother's efforts to pair her up with the sons of all her friends. Had her parents been able, they would have arranged a union for her years ago. But Neema had balked at the idea, having been less than enthusiastic about putting marriage and children before her career. She'd had plans that hadn't involved a partner and nothing her parents said or did had changed her mind.

Her last date had been with the son of her mother's hairstylist. An emergency room physician, he'd been nice, but annoying. His idea of an ideal relationship was a barefoot and pregnant spouse who had no ambition that didn't revolve around him and his needs. He couldn't understand why Neema would have wanted more. An hour into the meal, she'd been ready to leave. Once she was out the door, she'd vowed to never do that to herself ever again.

Davis had been attentive, and funny, and she imagined that if she'd been wholeheartedly honest with him, he would have been encouraging. Everything about him said that he would be supportive of her dreams and ambitions. When he had talked about his mother and his sisters, he had been proud of their accomplishments and respected that they wanted more for themselves. He considered that a favorable attribute for a woman to have, believing she could have it all if she wanted. But she hadn't been honest. She'd been evasive and omissive, purposely allowing him to believe that her future was in her parent's restaurant. That her dream was to carry on the family business. That she had no other aspirations, which was far from the truth.

As she pulled into an empty parking space and shifted her car into Park, Neema couldn't help but wonder what Davis would think of her if he were ever to learn the truth. How much would Davis Black hate her? Because in that moment, with all of it spinning like a storm wind in her head, Neema didn't like herself much at all.

Davis wanted to call Neema but tossed his phone to the other end of the sofa. He was feeling out of sorts, like a teenager with his first crush. Wanting to call Neema had him anxious and excited like it was Christmas Eve and Santa had promised him the best present. He chuckled softly as he reached for the device, deciding instead to send a quick text message to thank her for a wonderful evening.

There was no denying their attraction. Had anyone been paying close attention, they would have noticed that there was something decadent growing sweetly between him and her. Something that seemed to just rise out of nowhere to take control of their good senses and render them both foolish. Davis imagined he would claim that it was nothing at all and she would simply ignore any questions and comments about the two of them. But neither could ever honestly deny that their nothing was actually something, and it was bigger than either would ever be able to find the words for. It would mean admitting that their something left them tongue-tied and silly, imagining all kinds of what-ifs and maybes.

Davis held the phone in the palm of his hand for a good ten minutes, hoping for a quick response. When none came, he tossed the device back against the cushions. He imagined Neema was probably fast asleep. Then he felt bad that he may have disturbed her rest.

"What is wrong with me, Titus?" he said, talking to the large Rottweiler who lay sleeping at his feet. The dog lifted his head for a split second then lay back down, ignoring him. Davis sighed, a loud gust of breath blowing past his lips. He reached to scratch behind the dog's ears. Titus snuggled his muzzle against the palm of Davis's hand.

"She's pretty special, Titus," he said, talking out loud. "I can't wait for you two to meet each other. You're usually a pretty good judge of character, so I trust you'll let me know what you think about her."

The dog grunted. Or maybe passed gas. Davis wasn't quite sure which, nor was he interested in knowing. "A lot of help you are," he muttered as he gave the animal one last scratch as he stepped over him and headed for the bedroom.

Leaving a trail of clothes from the bedroom door into the master bathroom, he turned on the shower and waited for the water to warm before stepping inside. He kept playing the entire evening over in his head, trying to recall each gesture and every comment. It had been a good time. A really good time, although he sensed that she had been slightly reserved. He wasn't sure what to attribute that to because he sensed she had enjoyed herself as much as he had. At least, that was what he hoped.

Ending the evening and taking Neema home had been disheartening. He hadn't wanted to say good-night. He'd enjoyed talking with her. She had a keen sense of humor and a flirtatious spirit. She'd made him laugh and he'd found their conversations engaging. He'd been comfortable with her. So much so that he'd let his guard down, telling her things about himself that he would not have necessarily shared with just anyone.

Davis pressed his palms against the tiled wall and leaned into the spray of hot water. Closing his eyes, he tilted his head beneath the flow, allowing it to rain down the length of his body. He let himself fall into a moment of reverie, allowing his mind to clear.

Minutes later, he slathered his body with vanilla-scented soap suds. The aroma was clean and fresh, elevating his mood even more. As he wiped a loofah sponge across his skin, he thought about his next steps, considering where he and Neema might go for dinner after the gallery showing. Thinking about when he should call her next. And he thought of introducing her to his family, but promptly tabled that idea. He knew he was getting ahead of himself, yet somehow it felt right to consider the possibilities. Because Neema

Kamau had gotten under his skin, like an itch that was bone-deep and had his full attention.

The sound of glass breaking and the dog barking startled him. Cutting off the shower, Davis paused for a quick minute to listen. Titus was barking and growling, sensing a danger that Davis couldn't yet see. He grabbed a large white towel and wrapped it around his waist. Stepping into the bedroom, he moved to the nightstand and pulled a 9-millimeter pistol from the drawer. He did a quick check to make sure a round of ammunition was chambered.

He peered out the bedroom door, down the length of hallway toward the living room. Titus looked like a small bear, the hairs of his thick coat bristling around his large neck. He stood imposingly, his hind legs stacked back, his broad chest pushed forward, as if prepared to pounce. When he spied Davis, he barked again, the deep tone vibrating through the room. Davis eased in beside the dog, noting the broken glass littering the hardwood floor. Someone, or something, had shattered the sidelight of his front door.

Davis snatched the door open, the dog and he both moving through the entrance into the front yard. His weapon was raised as he checked left and then right. The street was quiet, nothing out of the ordinary catching his attention. Across the way, his neighbor's lights were on and he could see the elderly couple through their front window, the two watching television. He took a bracing inhale of the late-night air, holding it deep in his lungs before releasing it in a slow breath. Titus stood close to his side, panting softly. Giving him a gentle pat, Davis took one last look up and down the street before commanding him back inside the home.

Closing and locking the door, Davis surveyed the

mess. He couldn't begin to know who would have purposely vandalized his house. Turning from the foyer, he moved into the living room, trying to ascertain what had happened. And that's when he saw the bullet hole; a dead-center piercing of the painting hanging on the wall beside his fireplace.

"There were two shots fired," the police forensic specialist reported to Detective Armstrong Black. "They entered from the outside through the sidelight. One lodged in the painting and the other lodged in the wall beside the painting's frame."

"Mom gifted me that painting," Davis snapped. He stood with his arms folded, his annoyance clearly evident. "Now there's a canyon-size hole in the middle of it."

"You're lucky there's no hole in you," Mingus snapped back.

Davis had called the police, his brothers showing up on his doorstep with a quickness that would have surprised others. Armstrong had immediately taken up the investigation, barking out orders to the officers reporting to him. Mingus and Ellington had arrived in the same car, both hovering over Davis as if he'd been shot. When their father arrived, Davis knew that, despite his assertions that he was okay, there would be no dismissal of the seriousness of the situation.

"What do we have?" Superintendent Black asked, looking from one to the other.

"Two shots fired," Armstrong answered. "It appears to have been a drive-by. We're pulling all the camera footage in the area now to see if we can find anything."

"Did your doorbell camera catch anything?" Jerome asked, shooting his youngest son a look.

"I haven't had a chance to install it," Davis said, suddenly feeling like he was headed into an interrogation. "It's still in the box."

"Your mother and I didn't give it to you to keep in the box." His father's gaze narrowed. "So, who'd you piss off this week?"

Davis shrugged. "I don't have a clue who would do something like this."

"Mingus said you had a date tonight. What do you know about this woman? She doesn't have a scorned boyfriend or lover who might have it in for you, does she?"

"No," Davis said. He cut his eye toward Mingus, his brother avoiding his stare. "She doesn't have anything to do with this."

"You don't know that," Armstrong interjected.

"Yes, I do," Davis retorted, his curt tone moving them all to stare at him.

Mingus chuckled. "It's like that, huh?"

"Shut up, Mingus!" Davis snapped.

The brothers all shot each other a look. An awkward silence rippled around the room. Jerome threw his hands up in frustration. "I'm not sure what's going on, but we don't need you boys at each other's throats right now. Mingus, see what they're saying in the streets. If someone's put a hit out on your brother, I want to know about it yesterday."

Mingus nodded. "Yes, sir. I'm on it."

"Where's Parker?"

"Stomach flu," Armstrong answered. "I'm keeping him in the loop."

"I expect you to run point then. Pull whoever you need to help you. And let's keep the lid on this. I don't want the media running with some story that may ruffle someone's feathers and put your brother in greater harm."

"Is all this necessary?" Davis asked. His father shot him a look that made him take a step back, his lips pursed tightly together as he fell silent.

"You must have a death wish," Ellington muttered under his breath.

The brothers all chuckled as Davis eyeballed the ceiling.

Jerome shook his head. "You just keep your head down and try to stay out of trouble, please," he said, reaching to pull his son into a tight hug and tapping him on his back. The relief that flooded the patriarch's body was corporeal, feeling as if it slapped the wind from Davis's lungs.

"And let's try to figure out who did this before we tell your mother. I don't need her worrying."

"Yes, sir," the brothers all echoed in unison.

Tiger shoved the last bite of a donut into his mouth. He was following a thread of messages on his cell phone when he jumped with excitement.

"What?" Neema quizzed as she looked up from her device and a game of Candy Crush.

Starting the engine, Tiger tossed his cell phone into her lap. "There's police activity at the alderman's house."

"Which alderman?" Neema snatched up the phone to read the message. "What activity? And why didn't it come across the police scanner?"

For the casual observer, the text was cryptic at best, one of Tiger's informants in the police department sending him the tip. Neema knew enough to decipher the message:

911 at home of official Black. No eyes. Powers keeping it in the family.

Neema knew that the "official" was Alderman Davis Black and the "powers" were probably his father and brother, senior members of the police force. Suddenly her nerves were on overload. Why were the police at his home? And why were they trying to keep it from getting out? What had happened to Davis?

Minutes later, Tiger pulled his car in behind a Chicago police vehicle. "Let's see what we can find out," he said as he shut down the engine and swung open the door.

"I'm going to let you handle this one," Neema said, fighting to keep anxiety out of her voice. "It's your turn. I grabbed the last byline."

"You sure?"

"Take it," she said. "I'll make a few calls and see what I can find out from here."

"How does that work?" her friend said sarcastically.

"You're not the only one with contacts in the police department," she said.

Tiger extended his hand and they bumped fists.

"Hurry back," Neema advised. "If the story's good, we can make the morning paper."

Tiger gave her a thumbs-up, slammed the door, and headed for the officers standing on the front lawn.

The night was clear, a full moon and a spattering of stars illuminating the dark sky. The neighbors were awake, everyone's porch lights on as they peered out through their windows to see what was going on. The streetlights were bright, and all of it came together to make visibility easier. Neema slid down in the seat, pulling the baseball cap she wore low on her head. She was grateful for the tinted windows as she peered past the brim, eyeing the officers that moved in and out of the home's front door.

Davis suddenly stood in the entrance and Neema gasped. Loudly. He was standing shirtless, despite the chill in the air. He was even barefoot, only wearing a pair of gray sweatpants. His lean frame was ripped, rock-hard muscles beneath taut skin. He was beautiful, she thought as she imagined her palms pressed against his broad chest. She bit down on her bottom lip to stall the wave of emotion that had flooded her feminine spirit. He was also alive, and seemingly well, and for that she released a sigh of relief. But his expression was pained, and Neema sensed that whatever had happened had unsettled him.

He suddenly seemed to be looking in her direction. She sank lower in the seat and whispered a silent prayer that she wouldn't be discovered. She'd be devastated if she were outed before she had an opportunity to explain. And she couldn't begin to imagine what he would think to discover her this way. It was then that she saw the large Rottweiler at the edge of the lawn. The dog was sniffing the grass before lifting his back leg to christen an overgrown holly bush. He was solid muscle with a short, black coat and distinctive rust markings. Davis spoke and the dog moved swiftly behind him, the two disappearing into the home. Neema released the breath she hadn't realized she'd been holding.

Tiger suddenly flung open the driver's-side door, almost throwing himself into the seat. "I got it," he said as he started the engine.

"What happened?" she asked.

"Drive-by shooting. It took out the alderman's door, but no one was injured."

Neema gasped. "The door?"

"Well, you know, that decorative glass on the side.
I could never figure out what the attraction is. As far
as I'm concerned, it's nothing but a peephole for nosey
neighbors!" He shrugged.

Neema shook her head. "Do they have any leads?"

Tiger shook his head. "No, and top cop himself put
out a gag order. The official word is that they have no
comment."

"You plan to write it anyway?"

"Nope! I got an exclusive. When they're ready to release the information, we get first dibs."

"They promised you that?"

"Lieutenant Black promised me that." He handed
her a business card.

The simple black-and-white card embossed with the
city emblem listed Lieutenant Parker Black's name and
telephone number. On the back of the card, someone
had written a cell phone number in red ink.

"He's here, too?"

"No, his detective brother. Army...or Armor...some-
thing." He shrugged dismissively.

"Armstrong?"

"Yeah, that's it. He's heading the case and assured
me that if we kept a lid on it for now, he'd give us the
exclusive *and* an interview with the alderman. They say
both brothers are good for their word."

"They?"

Tiger gestured toward the team of officers milling
around on the sidewalk. "They speak quite highly of
them and the alderman."

Neema gave him a nod as he pulled out of the parking space and onto the road. She wasn't expecting it
when Tiger paused to toot his car horn, lowering the

passenger-side window to give his friends in blue a
wave. Before she could hide her face behind her cap,
she locked eyes with a man she recognized from the
restaurant. He had been there with Davis the night he'd
met Balducci.

There was no missing their similarities. Like Davis,
he stood tall, appearing well over six feet, with the same
rich complexion that was a warm tawny with just the
barest hint of mahogany undertones. They had the same
chiseled features—sculpted cheekbones and strong jaw-
lines. Both men had solid builds and broad chests and
shoulders. This brother seemed rougher around the
edges, his hair cropped close, his beard scraggly. He
wore black denim jeans, a collarless black shirt and a
black varsity jacket. He met her stare, his expression
hiding any trace of emotion.

Recognizing Davis's brother, Neema's head snapped
abruptly as she turned from his dead stare. And from
the narrowed gaze, Neema instinctively knew Davis's
brother had recognized her, too.

Chapter 6

Neema's nerves were on overload. There were two text messages from Davis. The first had come shortly after their dinner date. The second had come just a few minutes after she and Tiger had pulled away from his home. She hadn't answered either. She was feeling guilty and she wasn't even sure what he knew. She also didn't want to know. Not before she had a chance to get her story together so that she didn't look as bad as she was feeling. It was her worst-case scenario and she hadn't prepared a contingency for when it all went bad.

"Neema?"

Her name being called startled her out of the trance she'd fallen into. She looked up to see Tiger staring at her intently. "I'm sorry. You said something?"

"I asked if you wanted a donut with your coffee," he repeated, gesturing at the entrance to the twenty-four-hour Dunkin' Donuts shop. "Where'd you go?"

"Sorry, I was just thinking about the shooting."

"You mean the one we're not supposed to know about?"

"Whatever. Who do you think has it out for the alderman?"

Tiger shrugged. "Who knows? I'm thinking, with his family, he probably has more enemies than he has friends."

"I don't know about that. He's a nice guy."

"How do you know?"

"I don't *know him* know him," she said, a little white lie rolling off her tongue. "From what little I do know, he just seems like he'd be one of the good ones."

Tiger shrugged. "Whatever. About those donuts, I'll just get a mixed baker's dozen."

"That works," she replied.

As Tiger lumbered into the donut shop, Neema reread Davis's two messages. The first was a short-and-sweet thank-you note, lauding their dinner date and the good time he'd had. The second was a question: Davis asking about his proposed plans for their second date. It concluded with his imploring her to call him the next day when she had an opportunity. Neither gave her a sense of foreboding, so maybe, she thought, just maybe things hadn't fallen apart. Maybe there was still time for her to tell Davis the truth before his brother outed her. Maybe, she mused. And then again, maybe it was all wishful thinking.

Davis couldn't contain his excitement when he saw Neema standing outside the Taylor Gallery. They had agreed to meet when his last meeting had run over. The two had talked a few times since their first dinner date. Neema had called him the following day and they'd slid into a comfortable routine, chatting in the early morning before his day started and again at night before drifting off to sleep.

He was in awe of the ease between them. He enjoyed the conversations that sometimes challenged his sensibilities, and hers. Debating gender roles, politics and pop culture with her was always engaging. He'd discovered that she had an affinity for all things chocolate, lilies were her favorite flower and she was not a fan of roller coasters. And she made him laugh. They laughed often and easily, gut-deep laughter that left him feeling immensely blessed.

He hurried down the block, pausing once to shake hands with a constituent who stopped him to express her appreciation for his efforts. The elderly woman had his fingers clamped tightly between hers as she pumped his arm eagerly.

From where she stood, Neema tossed him a wave of her hand. Her own eagerness lifted her smile, joy shimmering in her dark eyes. She watched as he politely acknowledged the senior citizen who blocked his path. Neema was giddy and there was no denying how much she wanted to spend time with him.

She had finally gotten up the nerve to call him, ready to explain herself, if necessary. But Davis hadn't questioned or accused her of anything. He'd been happy to talk to her and their conversations had been enlightening. They'd talked for hours over the last few days, getting to know each other's idiosyncrasies and discovering all they could as they shared experiences. Her excitement at the prospect of being with him again was palpable and it took everything in her not to jump up and down like a toddler with a new toy.

Davis moved swiftly toward her, grinning from ear to ear. Neema's own smile widened as he reached her side. He stopped abruptly, as if reluctant to pull her into a hug, but wanting to draw her into his arms. The moment was suddenly awkward and they both laughed.

"Hey there," he said, greeting her warmly.

"Hi, Davis. It's good to see you."

"I'm glad you could make it."

"Me, too."

"Shall we head inside?"

Neema nodded, taking the hand he extended to her. As he entwined her fingers with his own, she felt her knees begin to quiver and heat flood her entire body. She sensed that Davis felt it, as well. "I can't remember the last time I was this excited," she said.

Davis met her stare. "This ranks right up there with our dinner the other night for me."

Neema squeezed his hand, her bright smile like the gentlest caress.

There was a nice crowd gathered inside the gallery. The space was warm and welcoming, bright white walls adorned with bold splashes of framed color. The paintings were exquisite, traditional portraits of people in the neighborhood executed in vibrant monochromatic colors that spanned the color wheel.

Davis gave her a slight tug and gestured with his head in the direction of the artist. Neema turned to look where he was leading her. Gaia Russo stood off in the corner assessing the art patrons who had come out to support her. She was long and lean, with a bohemian aesthetic. Her thick blond hair had been dreadlocked, and she had piled it high atop her head, the strands adorned with gold trinkets. She wore a velvet dress in a deep shade of burgundy that was embroidered with colorful birds and flowers. She was very pretty with a picture-perfect smile that filled her face when she laid eyes on Davis.

She tugged him into a deep hug and held on, murmuring something in his ear as Neema stood politely by.

When the other woman finally released him from the hold she had around his neck, he introduced them. "This is my friend, Neema. Neema, this is Gaia. Gaia is the distinguished artist being honored tonight."

"I don't know how distinguished I am," Gaia responded, laughing heartily. She reached to give Neema a hug. "It's a pleasure to meet you. Any friend of Davis's is a friend of mine."

"It's nice meeting you," Neema responded. "And I love your work!"

"Thank you. Let me give you both a guided tour."

Gaia led them from corner to corner, showing off her artwork. She took the time to explain the who and what of each piece, a story behind the designs that best expressed her talent. Both Davis and Neema were duly impressed with each painting, recognizing many of the faces, including a portrait of Davis done in turquoise blue.

"What do you think?" Gaia asked her, her arms folded over her chest as they stood studying the image.

"It's wonderful," Neema said.

Davis shrugged. "I don't know. I don't look like that, do I?"

"She definitely captured your good side," Neema said.

Davis shook his head, chuckling softly. "I guess that means I'll have to buy it."

"Actually, it already sold," Gaia said. "I do believe your mother purchased it."

His eyes widened, his words edged in surprise. "My mother? She's been here?"

"She was here yesterday as we were hanging the exhibit."

"And you let her buy this one?"

"We are talking about *your* mother, Davis. You do remember her, don't you?" She turned to Neema. "His mother is quite formidable. No one *lets* her do anything."

Neema smiled. "I haven't met her yet, but I look forward to it."

"You'll like her. And if she likes you, you'll have an advocate for life. She's always been very supportive of me and my son."

Davis turned to Neema. "Do you have a favorite painting?"

"I really like the images of the children. The little boy in purple, and the one in green, are incredible. That smile on his face is pure joy!"

"That's my son, Emilio" Gaia said, pride glowing in her blue eyes. "He's also the little boy in red and the boy in orange."

"I'll take all of those," Davis said.

Gaia's brow lifted in surprise. "All four of them?"

Davis nodded. "They're still available, right?"

"They are. When did you start collecting?"

"You say that like I never had an appreciation for art. I'm insulted."

"I know you, remember? How many times did we argue about collecting art being an investment versus a hobby? You were always cheap."

"I prefer frugal."

Neema watched their back-and-forth with amusement. She, too, was curious about his purchase, surprised that he'd come intending to buy something. Not once had he mentioned an interest in collecting artwork.

"So, do you want the sale or not?" Davis was saying.

Gaia laughed. "Of course. If you want them, they're yours."

The gallery director, a short man with a goatee and lazy eye, seemed to swoop in from nowhere, sensing a sale was on the horizon and wanting to make sure they didn't lose it. "Excuse me. I don't mean to interrupt, but if I can steal Gaia away. There's a couple who'd like to talk to you about the lavender lady."

"Not a problem," Davis said. "I'd actually like to finalize my sale if one of your staff can help me with that?"

Gaia nodded. "Alderman Davis would like to buy the four *Sons*."

"Of course!" the man exclaimed excitedly. "If you'll follow me to my office, I can take care of that for you."

Davis pressed a gentle hand against Neema's forearm. "This shouldn't take long and then we can go grab something to eat. If that's okay?"

"That's fine. I'll be here," she said sweetly.

Neema moved to the corner that Gaia had vacated, the spot giving a full view of the gallery space. It was an eclectic mix of patrons, crossing all socio-economic levels. She recognized a few local politicians, three small business owners and one public school administrator. It was easy to discern who was there to support the artist and maybe buy some art, and who was there for the free wine and cheese plate.

Neema felt his stare before she saw him. And when she saw him, her anxiety level rose tenfold. Davis's brother stood by the door, eyeing the crowd from the other side of the room. He was dressed in black from head to toe and he looked quite intimidating. He was staring directly at her and she began to shake, wishing the floor would open up so she could fall into it.

His gaze shifted first, turning toward the offices as Davis stepped out the door. Neema's eyes followed and they both spotted the woman at the same time. It was the woman who'd been at the restaurant the night Davis had met with Balducci. The stunning redhead who'd left before their meal. Neema had noticed her when she'd entered the restaurant with Balducci but had missed her departure.

She watched as Davis recognized her, as well, unable to hide his surprise. There was a moment between the two and Neema sensed he wasn't comfortable. The redhead, on the other hand, seemed extremely comfortable as she sauntered directly to his side to greet him. She pressed a manicured hand to his chest and leaned her body against his to whisper something into his ear. The color seemed to drain from Davis's face as he whispered back. The exchange was brief and visibly disconcerting. She then blew him a kiss and headed out the door.

Davis hesitated, as if trying to collect himself, or maybe to decide his next move. His eyes darted back and forth, and his expression was tense. When his brother stepped up in front of him, blocking her view, Neema felt her stomach flip, feeling like her last meal might come back up. She leaned against the wall, needing it to keep her from falling. She continued to watch as the duo stood huddled together for a good few minutes before turning their attention to the room.

Before she could catch her breath, the two men were headed in her direction. Davis didn't look happy. She could only begin to imagine what his brother may have had to say about her. She wasn't sure what was coming or how she'd have to handle it. She took a deep breath and held on.

Davis moved to her side, an arm sliding possessively around her waist. His smile had returned, replacing the strife on his face just minutes earlier. "I'm sorry. I didn't mean to take so long."

"It's fine," she said. She instinctively stepped closer to his side, sliding easily into his body heat. "Are you okay? You look frazzled."

He shrugged. "I'm good," he said unconvincingly.

Neema's gaze shifted to the other man.

Davis continued. "Neema, I'd like you to meet my brother. This is Mingus. Mingus, this is my new friend, Neema Kamau."

Neema gave him a nervous smile. "Hi, it's a pleasure to meet you."

"Have we met before?" Mingus questioned, his gaze narrowed ever so slightly. "You look familiar."

She nodded. "Not officially, but you were at my family's restaurant with your brother the other evening. I was working that night. You probably saw me there."

Mingus gave her a nod. His expression was stoic, but something shimmered in his eyes. Something that exacerbated Neema's already jittery nerves.

"We may have run into each other another time, too," she said.

"My brother gets around, so anything is possible," Davis interjected, oblivious to the rise of tension between the two.

Mingus didn't say anything, his silence speaking volumes. Neema slowly smiled, her eyes still locked on his face.

"Neema and I were just headed out to get some dinner. Would you like to join us, big brother?"

Mingus shook his head. "I have to pass. I have work to do tonight. You two go have fun." He gave his brother a fist bump. He gave her one last look. "I'm sure we'll meet again, Neema. In fact, I'd bet on it," he concluded before making an about-face.

Neema took another deep breath. Despite the Hail Mary that Mingus had just afforded her, she was suddenly feeling like her good time may have come to an abrupt end.

"We should be going, too," Davis said, gesturing toward the door.

"Do you need to say goodbye to Gaia?"

"We're good," he replied, throwing a glance at the young woman who stood in the midst of admirers, explaining the why behind another painting. "I'll give her a call in a day or two."

"What about your paintings?"

"They'll deliver them to my office when the show is done."

Neema moved to the painting of Davis. The imagery was hauntingly beautiful. Gaia had captured his quiet spirit in the vibrant turquoise color. He was staring off into the distance, his expression contemplative and serious. Her affection for Davis was evident in every stroke. The reflection gave viewers pause and provoked conversation.

"It really is a beautiful painting," Neema said. "I lost count of the people who wanted to buy it and were disappointed. Did you pose for it?"

"No," Davis said with the shake of his head. "Gaia used an old photograph."

"I really like her. She's an amazing talent, and she's very sweet."

"She has moments," he said, one eyebrow quirked.

"But why don't we get out of here? I'm ready to get something to eat."

Neema smiled. "That sounds like a plan to me!"

Davis reached for her hand, holding tightly to her as they crossed the room and headed out the door.

Despite his best efforts, Davis was having a hard time focusing. He was wearing his emotion on his sleeve and he was certain Neema could read his angst. Things had started out smoothly at the gallery. Buying paintings for Balducci had been easier than he'd initially imagined, right up to the moment Ginger had brushed up against him to whisper in his ear.

He'd been shocked to see her there and he hadn't done a good job hiding his surprise. He recalled their conversation, allowing it to play over and over again in his head. Ginger had leaned her body against his, standing so close that her perfume had burned his nostrils. She'd purposely teased him, dragging her manicured fingers down the length of his chest, and then she'd whispered in his ear.

"Don't trust him," she'd said. "Balducci doesn't care about his daughter. He's setting you both up."

"What do you mean?" Davis had whispered back, concern rising like a tsunami about to crush a shoreline.

"Just be careful," Ginger had reiterated. Then, like that, she was gone.

The entire exchange had left him looking like a deer in headlights. It had shaken him far more than he wanted to admit. Trying to maintain his composure had been challenging at best. Mingus stepping in had kept him from completely embarrassing himself. And now he couldn't stop thinking about Ginger's warning, a sense of foreboding knotting his intestines.

"Do you want to talk about it?" Neema was asking, pulling him from his thoughts.

They were sitting in a booth at Original Soul Vegetarian restaurant, the East 75th Street eatery being one of Neema's favorites. She had recommended he try the battered tofu, down-home collard greens and corn bread. Davis hated that he couldn't get out of his head to enjoy the meal and the company.

"I'm sorry, Neema. I didn't mean to bring the mood down."

"You haven't, but you look like you could use a friend right now."

Davis gave her an appreciative smile. "Thank you, I just…it's…well, I…" he stammered, not sure what he wanted to share or say. His encounter with Ginger had thrown him and he was finding it difficult to dismiss her warning.

Neema persisted. "Does this have something to do with your friend? The redhead from your dinner meeting the other night?"

"Her name's Ginger. But we are not friends. I really don't know her. We met for the first time at my meeting with Mr. Balducci."

"Oh! It seemed like you two were well acquainted."

"No, not at all. She's was…well…" He turned a brilliant shade of red as he realized how it must have looked to everyone else in the room with Ginger up against him like they were lovers in a relationship. He suddenly felt like a complete and total jerk. "Neema, I am so sorry. I didn't mean to be disrespectful. I didn't realize Ginger would be…" His voice fell off and he shook his head, unable to find the words to describe Ginger's behavior. "I definitely didn't mean to embarrass you, if I did," he concluded.

Not that she would admit it, but Neema had been in her own feelings about the close encounter. Something like jealousy had swept through the pit of her stomach as she'd watched the two of them together. The other woman's boldness wasn't something she witnessed often, and it had been off-putting. In conjunction with her anxiety about his brother Mingus outing her, it was a wonder she was still standing, she thought.

"I wasn't embarrassed," Neema said aloud, "not for myself, anyway. But I could see that you weren't comfortable."

"I wasn't, and I admit I probably didn't handle it well."

Neema giggled. "She's definitely thrown you off your game. My grandmother once said that women of questionable virtue can easily take a man to his knees and, once there, him being able to get back on his feet becomes a challenge he won't always win. I didn't understand it then, but it's starting to make more sense."

Davis paused to give her comment some thought before he answered. "I imagine your grandmother probably had a lot of wisdom that she shared. Is she still living?"

"No. She passed a few years ago. My mother took up the mantle and now I get regular tidbits of wisdom from her."

"I'm sorry to hear about your grandmother. I imagine she was a very special lady," he said, reaching across the table to hold her hand.

His touch was warm and gentle, and slightly disconcerting. Neema found herself staring at the length of his fingers as they slowly stroked hers. Heat simmered beneath his fingertips, sending waves of warmth through

her body. She took a deep inhale of air and answered.
"She was. And she would have liked you!"

"I have that kind of effect on mothers. They tend to
like me a lot." His smile was smugly teasing.

"I imagine they do!" Neema said, laughing heartily.
"So why are you still single?"

Davis sat back in his seat, crossing his arms over his
chest. "Why am I still single? Good question!"

"Do you have a good answer?"

"I'm still single because I believe marriage is forever,
and for me, forever requires the right woman. What's
your excuse?"

"I haven't found the right man."

"Then it's a good thing we found each other when
we did!" Davis said. He was grinning from ear to ear,
his mood having shifted substantially.

Amusement flushed Neema's face. "You're quite the
comedian, Mr. Black."

Davis leaned forward, clasping both of her hands beneath his own. He stared into her eyes, his gaze sweeping her face. His tone dropped like a seductive breeze
between them. "I'm very serious, Ms. Kamau. I like
you. I like you a lot, and I'm excited to see where we
can go with this relationship."

Her breath caught in her chest and Neema had no
words. She chuckled softly.

Me, too, she thought to herself. *Me, too!*

Chapter 7

"Hey," Mingus said, startling Davis as he entered his home. His brother was sitting in Davis's living room, his feet propped on the coffee table, a tumbler of bourbon in his hand. It was dark, only a faint stream of moonlight shining through the sliding-glass doors that led to the rear deck.

Surprised, Davis jumped, cussing loudly. "You just scared the crap out of me!" he snapped as he switched on a lamp, illuminating the room in white light. "What the hell are you doing here?"

"Just checking on you. I also wanted to check your security. It's seriously lacking, by the way."

"I've never had reason to be concerned about my safety."

"Someone shot at you the other night. I think it's time to be concerned. I'll send a team over tomorrow to secure the house. And you need to remember to turn on your alarm."

Davis dropped into a leather recliner. "Yeah, whatever."

"How was your date?"

"What date?" He gave his brother a look, not interested in the interrogation that he felt was coming.

"She's cute."

"She is. I think she's absolutely gorgeous."

"What do you know about her?"

"I know that I really like her and that we're taking our time getting to know each other."

Mingus went quiet, pulling his glass to his lips to sip on his beverage.

Davis could see his brother's mind working, the gears in his head on overload. "What do you know?" he finally asked.

Mingus shrugged. "Nothing…yet."

"But you think you know something?"

"I think you just need to be careful. There's a lot in play right now and I'm not sure we know who all the players are."

Davis took a deep breath. "Neema's good people. She wouldn't hurt me."

"So, you trust her?"

"Obviously we're still getting to know each other, but yeah, I do."

"Okay." Mingus refilled his glass from the bottle that sat on the coffee table. He took another slow sip.

"You don't think I should?"

"Again, I think you just need to be careful."

"What do you think I need to do about Ginger? She seemed insistent that I not trust Balducci. It's got me concerned."

"I'm working on that. Word on the street is that she's risen quickly up the ranks in his organization. When he's not giving orders, she is. He's not making many moves these days that she doesn't have her hands in. You might not remember, but she was part of the trafficking case that Armstrong and Danni broke last year. She got a sweet immunity deal to flip on Balducci's son."

"And he made her his number two?"

"I didn't say it made sense."

"So, what should I do? She said I need to be careful, but I'm not sure what I need to be concerned about."

"Just be smart. Keep your eyes and ears open, and don't take any unnecessary risks."

"You sound like Mom and Dad now."

Mingus shrugged. "Whatever! Just don't do anything stupid."

"Does Armstrong have anything on who shot up my door?"

"Nothing new that I'm aware of."

Davis leaned forward in his chair, his elbows resting against his thighs. He dropped his head into the palms of his hands, trying to make sense of what felt like nonsense. Whatever was going on felt so much like nothing. His agreement to help Balducci wasn't supposed to be about anything but helping Gaia. His friend was ten grand richer and her father now owned four paintings of his grandson. Someone had shot at him and Davis didn't have a clue why. Was it random? Just one more notch on the criminal belt that plagued the city of Chicago daily? Or had he been targeted? And if so, why? What he did know is that none of it made an ounce of sense.

Mingus seemed to read his mind. "We'll figure it out," he said as he got to his feet, leaving his glass on the table. He moved toward the front door.

Davis thought about Neema and the concern that

had seeped from her eyes. She'd been genuinely worried about him, sensitive to his mood and determined to help him feel better even though she hadn't had a clue what his problem was. She'd asked and he'd avoided her questions, unable to explain without violating the promise he'd made to others. He was becoming adept at being evasive, but keeping secrets was not how he wanted to start their relationship. Especially when he wasn't doing anything wrong that really needed to be kept secret. At least, nothing that he was aware of.

He looked up at his brother. "I hope so, big brother. I really hope so."

"I think I messed up," Neema said, cutting her eyes toward Tiger. Her friend was watching a YouTube video on his cell phone, the duo taking their first break of the evening.

"What did you do?"

"I met someone. A really great guy."

"I knew it!" Tiger exclaimed excitedly. "So, what did you do?"

"He thinks I'm a full-time waitress."

"Why?"

"He has a high-profile position with the city and when I first met him, I thought there might be a story there. I kind of went undercover."

"You lied to him."

"I just didn't tell him the whole truth."

"And now you like him."

"I do. I really like him. More than I ever expected to like him. I can actually see us being in a relationship."

"Yep! You've messed up!"

"You aren't much help."

"So just come clean," Tiger said.

"I've been thinking about that. Trying to figure out how to do it without seeming like a horrible person. Because I feel horrible."

"How long have you two been seeing each other?"

"Not long. Not long at all."

Tiger tossed her a look. "I'd just tell him. What harm can it do? At least you're not married for five years with two kids and you have to tell him a secret you've been holding on to since the day you met. Now that would not be cool!"

Neema shrugged, not answering.

"Who is he?" Tiger questioned. "Is it someone I know?"

"You don't know him."

"I bet I do. That's why you don't want to tell me."

"Exactly."

Tiger laughed. "Look, you know better than anyone that I don't do relationships well. Hell, my marriage is only working because of Heather. She's the glue that keeps us together. She tells me what to do and I do it. It works, and we're both happy. At least, I'm happy and I think she's happy. You should talk to her. Do that girlfriend thing you women like to do. She'll confirm that you really screwed this one up and then give you great advice on how to fix it."

"Maybe I will. I just know I need to make things right."

"It's not the new city clerk, is it? I heard he was single."

Neema rolled her eyes skyward. "It's not."

"That district attorney with the unibrow?"

Neema laughed. "Not him, either."

"That's good. I don't know if I could do a double date with him and that furry creature on his face."

"You're such a fool!"

"I'm honest," he said. "Besides, if you'd just tell me, we wouldn't have to play this game."

"I'm not telling you, Tiger."

"If it is the DA, I understand perfectly. I wouldn't tell that, either."

A call suddenly came in over the police scanner, a dispatcher announcing a domestic dispute and hostage situation. The two listened as Neema adjusted her seat belt and Tiger downed the last of his coffee. He started the ignition and pulled the car into traffic. "It's that dude running for mayor, isn't it?"

Neema shook her head. "I said I'm not telling."

"Well, did you at least get a story?"

When Neema hadn't been thinking about getting a story, she was trying to piece together a story. For three days, she'd worked the night shift, then spent the morning helping her parents prep the restaurant for the day. Right after lunch, she hustled from point to point seeking answers to the whys of Alexander Balducci and Davis Black. Everyone she talked to or questioned had nothing but good things to say about the alderman and with the exception of Davis's father, no one could connect the two men to each other. Between her research and work, she searched out moments to talk to Davis.

Chatting with Davis had become the highlight of her day. Hearing his voice over the telephone made her happy even if the conversations were short and brief. Syncing their schedules had become a challenge that neither could master despite their best efforts. She'd been surviving on quick naps in the late afternoon and early evening, and then her night and day would start all over again. Davis still believed she was spending her time doing daughter duty, and she had no idea how to change the narrative so that it made sense without looking like she'd lied outright.

Just tell him, she thought to herself. She and Davis had found an hour between his town council meeting and her day job to catch up with each other. Davis had been sharing details of his morning. He'd met with senior citizens protesting the redistricting of a public park, and the teacher's union threatening to strike. There'd been lunch with city clergy and stacks of proposals that had required his attention. Then he'd had dinner with his brothers, calling her before he had to be at the monthly council meeting.

"There are some days where I'm better at schmoozing than others. Today was not one of them. I couldn't get a smile out of those old women to save my life!" Davis said with a deep laugh.

Neema laughed with him. "You were probably trying too hard. Some things you need to let evolve organically. With older people especially. You just have to let them do what they do."

"There aren't enough hours in the week. Those women would take up most of them to tell you about their gout, their joint pain and their hemorrhoids. I've never heard anyone complain about their health issues as much as those old women complained! But enough about me. How was your day? Are you still at the restaurant?"

"No. I had to run some errands for my father. Once I'm done, I'll head back to help them clean the kitchen and close up."

"When do you have off again? I'd really like to see you."

"I have to work tomorrow, but I'm free the day after, I think."

"I'd love to cook dinner for you, if you're available?"

"You cook?"

Davis laughed again. "Why do you say it like that? Like you're surprised I'd be able to cook."

"I don't know. It just…well… I just wasn't expecting it."

"I'm insulted! I happen to be a very good cook."

"It wasn't meant to be an insult. I'm actually excited to see what you can do."

"Well, good, because I plan to show off my culinary skills. When I'm done, you'll be apologizing for doubting me."

"We'll see…" Neema joked softly.

"I need to run, but I'll try to call you after my meeting."

"Good luck tonight," she said, wishing him well before disconnecting the call. A gust of warm breath passed her lips, her whole face twisting into a frustrated pout. Another opportunity to tell him the truth had passed her by yet again.

Chapter 8

When his office door swung open, Davis looked up in surprise. With nothing scheduled on his calendar, he had not been expecting anyone and had been lost in the mountain of paperwork across his desk.

Gaia's bright smile led the way as she and her son, Emilio, waved in greeting. "Hey there!" she said cheerfully.

"Hi, Uncle Davis!" Emilio rushed to Davis's side to give him a hug. The youngster had shot up an inch or two since the last time Davis had seen him. He was lanky, more arms and legs than torso, with his mother's warm coloring and a head of blond curls. Davis had always thought him a beautiful melding of his two parents, but for the first time he noticed the boy's resemblance to his grandfather.

The two pounded fists. "Hey, dude! What's up?" Davis said.

"We brung your paintings," the boy answered.

His mother corrected his grammar. "We brought the paintings. Not 'brung,'" she scolded.

"You did?" Davis gave Gaia a hug.

"I hope this isn't a bad time?" she said.

"It's fine. I just wasn't expecting to take possession this early. Doesn't the show hang for another week or two?"

"For the next month, actually. But I switched them out with new work. Trying to maximize my sales as much as I can."

Davis nodded. "I get it. Smart move. Let me help you get them out of the van."

Gaia shook her head. "Nope! I can manage. It's part of the customer service. I can even hang them for you if you want me to."

"That's not necessary." Davis paused, seeming to choose his words carefully. "I'm actually gifting them to a family friend. Do you know Alexander Balducci?"

"I know the name, but I've never met him," she said nonchalantly, not reacting at all to the disclosure.

Davis took a deep breath, released it slowly. "He's a good friend of my father's. They've done some real estate investments together. The two of them are looking for local artists to showcase in the public spaces of one of their new skyscrapers, and I thought these would be a perfect addition."

Gaia grinned. "Thank you! That's so cool."

Emilio interrupted. "Uncle Davis, can I play a game on your computer?" He sat in Davis's chair, swinging his long legs back and forth.

Davis nodded. "Knock yourself out, kid. I'm going to help your mom."

"Really," Gaia said, "I can do this myself."

"I know you can, but you don't have to. So stop arguing."

She rolled her eyes as she headed out the door, Davis on her heels. "Fine. Then you can tell me about your friend Neema. How is she?"

Davis grinned, his smile pulling from ear to ear. "She's good. I'll see her later tonight."

"I like her. Is it serious?"

"It's…well…it's still developing."

"She likes you. You could see it all over her face."

"I really like her, too, and I don't want to mess it up. You know better than most that I can sabotage a relationship."

"I wouldn't say that. You were never ready for a serious relationship, and you were always up-front and honest about that. I wouldn't call that sabotage. When it looked like it was getting serious, you just backed out and, usually, you did it nicely. Although there was that one time…." She grinned, her brow rising as she tossed him a look. "What was that girl's name?"

Davis groaned. "Don't remind me. Linda had some serious issues."

"She didn't want to let go. She was determined she was going to be Mrs. Davis Black."

"I had to get a restraining order against her, it got so crazy," he said, thinking back to the bombshell who'd made his life a living hell for months after he'd broken it off with her. They'd been introduced by a mutual friend, and for the first few weeks he'd enjoyed their time together. Then she'd started planning his future, wanting to dictate every aspect of his life. When he'd discovered she'd been deleting messages off his answering machine and trying earnestly to keep him from his family and friends, he'd dropped her. But despite his efforts to walk away, she'd hung on for dear life. The last he'd heard, she'd married an investment banker and now had three kids.

"I didn't get that kind of vibe from Neema. But I told you from day one that Linda was not the one for you. I didn't like her at all."

"No one did. Even my mother didn't like her, and my mother can find the good in everyone."

"That's why I love your mother so much."

Davis changed the subject. "So, what's going on with you? Dating anyone?"

"I am solely focused on my child and my career. I have no time for dating."

"You know what they say about all work and no play."

"I know what eviction notices, late payment notices and bills due look like. Playing can't help me with that. That's one reason why I need this show to do well or I was going to have to give up this dream and stick to a regular nine-to-five job to keep supporting Emilio."

"His father hasn't helped?"

"His father has taken the definition of deadbeat to a whole other level. Emilio hasn't even gotten one holiday card from that fool since he was born. As far as I'm concerned, his father is dead to us."

"I'm sorry to hear that. I expected more from Carl."

"Carl isn't the man you and I once knew and loved. His heart is as cold as ice as far as we're concerned."

Gaia passed him two of the four paintings, each carefully wrapped in brown paper and bubble wrap. She closed the door to her minivan. Clasping the other two in her hands, she led the way back into his office. Her son still sat where they'd left him, gone from playing a game to watching a cartoon on YouTube. He looked up and gave them both a slight wave as they entered the office.

"Just rest them here," Davis said, leaning the artwork against the wall.

"I really do appreciate this," Gaia said. "I can't begin to tell you how much this means to me."

"I'm glad I could be of help. If I can do more, I definitely will."

Gaia hugged his neck. "You've always been good to me. There's a special place in heaven for you, Davis Black."

Davis chuckled. "Let's just hope I have no use for it any time soon."

Neema rang Davis's doorbell promptly at seven o'clock. She'd arrived some thirty minutes earlier and had sat in her car watching the clock. She'd been a bundle of nerves, undercurrents of excitement coursing through her like little shimmers of fire building to a large flame.

As Davis pulled the door open, there was no denying that both were excited to see each other. Glee bubbled like a tidal wave between them, the wealth of it feeling combustible as Davis wrapped his arms around her in a warm hug.

"Welcome to my humble abode," he said as he finally released the hold he had on her. He stepped aside, bowing ever so slightly as his arm waved in a gallant gesture for her to enter.

Neema laughed. "Very nice," she said as she took in the open space.

"I have to credit my mother and sisters for the décor. Before they took control, there was only a battered couch and a table I'd fashioned out of an old tire and a piece of plywood."

"I'm sure that was cute."

"It was college-dorm-room fancy," Davis said with a chuckle.

"It sounds like it. I'm sorry I missed that!"

"You really didn't miss much."

They laughed heartily, any ounce of tension dissipating.

Neema moved further into the foyer and then came to an abrupt halt. Davis's dog sat obediently, eyeing her cautiously. He looked even larger and more intimidating than Neema remembered.

"Hi there," she said, tossing the animal a wave of her hand. "Aren't you a big boy!"

Titus cocked his head to the side, his ears perking up as he continued to assess her.

"You're not afraid of dogs, are you?" Davis asked.

Neema shook her head. "Not usually, but then it's not often I'm around a dog as large as that one."

Davis chuckled. "This is Titus. He's nothing but a big teddy bear. Just extend the back of your hand and let him smell you. Once he knows your scent, he'll probably ignore you."

She nodded as Davis called the dog to his side.

Titus came eagerly, his stubbed tail wiggling from side to side. Neema smiled as she extended her hand and let him sniff. When he nuzzled his nose into the palm of her hand, she moved to rub the top of his head.

"He likes you," Davis said, exhaling a sigh of relief at the exchange.

"He's beautiful." Neema knelt to hug the dog's neck. "How long have you had him?"

"Nine years. My sisters gifted him to me for my twenty-first birthday. He was tiny back then."

"He's very sweet," Neema said, standing.

"Titus. Bed," Davis commanded, pointing to the back of the home.

The dog hesitated for just a second then turned, disappearing down the hallway.

"Please," Davis insisted, "have a seat and make yourself comfortable. Dinner's almost ready. Would you like a glass of wine?"

"I think I'll pass for now. Is there anything I can do to help?" Neema asked.

"Just talk to me while I get the food on the table."

Neema rested her purse on an end table and followed him into his kitchen. The room was a chef's dream with stainless-steel appliances, white cabinets and marble counters. Something simmered in a saucepan on the stovetop and he'd set his dining room table with two place settings. She was duly impressed as he moved easily around the kitchen, seeming comfortable in the space. She moved to the counter and took a seat on one of the stools as Davis washed his hands.

"Something smells really good! What are we eating?"

"Well, I thought we'd start with a warm kale salad with bacon, dates, almonds, crispy shallots and grated parmesan. For the entrée, I'll be serving pan-seared scallops with a bacon cream sauce and mushroom risotto. And for dessert, I made my famous sticky toffee pudding with molasses sauce."

Neema was wide-eyed as she stared at him in awe. "I think I just gained ten pounds," she said jokingly.

"You didn't believe me when I told you I was going to prepare a feast."

"I didn't know you were that skilled a cook."

"I can burn in the kitchen!"

"So, I see."

"Just wait until you taste it. The pudding is melt-in-your-mouth perfection. And I made extra in case you want a second helping. Because I know you'll want seconds!"

She pointed. "No, I mean I see you can burn...something's smoking in your oven."

"My croutons!" Davis cussed as he rushed to the appliance and snatched open the door. He grabbed an insulated mitt from the counter and pulled a baking pan from inside. Small cubes of black ash smoldered, the rank scent of burned garlic rising in the room. He dropped the pan into the sink and turned on the cold water. A low hissing sound followed by steam billowed upward. Davis turned toward Neema, his face a crimson shade of red. "This is not what I meant when I said I could burn."

Neema laughed. "I'm sure it tastes better than it looks," she said.

Davis shook his head. "Now you're just being mean!"

Minutes later, they sat at the dining room table, Davis having served the first course of what would prove to be one of the best meals Neema had ever eaten. Despite the mishap with the first batch of garlic-infused croutons, the second toasting proved to be on point. The salad could easily have been a meal all on its own. The scallops were fork tender, surrounded by a sauce that made Neema want to lick her plate. The dessert was heaven in a bowl. Davis had outdone himself.

The conversation was engaging, the two catching up with each other's lives. More than once Neema thought about telling him about her job at the newspaper, but when she couldn't find the right segue into the subject, she changed her mind. Instead, she talked about her parents, the last book she'd read, the changing state of politics, and why women in relationships needed to maintain a degree of autonomy from their partners.

"I'm not one of those women that does matching his and her T-shirts. It rings false to me. Like a couple is trying too hard to be a couple."

Davis shrugged. "I'd do it if it made my partner happy, but no, I'm not going out of my way to coordinate our outfits. However, I do think that when two people have been together for some time, that coordination happens naturally. My parents are notorious for wearing the same color when they go out, and it happens without them trying."

"See, that I can understand, but if you're spending weeks searching for the same his and her leopard-print shirt to wear to date night—" she shook her head "—then something's not right."

"To each his own. What works for some might not work for others."

"I agree."

"So, tell me…" Davis started, pausing to take a sip of his wine before continuing. "What are your expectations when it comes to a man and relationships?"

"Interesting question," Neema said as she sat back in her seat. She took a deep breath, holding it for a split second before letting it out slowly. "I expect kindness and respect. I want to be in a relationship with a man who is genuinely compassionate toward others. Who isn't self-centered, and who supports me. I also want to be romanced. And I want affection. I think emotional intimacy is as equally important as physical intimacy.

It's also important that any man I'm committed to has a vision for his future that aligns with my own."

"And what's your vision?"

"I want a family. Children. At least two, maybe three. I also want to be in a partnership where my opinion is equally as important as his, even if he feels that as head of the family, he should take the lead."

"Having a big family... I've always imagined myself with a big family." Davis gave her a soft smile, the wealth of it shimmering in his eyes. "I want children. At least three. And I agree that a relationship should also be a partnership. I also think that honesty and trust are important. I would find it very difficult to be with a woman I can't trust."

Neema nodded, her gaze dropping to her plate as she gave him a quick smile. A knot tightened in the pit of her stomach and a little voice screamed in her head. *Tell him!* She closed her eyes for a brief moment, then opened them to stare up at him.

"Can I get you something else to eat?" Davis offered as he stood from the table and began to clear away the dishes.

"I'm stuffed," Neema said as she joined him. She reached for a dish towel to dry the few dishes he had begun to wash by hand, the others placed in the dishwasher. "But that was so good!"

"There's more pudding if you want it."

"I do, but I couldn't eat another bite."

"How about I wrap it up and you can take it home for later?"

Neema bobbed her head. "I like how you think."

"I need to make sure you're thinking about me later."

Neema laughed. "Thinking about you won't be a problem. I think about you all the time." She clamped

her lips closed, the words having slipped off her tongue
before she could catch them.

Davis smiled. "Well, that makes two of us, because
I haven't been able to get you off my mind, either."

An awkward silence rose full and abundant between
them. Neema folded her dish towel and rested it on the
counter. She wasn't quite sure what to say next, so much
spinning through her head.

Davis seemed to read her mind. "Let's go into the
living room and sit," he said as he clasped her hand
beneath his. His palm was warm against the back of
her fingers.

Neema followed as he led the way. He sat on the
sofa and she settled down next to him. He had turned
on his stereo earlier and the soft lull of someone's jazz
played in the background. A fire burned in the fireplace and only one lamp illumed the room. The ambience was seductive and comfortable. For another good
hour, they sat and talked, chatting about everything and
about nothing. The mood was comfortable and they
were both content.

"Did you pass notes in school?" Davis questioned.

Neema laughed. "No. I was a model student."

"Well, I did." He reached for the pad of paper and a
pen on the coffee table. His expression was smug as he
scribbled something across the page. He tore the sheet
from the pad, folded it in two and then folded it again.
He pretended to look the other way as he slipped the
note to Neema.

As she pulled the message into the palm of her hand,
he stood abruptly and moved to the front door where
Titus stood in want of his attention. He opened the
door and Titus ran out into the yard. Davis stepped
outside with him. While they were gone, Neema un-

folded the piece of paper and read it once, twice, and then a third time. Reaching for the pen, she checked a box and folded it back, laying it on the seat Davis had just vacated.

Minutes later, when the two returned, she met the look Davis was giving her with one of her own, amusement dancing in her eyes.

Retaking his seat beside her, Davis reached for the slip of paper and unfolded it, grinning broadly as he read it out loud. "'Neema, will you be my girlfriend? Check yes or no.'" A large X marked the yes box. He pumped his fist in the air. Titus barked, his excitement reflecting his master's.

Neema laughed. "You are too silly!"

"It's easy to be myself with you, and I try not to take myself too seriously. I've also been known to make a complete fool out of myself, so you've been warned."

He took up the notepad and scribbled a second message, folding the paper before passing it to her.

Neema gamely rolled her eyes heavenward as she opened and read it. She lifted her eyes to meet his. Delight shimmered in his gaze as he stared at her curiously. She wanted to laugh and jump with joy, but didn't, feigning indifference instead. She shrugged.

"Maybe," she said, her voice dropping an octave.

Davis laughed. "Maybe? That wasn't an option. You need to check yes or no and then sign it so it's official."

"Sign it?"

"Yes, it definitely requires a signature."

"I don't know about that," she said. "Let me read it again."

Neema sat back against the cushions, pretending to read the note a second time. She tossed him a look then shifted her eyes back to the piece of paper. Finally, she read it out loud. "'Neema, may I have permission to kiss you Check yes or no.'"

"See," Davis said, pointing. "There's no maybe there."

"But what if I'm not sure, then it will be maybe."

He shook his head. "You're sure. You knew the answer before I even asked the question. Yes or no?"

She chuckled. "That's arrogant of you."

"I prefer confident. So, yes…or no?"

Neema reached for the pen, ticked a box and passed the sheet of paper back to him. She smiled smugly as she folded her arms over her chest and crossed one leg over the other.

Davis's bright smile grew brighter as he read it. He refolded the note and slid it onto the coffee table. Then, just like that, he changed the subject.

"Do you want wine?"

Confusion blessed Neema's face. "Wine?"

"I was going to refill my glass," he said as he stood, gesturing with the crystal goblet.

"No, thank you," Neema said.

She watched as he made his way into the kitchen. Titus watched him leave and then suddenly moved to her side, laying his massive head in her lap. She scratched behind his ears. "Your daddy thinks he's funny," she murmured softly.

Titus grunted in agreement and Neema leaned to press her forehead to his. "We're going to be good friends, Titus."

Davis returned a few short minutes later with a full glass of cabernet sauvignon. He looked like he hesitated a step as he spied her, and his dog, cradled comfortably together. He shook his head. "I can't turn my back on him for two minutes before he's trying to steal my girl." He dropped down onto the other end of the sofa.

"He knows you're slipping on the job."

Davis choked, laughing gleefully. "Slipping?"

"What happened to my kiss?"

He was still chuckling. "Oh, it'll come when the moment's right. I just needed to secure permission so that when it happens, we'll have gotten that out the way."

"Titus just went for it," she said as she nuzzled her cheek against the dog.

"Titus doesn't have the finesse I have. But you'll find that out when the time's right."

Neema's smile pulled full and wide across her face. Before she could respond, Davis's cell phone rang, vibrating harshly against the tabletop.

He leaned to see who was calling, then apologized. "Sorry," he said. "I need to take this." He stood again and moved into the kitchen to take the call. His voice was hushed, and he whispered hurriedly, seemingly thrown off guard by whoever was calling. Minutes passed and Neema sensed the conversation was intense.

When he finally returned, he apologized a second time. "I'm really sorry, but I have to cut our evening short. I need to run to my office."

"Is everything okay?"

"I'm not sure. That was Gaia. She said it was urgent and she needed to speak with me. Something has her upset and she sounded scared."

Neema nodded; a slow, methodic up and down bob of her head.

"I'm so sorry," Davis repeated. "I'm not sure how long I'll be." He hesitated for a minute, something about her expression giving him pause. There was an obvious moment of contemplation as he appeared to ponder the logistics of what he wanted to do and what he needed to do. He continued. "I'd invite you to ride along, but I'm sure Gaia wouldn't appreciate it. I hope you understand."

Neema stole a quick glance at her wristwatch. She really did need to stop by the restaurant to help her mother close since her father was out of town visiting a restaurant supplier. She nodded her head. "I do and I wouldn't want to intrude. It sounds personal, and Gaia might be offended if I just tagged along."

She stood, brushing her hands down the front of the denim skirt she was wearing. "Call me later?"

"I will," Davis said, nodding. "Let me grab your pudding."

"I definitely don't want to forget that."

"Think of me when you savor that first bite."

She laughed as he grabbed the plastic container off the counter and moved swiftly back to her side. He stepped in close, the nearness of him igniting a wave of heat that was welcome and unexpected. Neema took a deep breath, inhaling his scent wholly into her lungs. He wore Acqua di Giò, and smelled of rosemary, fruity persimmon and warm Indonesian patchouli. It was heavenly, she thought to herself.

"Thank you," she whispered. "I really had a great time."

"You're welcome. Let's plan on doing it again soon," he said as he brushed his finger against the line of her profile.

His touch sent shivers down the length of her spine.

"I'll cook for you next time."

"That's a deal," Davis responded.

Neema eased past him, heading to his front door.

"Please do call me," she said, turning back to him. "There's something I want to tell you."

"Do you need to talk now?"

She shook her head. "Later. Go support Gaia and we can talk when you have more time." She gave him a warm hug. "You have a good night."

As she stepped out of his arms, turning toward the door, Davis called after her.

"Yes?"

He moved close a second time and leaned in to press a damp kiss against her cheek. He let his lips linger on her skin, his breath warm and teasing. His touch was like a whisper of silk gliding against satin and it left her breathless, frozen in place. It took a moment for her to snap out of it. When she did, she whispered goodbye a second time, spun on her heels and scurried out the door.

Davis had known his dealings with Alexander Balducci would eventually blow up in his face. He hadn't expected it to happen so soon. Gaia knew. He didn't know how, but she knew. He'd heard it in her voice.

The conversation had been short and abrupt, Gaia demanding he meet with her right then and there. Her request had been cryptic, giving him little to go on. There had been a fury wrapped around her words that only someone who knew her well could have detected and Davis knew her well. His friend had worn her emotions like a shroud and bitterness had fueled her demands. Her jaw had been tight, her teeth clenched together and she had spat her words. He had thought to put her off, to deal with her another time, but then she began to cry. Her tears had tugged hard on his heartstrings and he couldn't refuse her. He'd had to disappoint Neema instead and that had him feeling like a complete and total jerk. It was not how he had hoped to end what had been a near perfect evening.

As he pulled in front of his South Keeler Avenue office, he noticed the Pentecostal Church of Holiness on the corner was holding service, the number of parked cars on the street almost double. Gaia's minivan was parked across the street, but she wasn't sitting inside. He thought it odd but pondered she might have taken a walk. The neighborhood wasn't necessarily unsafe after dark if you were familiar with the area, and Gaia had been raised two blocks over.

He exited his car and sauntered over to hers just to be sure he hadn't missed her behind the tinted windows, but the vehicle was empty. He crossed back to the other side of the street, heading toward the front of the building. That there was no light shining from inside gave him pause. He was almost certain he had left a desk lamp on before he'd left for the evening. But maybe he hadn't, he thought. Maybe he only thought he had. He had been in a rush to get out the door, leaving early to prep for his date with Neema. As he neared the front door, the motion sensors outside should have also turned on, but the entrance way remained pitch black.

Voices chattering across the street drew his attention and he turned to eye two women wishing each other a good night as they hurried to their respective cars. The church service was finished and parishioners were beginning to exit the large brick cathedral on the corner. Turning back, Davis unlocked the door and stepped inside, closing the entrance after himself. He flicked the light switch on the wall, but nothing happened. *It must be a fuse*, he thought, trying to recall where the master breakers were located. He swore, profanity echoing through the late-night air. Using the flashlight app on his cell phone, he spun around, moving into the office space, and that's when he spied Gaia's body lying on the carpeted floor.

The moment felt surreal as Davis rushed to Gaia's side, calling her name in hope of a response. Despite the volume of blood that pooled on the floor beneath her, he felt for a pulse, ignoring everything that told him his dear friend was gone. Gaia was dead.

Davis fumbled with his cell phone, dropping it to the floor twice as he tried to dial 9-1-1. And that's when he heard the floorboards creak behind him. As he turned, catching the glimpse of a shadow in the dim light, some-one struck him in the back of the head. He dropped to his knees, the room spinning. Then a second blow turned everything black.

Chapter 9

It was a perfect storm, a rare combination of circumstances building to one monumental catastrophe, Davis thought. The police had found him passed out on the floor with a weapon in his hand and Gaia's dead body by his side. A forensics team was now making short work of every square inch of his office and he'd grown weary of answering the multitude of questions being asked repeatedly. His head was pounding, and his heart was splintered. His friend was dead, and it was apparent that he was at the top of the police department's suspect list.

"So, tell me again, why you asked Ms. Russo to meet you here at your office?" the uniformed police office asked.

Davis blustered a heavy sigh, frustration etched over his face. "I did not ask her to meet me. She asked me to come down here. She said there was something important she needed to discuss with me."

"And she was inside your office when you arrived?"

"That's correct. She was lying on the floor when I entered."

"Did she have a key, Alderman Black?"

Davis shook his head. "Not that I'm aware of. I never gave her a key."

"So how did she gain access to the building?"

"I don't know. The door was locked when I arrived. I unlocked it."

"We didn't find any signs of forced entry."

"I said I don't know. I don't know how she got in. I don't know who killed her. And I sure as hell don't know who hit me in the back of the head." His voice rose, the tension feeling like he might spew if pushed too hard.

"Where did the gun come from?"

"I purchased it legally and it was locked in my desk drawer."

"And you don't remember firing the weapon?"

"I didn't have the gun!"

"But witnesses heard gunshots minutes after you entered the building and we found you with the gun in your hand. How do you explain that?"

"I didn't fire my weapon."

The office narrowed her gaze, suspicion dripping from her eyes. "Were you and Ms. Russo in a romantic relationship?"

"I've told you multiple times. We were just friends. Now, I'm done. I'll gladly make a statement at the police department with my attorney present. But right now, I need to have my head looked at."

"Just a few more—"

"Officer, I'll take it from here," Parker Black stated. "Alderman Black has exercised his right to an attorney, and we don't circumvent the law. Please, have a medic come examine his head, then escort him to the hospital."

"Yes, sir, Lieutenant!" she responded, tossing Davis one last look before scurrying for the door.

Davis looked up, his brother standing above him. "I don't need…"

Parker held up a finger, stalling his comment. "I insist. Ellington's on his way and Dad's outside talking with the first officer on site." He squatted closer to his brother, lowering his voice an octave. "We have to be mindful of how this looks. We don't want the police department charged with showing favoritism."

"I didn't do this," Davis hissed through clenched teeth.

"We know that. Anyone who knows you knows that. But right now, it doesn't look good for you."

"So, what do I do?"

"Don't say another word until Ellington gets here. Not one word. The press is all over this and we can't risk any leaks or comments being misconstrued. We can't risk anything said being used against you. In a few minutes, we're going to let an ambulance take you out of here. You need to look like a victim, not a criminal."

"I am a damn victim!" Davis snapped.

Before Parker could respond, an EMS team entered the room, coming to Davis's side. Parker took a step back, gave his brother a nod and exited. Minutes later, when Davis came out on a stretcher, his father, Mingus, Ellington and Parker were standing at the rear of the ambulance, huddled together in deep conversation.

"You go with your brother," Jerome ordered, his eyes on Mingus. "Don't let him out of your sight."

"I'll meet them there," Ellington said, the patriarch giving him a nod of approval.

"This isn't going to go away quietly," Parker noted. "It's already being whispered that we need to recuse ourselves from the investigation and call in the Feds."

"That won't be necessary," Jerome said. "I'm going to assign Lieutenant Caswell to the investigation. He'll report directly to the mayor, not me. If no one named Black goes near this case, we should be able to keep the FBI out of it."

"Caswell couldn't find a murderer if the guy stood on his front porch and announced himself," Parker muttered. "I don't want to risk him running with circumstantial evidence and railroading Davis for a crime he didn't commit. Maybe we should call in the Feds. At least then he'll have a fighting chance to get to the truth. Whatever that may be."

There was a moment, the father and his sons looking from one to the other, as they pondered their options to help their kin. Jerome finally nodded. "Your call. I'll support whatever decision you make. If you want the FBI on this case, make the call. Right now, it sounds like we can use all the help we can get."

Jerome gave Davis a gentle tap as they lifted him into the ambulance. "It's going to be okay, son. I'll see you at the hospital," he said.

"Why is this happening?" Davis questioned as Mingus took a seat beside him in the ambulance.

His brother shook his head. "We'll figure it out. But right now, that's the least of your troubles."

"The cops think I killed Gaia. How much worse can it get?" Davis muttered.

Mingus shot a look over his shoulder before he leaned to whisper in his brother's ear. "Balducci thinks you may have killed his daughter. He's coming for you. That's how much worse it can get."

* * *

Davis didn't know when he'd fallen asleep or how long he'd slept. When he opened his eyes, he was in a hospital bed and connected to a series of monitors that beeped periodically. A nurse stood at his side, adjusting the drip for intravenous fluids. His eyes followed the plastic tube from the bag of saline to the back of his hand where someone had placed a catheter into his peripheral vein. He looked back at the nurse, who was smiling at him. She was an older woman who reminded him of bread dough. Her complexion was pale and she was round and plump.

"How are you feeling?" the rotund woman asked.

He shrugged, his mouth dry as he tried to speak. "What happened?"

"You have a slight concussion. Apparently, you passed out in the emergency room while the doctor was examining you. Your blood pressure was elevated, and they opted to keep you for observation. Your mother just stepped out to get herself a cup of coffee. Your brother ran to the restroom. I imagine your family will be back shortly. You've had a few visitors since you arrived."

"How long have I been out?"

"Since late last night. I just came on duty. My name's Arlina."

Davis nodded. "Thank you, Arlina."

"I'll be back in a while to check on you. I'll also let your doctor know that you're awake. As soon as he comes by and says it's okay, we'll be able to order you something to eat. I imagine you must be hungry right about now."

As if on cue, Davis's stomach grumbled. The nurse named Arlina laughed. "You rest. I'll be back shortly," she said as she opened the door and exited the room.

Davis pressed his head back against the pillow behind him. He closed his eyes as he took a deep inhale of air. Everything suddenly came rushing back to him and he felt his stomach bubble and churn with anxiety. The last few hours hadn't been a nightmare that he could wake himself up from. Gaia was dead and he was still a suspect.

"Davis?" His mother's voice pulled him from his trance and his eyes flew open, meeting her stare. Concern blessed her expression, her eyes misted with worry. Relief spread her smile bright and wide. "The nurse said you were awake. How do you feel?"

"I feel like crap. And I have a headache."

"Paul said you would."

"Paul's my doctor?" Davis questioned.

"He's been keeping an eye on you." His mother fussed around him, straightening the bright white coverlet and sheets that lay across his body.

"Where's everyone?"

"Mingus is in the hallway on his cell phone. Your father is at the station. Everyone else was here to check on you last night. I'm sure they'll be back soon. You had us all worried sick." She leaned to kiss his forehead, brushing her fingers against the spot where she'd just pressed her lips.

"Hopefully they'll let me go before then."

"Your father says you need to stay here as long as possible."

"I'm not doing that, Mom. I have a job to do and I need to make a statement about Gaia's death. Has anyone checked on Emilio?"

His mother took a deep breath. "Alexander took custody of his grandson."

Davis's brows lifted. "You know?"

"Alexander confided in your father and me. He's broken that he will never have an opportunity to forge a relationship with his daughter. He's determined to be there for her son."

"That poor kid. I'm sure he doesn't have a clue what's going on."

"He'll be fine. I plan to go over to check on him myself."

"Is that a good idea?"

His mother looked at him, her brow creased. "It's what we do for friends. No matter what the circumstances."

Davis shook his head. "Can you explain to me, please, how you and dad are friends with that man?"

"Things aren't always what they seem, Davis."

"So, he's not a friend?"

"He's a necessary evil," his mother said before changing the subject. "Your sister is interviewing assistants for you. Why didn't you let us know you needed help?"

"I can handle it, Mom."

"Humph! Well, Vaughan has found a few students she thinks will be perfect for the job, especially while you recover. If nothing else, there will be someone there to keep the office open."

Davis nodded, knowing there was no point in arguing. Although it was annoying at times, he couldn't deny that his family intervening whether they were wanted or not, often came in handy. He trusted that whomever Vaughan hired would be exactly who he needed to help him run his office. He also didn't have the energy to give it attention. He was more concerned about what was happening with the investigation. And he suddenly thought about Neema.

"Where's my phone?" he asked, lifting his eyes back to his mother.

"I'm not sure. The police may have it. Mingus will know."

"I need my phone. I need to call my new friend. She's probably wondering what's going on."

"You have a new friend? How do you have a new friend and not one of your siblings told me?"

Davis laughed. "Now that's a question I can't answer for you!"

"Someone's sleeping on the job. I should have gotten a full report by now. What's her name?"

"Neema. Neema Kamau. Her father owns that African restaurant that Dad likes so much."

"I know Mr. Kamau. He's a very nice man. I didn't know he had a daughter. Will you be bringing Neema to Sunday dinner soon?"

"Soon. Maybe. If this situation doesn't scare her off."

His mother smiled. "If it does, then she definitely isn't the woman for you."

Davis shrugged, the two of them falling into a moment of quiet. He broke the silence with a question. "Aren't you going to ask me if I did it?"

"If I know anything about you, Davis Harper Black, it's that you did not *kill* anyone. Most especially someone you loved and cared about. That's not a question I will ever need to ask. I know you didn't hurt Gaia."

"No, I didn't," he replied, "but I do need to try to figure out who did."

Neema woke in a surly mood. She'd sat up until well after midnight hoping that Davis would call and when she'd finally given in and called him, there had been no answer. No answer. No return calls. No text messages. He'd gone radio silent and she was feeling out of sorts about it. She had never been the jealous type, but knowing that Davis had gone to spend time with another woman had that green-eyed monster stalking her spirit. He and Gaia had history and their connection was undeniable. Neema wasn't quite sure what she and Davis had just yet beyond the desire to take their new friendship farther.

She pressed her hand to her cheek where he had kissed her. She knew she was only imagining things, but it felt as if his touch was still there, still tingling, still sweeping heat through her feminine spirit. It had been a perfect first kiss, and it had left her wanting more.

Throwing her legs off the side of the bed, she stood, stretching her arms up over her head. With her fingers reaching for the ceiling, she held the stretch for a good few minutes. She bent forward at the waist, her hands sweeping the floor. Pulling her elbows back against her sides, she rolled her body upward, slowly unwinding each of her vertebrae until she was standing straight again.

As she headed toward the bathroom, she reached for the television remote, turning it on to catch the morning news. She was just about to brush her teeth when she heard the newscaster announce a forthcoming story about the city alderman as soon as they returned from a commercial break. She brushed, rinsed and spit, then stepped back into the bedroom. She dropped onto the corner of the bed. Her heartbeat was suddenly racing, anticipation curdling in the pit of her stomach. Intuition told her something was seriously wrong. Her sour mood nosedived at the news anchor's next words.

"A local politician has been hospitalized after a late-

night shooting left one person dead. Good morning, everyone, and thank you for joining us this morning at seven. I'm Mark Miller and this is ABC7 Chicago."

The news anchor was familiar, a man Neema had interviewed a year earlier for a piece on local celebrities. He was balding, an unsuccessful comb-over failing to hide the spot of flesh on the top of his head. The newscaster continued. His expression was smug as he stared into the camera.

"A shooting last night left one person dead and another hospitalized this morning. Local politician Davis Black, the elected alderman of the twenty-fourth district, was found injured early this morning in his office after reports of shots fired. A second victim was pronounced dead at the scene. The ABC7 team's Wesley Wallace is reporting live from Northwestern Memorial Hospital."

A well-dressed news reporter stood on the sidewalk near the hospital's parking lot. He wore an expensive wool suit and polished leather shoes. His voice was nasally, sounding like he had a perpetual cold. Neema found it slightly disconcerting.

"Mark, police have confirmed that a young woman was pronounced dead at the scene of a shooting on South Keeler Street, in the office of Alderman Davis Black, son of Chicago's police superintendent. Cook County EMS reported Alderman Black was transferred here to the hospital with non-life-threatening injuries. The victim, who has not yet been identified pending notification to her family, and Alderman Black were known to each other. Neighbors living near the scene say they are still in disbelief."

The camera shifted to a scene previously recorded in front of the alderman's office.

"I've never seen anything like this," a woman identified as Betsy Trevino was saying. Betsy held a small black dog in her arms and the dog was dressed in a pink tutu. "I just think it's sad. It's sad that people do this kind of thing. Mitzi and I—" she gestured with the dog "—normally walk this stretch twice per day and usually it's very peaceful."

The clip ended and Wallace continued. "The alderman's office has not yet issued a statement, but sources say he's stable and recovering from his injuries. It's anticipated that he will be released within the week. Detectives are still working to find out what led to the shooting, but do say they are questioning a person of interest. We will bring you more as this story evolves, Mark."

Neema depressed the volume button on her television remote, silence filling the space. She reached for her cell phone and tried Davis's number one more time. It rang once and went directly to voice mail.

She was suddenly shaking. The news report was just vague enough to capture everyone's curiosity and just precise enough to leave them wondering how Davis Black figured into the crime without being outright guilty. She imagined that every reporter who worked that beat was trying to break the story and get the facts. How they'd managed to keep it on the low until daybreak left her questioning just how well connected the Black family was to the press. She hadn't heard anything on the police scanner and even Tiger's informant had failed them.

Neema jogged to her closet to find something to wear. Davis might not be answering his calls, she thought, but she knew where to find him. And right now, she needed to lay her eyes on him to know that he was well.

* * *

When his father and brothers arrived, Davis's mother kissed him on the forehead and excused herself from the room. There was a hushed exchange between his parents; Davis sensed an air of tension between them that both were trying to hide. He shot his brothers a look, the lot of them taking stock of the moment. When the door closed behind the matriarch, his father seemed to breathe a sigh of relief.

"Is everything okay with you two?" Davis questioned, asking what they were all thinking.

Jerome looked from one to the other. He nodded his head. "Everything's fine. Your mother is just concerned about you." He changed the subject. "So, where are we? I have to update the mayor after lunch this afternoon."

Parker took a seat on the edge of the bed. "I've turned the case over to the FBI. They're sending a team later today to take over the investigation. They're going to want to talk to you, but we'll hold them off until after you're out of the hospital."

"They'll need to schedule that through me," Ellington said. "You have legal representation and you are not to talk to anyone about this case without me being there."

Davis looked confused. "The FBI? You're not going to handle the case?"

"Letting the FBI take the reins doesn't mean we aren't going to investigate. It means what we do will be off the books and when we find what we need, we point them in that direction," Parker said.

"It avoids the look of any impropriety," Jerome said. "No one will be able to accuse us of hiding anything because you're my son."

"Right now, though, we have more questions than

we do answers," Armstrong interjected. "First, someone does a drive-by on your home and now this. It can't
be coincidental."

"Tell us what you remember," Parker said, directing
his question toward Davis.

"Gaia called me. She was furious. She said she
needed to see me immediately. I asked what was wrong
and she responded that I already knew and she wanted
answers. I automatically assumed that she was talking
about Alexander Balducci."

"What's he got to do with this?" Armstrong asked.

"It's complicated," Jerome answered. "And Davis
isn't at liberty to say anything more."

Davis and his father exchanged gazes, the patriarch's
stare feeling like a warning.

The brothers all seemed to be trying to read the moment. All of them except Mingus, who looked like his
mind was racing to put two and two together but coming up with three instead of four.

"Did she mention him directly?" Parker asked.

Davis shook his head. "No. She just said that she had
trusted me and asked how I could do that to her, and
then she started crying. That's when I agreed to meet
her. She said she was headed to my office and would
see me when I got there."

"Did you understand what she was talking about?"
Parker queried.

Davis gave his father another look and nodded.

"Where were you when she called?" Armstrong
asked.

"Home. Having dinner with Neema."

"Who's Neema?" Ellington questioned.

"His new boo thang," Mingus muttered, amusement
dancing in his eyes.

Davis rolled his eyes at his brother. "She's a friend."

"Did you say anything to her?" Parker asked.

"I did. She met Gaia at her gallery opening last week. I told her Gaia was in trouble and I needed to go help her. I wanted to invite her to tag along but we both agreed that it wasn't a good idea."

"I just bet she did," Mingus muttered under his breath.

"What's your problem?" Davis quipped.

Mingus held up his hands as if surrendering. "No problem here."

"Something we need to know about her?" Armstrong asked, looking from Mingus to Davis and back.

"No!" Davis snapped. "She doesn't have anything to do with this."

Mingus stood silent, not bothering to respond. Davis suddenly found the look his brother was giving him disconcerting.

"Let's move on," Ellington intoned. "We can come back to baby brother's love life."

"No, we won't," Davis said. "Let it go, please."

"So…" Armstrong continued, "you ended your dinner and left to meet Gaia. Did you make any stops?"

"No. I went straight to the office. It was just after ten o'clock when I arrived. Her minivan was parked across the street and I checked to see if she was sitting inside, but she wasn't there. I figured she might have taken a walk up the street when I didn't see her standing in front of the door."

"So, from the time you got her call till you left to meet her, was how long?"

"Maybe an hour at most. If that."

"Anyone see you?"

Davis shrugged. "Church was just getting out across

the street. There was a group of women standing beside the car parked in front of Gaia's van. I'd heard them talking just before I opened the office door."

"Then what?"

Davis took a deep breath before continuing. "I unlocked the door and went inside. I tried to turn the lights on, but they didn't work. I thought it might have been a fuse. That's when I found Gaia on the floor."

"You saw her? I thought it was dark?" Ellington asked.

"I had the flashlight app on my cell phone engaged."

Ellington nodded. "Then what?"

"I went over to check for a pulse. Then I saw the blood. I was trying to dial 9-1-1 when someone hit me in the back of the head."

"There was someone else there?" Armstrong asked.

"Yeah. They were inside."

"You sure they didn't walk into the building behind you?"

"I'm positive. I locked the door after myself. Whoever it was, was already there."

"Do you have any idea who it might have been?" Mingus asked.

"No," Davis said firmly. "I don't have a clue."

"Who found him?" Ellington asked.

Parker took up the recap. "We received a 9-1-1 call from an Eloise Harper, who said she heard gunshots being fired in the alderman's office. Two police units were dispatched to the scene. On entry, Officer Patrick Owens and his partner, Tyson Forde, found Davis regaining consciousness. He had what is presumed to be the murder weapon in his right hand.

"We're still waiting for Forensics to confirm that, but two bullets had been discharged and the casings were found on the floor beside the body. Gaia took two shots to the chest, one pierced her heart, killing her instantly."

"You said the weapon was in his right hand?" Mingus challenged.

Parker nodded. "That's what the officers both wrote in their reports."

"Davis doesn't shoot with his right hand. I always give him a hard time about it when we go to the gun range."

Davis nodded. "I do almost everything with my left hand except write. I only write with my right hand."

"He's done that since he was a baby," Jerome interjected. "He's always been ambidextrous."

"The prosecution will argue that his ability to use both hands equally well negates the argument that because he usually only uses his left hand, the gun being in his right hand doesn't mean he didn't fire it," Ellington said with the shake of his head.

"You already have them prosecuting me and I haven't been charged. Do you really think they're going to charge me?" Davis asked, a look of astonishment on his face.

"It's all conjecture at this point. Just relax."

"So, right now, everything we know is circumstantial," Jerome said. "What do we have so far than can refute the evidence the district attorney's office thinks it may have?"

"We've issued a warrant for any camera footage in a two-mile radius," Parker said. "And we're questioning the witnesses who claim to have heard the gunshots."

"Claim?" Ellington asked.

"The officer who spoke with the 9-1-1 caller says there is something off about her statement, but she couldn't put her finger on what it was. She just said that she didn't trust it."

"See what you can find out about Eloise Harper," Jerome instructed, his eyes locked on Mingus.

Mingus nodded. "Get me the names of all the witnesses," he said to Parker.

"We need to figure out how Gaia and her killer got into the building. Who else has keys? And I want to know what the deal was with the lights. Who cut them off and how?" Armstrong noted.

"It's about the details," Parker interjected. "It's too neat not to think that someone didn't make a mistake."

"Do you have any idea who would want to do this to you?" Jerome questioned.

Davis shook his head. "No, sir. I don't."

"Mingus, find out what you can about Gaia, too. See if you can retrace her steps before she arrived. Maybe this is about her and not about Davis at all," Armstrong added.

"Will do."

"I need to help. I need to get out of this bed and…" Davis was saying before there was a knock on the room door and Simone pushed her way inside.

Vaughan followed on her heels. "Hey," she greeted.

The two sisters paused to give their father a kiss before pushing past their brother brigade to get to Davis's side.

"You look a million times better," Simone declared. "When we left earlier, you didn't have any color. I've never known you to be that pale."

"I'm starting to feel better," Davis said.

"We were worried," Vaughan added.

"Where's Mom?" Simone queried, looking around the room. Her hand rested against her abdomen, the first hint of a baby bump beginning to rise beneath her fingers.

"Your mother had to be in court this afternoon," Jerome said. "She'll be back later."

"She left about an hour ago," Davis said.

"So, have you guys figured out what happened yet?" Vaughan asked.

Before any of the brothers could answer, there was another knock on the closed door. Mingus stood closest, so he reached to pull the door open. There was a moment of hesitation as he blocked the entrance.

"Who is it?" Davis asked, everyone turning to stare.

Not bothering to respond, Mingus's face blanked as he stepped aside to let Neema enter the room.

Chapter 10

Neema hadn't known what to expect, but she hadn't anticipated walking in on the family reunion Davis was hosting in his hospital room. She suddenly felt like a lab experiment as the Black family stood staring at her. She carried an oversize bouquet of flowers in one hand, so lifted the other in a slight wave, forcing a smile onto her face to hide her discomfort. "Hi," she said softly. "I didn't mean to interrupt."

"Neema!" Davis straightened excitedly, waving her into the room. "You're not interrupting at all. Please, come in!"

She moved closer to the bed, acutely aware of the looks his gathered family was giving her. Simone and Vaughan both swept appraising gazes from her head to her feet, eyeing the casual slacks, white blouse and black-and-gray tweed blazer she wore. A bright scarf in shades of green and fuchsia had been wrapped around her neck. Her shortly cropped hair had been recently cut and she had adorned her face with just a hint of makeup.

Moving to Davis's side, she was surprised when he reached out to hug her, the public display of affection moving everyone in the room to eye them both curiously.

"I tried to call first," she said as she set the flowers on the table by his bedside, "but no one answered your cell phone and the hospital was restricting your calls. I took the chance that I wouldn't be intruding."

"I'm glad you came," Davis said. He had hold of her hand, entwining his fingers between hers as he held on tightly. "I don't have a clue where my phone is." He pulled the back of her hand to his lips and kissed her gently.

Smiling, Neema swept the room with her eyes. "Hello, everyone!" she said, self-conscious about being watched.

Jerome cleared his throat. "Son, aren't you going to introduce your friend?"

"I'm sorry," Davis said. "Everyone, this is my friend, Neema Kamau. Neema, this is everyone!"

The patriarch shot his son an annoyed glare. "It's nice to meet you, Neema. I'm Jerome Black," Davis's father said, his voice a deep baritone. He held her hand between both of his, gently patting the top of her fingers with one as the other held the appendage firmly.

There was no missing the resemblance to his children. His sons had not only inherited their father's good looks but also his height and athletic frame. The patriarch was one distinguished man with salt-and-pepper hair and a full beard and mustache. He reminded Neema of the actor Sean Connery, but with a complexion that was a rich, chocolate brown.

"It's very nice to meet you, sir."

Parker extended his hand. "I'm Davis's brother Parker. And this is Armstrong, Ellington, and Mingus."

"We've met," Mingus said. He stood with his arms folded over his chest and leaned back against the wall.

"I'm Vaughan, his oldest sister." Vaughan stepped forward to shake Neema's hand.

Simone was still staring, her gaze narrowed. "Have we met before? I'm Simone, by the way."

"I don't think so," Neema said. "But your brother has told me a lot about you. Congratulations on the new baby!"

Simone gave her a slight nod. "My brother hasn't told us anything about you. How long have you two been dating?"

Neema shot Davis a quick look.

"Don't start, Simone. You are not about to interrogate Neema."

"I just asked a question. Not sure why you want to hide."

"No one's hiding."

"Leave your brother alone," Jerome admonished. "Neema, Davis, we're going to take off and give you two a moment. I hope we'll see each other again, young lady."

"Thank you, sir," Neema responded.

"Well, we just got here," Vaughan complained.

"And you're just leaving," her father snapped back. "Your brother needs his rest, and we need to get out of the way before the hospital throws us out. You know there're only supposed to be two people in here at a time."

"Maybe for other families," Simone muttered under her breath.

"Excuse my sister," Davis said. "She never acts like she's had any home training."

"Excuse you," Simone countered. "I just say out loud what everyone else is thinking."

"You talk too much," Jerome said. "You girls come on, let me buy you lunch."

"Ohhh!" Vaughan squealed. "Daddy's buying lunch. My day just improved tenfold."

"You buying us lunch, too?" Armstrong asked.

Their father gave him a look. "You boys have a case to investigate. This is a daddy-daughter adventure."

They all laughed.

"I thought I'd try," Armstrong said, shrugging his shoulders.

"Davis, we'll be back later," Parker said. "Neema, it was nice to meet you."

Neema gave him a smile.

"I hope we'll see you again soon, Neema," Ellington said.

"Maybe at Sunday dinner?" Vaughan interjected. "I'm sure our mother would love to meet you."

"We'll see," Davis answered. "I don't need you vultures trying to scare her away."

"Ignore him," Vaughan joked. "He loves us."

Neema giggled. "It was nice to meet you all."

Simone was still staring at her intently. "I'm sure I know you from somewhere," she said. "It'll come to me."

"Goodbye, Simone," Davis said. "Love you!"

Simone leaned in to kiss her brother's cheek. "Love you more, baby brother."

As the family exited the room Mingus still stood, his expression frozen, his mood unreadable. He and Davis exchanged looks.

"I'll be okay," Davis said, almost reading his brother's mind.

Mingus nodded. "Remember what Ellington said. If, and only if, he's present."

Davis's gaze narrowed and his brow furrowed as he comprehended what his brother was trying to say without speaking the words. He nodded. "I understand," he said. "Don't worry."

Mingus swung his eyes toward Neema. "Good to see you again," he said.

"It's good to see you, too," she answered.

The noise level in the room dropped substantially and Neema and Davis found themselves alone together. He tugged her arm gently, pulling her down beside him on the bed. He still clutched her hand, not wanting to release the grip he had on her fingers. Her skin was warm against his and he hadn't realized just how much he'd craved her touch until he needed to think about letting go.

"I'm so sorry about that," Davis said. "My family can be a bit overbearing sometimes. They can take some getting used to."

"They're protective. That's not a bad thing."

"Spend some time with my sisters and you may change your mind about that. I'm sure you and Vaughan will be good friends in no time. Simone is going to make you work for it. She's just difficult for the sake of being difficult, and she's gotten worse since she got pregnant."

"They both seem very nice."

Davis laughed. "You're just being kind."

"Really, they were fine. It was nothing you won't have to go through with my family. I have cousins who are worse than my father."

Davis pressed his palm to the side of her face, staring into her eyes. "I missed you," he said.

"I missed you, too. I was worried to death that something horrible had happened. The news said there was a shooting, a woman was dead and you were hospitalized."

Davis took a deep breath and nodded. "Someone killed Gaia." The words caught deep in his chest and he suddenly felt like crying. He shook the sensation away, wiping at his eyes with the back of his hand. "I'm sorry."

"Don't apologize for how you feel. You have every right to your emotions. And I am so sorry about Gaia. I know how much you cared about her. And how much she cared about you."

He nodded again, still at a loss for words.

"What happened?" Neema asked, genuine concern in her voice. "Was it a robbery?"

Davis hesitated for a split second, his brother's warning not to discuss the case ringing in his thoughts. He hesitated and then he made a decision he knew none of his family would approve of, but one that solidified how he was feeling and what he wanted. He trusted Neema. He wanted her to trust him. If they were ever going to build anything significant between them, he needed to be open and honest and vulnerable. There wasn't room for secrets and lies between them.

"I don't know. When I arrived at the office, Gaia was dead. Then someone hit me in the back of the head. When I came to, the scene had been staged as if I was the one who shot Gaia."

Neema gasped. Loudly. "That doesn't make sense. Why would someone do that?"

"I don't know. That's what my brothers are trying to figure out."

"They're investigating the case?"

"Not officially. Officially, the case has been turned over to the FBI."

Neema nodded, trying to process what she'd just heard. It hadn't been at all what she'd expected and, if she were looking for a story, it was everything. But she wasn't looking for a story. At least, she thought, she didn't think she was. It definitely wasn't the priority it had been when she'd first met Davis. In this moment, Davis was everything and more than she could have ever imagined. She couldn't be that person if she wanted a relationship with him, and she wanted to see what they might be able to make of whatever was happening between them.

She reached out and wrapped her arms around his neck, hugging him close. "I am sorry about Gaia, but I'm glad you're okay."

"I'll be fine. Doctors say I have a slight concussion and my blood pressure was high when they checked me in. I was also slightly dehydrated. Hopefully, my numbers are improving and they'll let me go home tomorrow. I'm sorry you were worried. I would have called, but…well…" He paused. He took a deep breath. "There's so much I want to tell you."

Neema shushed him as the monitor beeped to indicate a rise in his blood pressure. "You just need to rest. We have plenty of time to talk."

"I hope so, Neema. You're something special and I really care about you. I like *us* together. I like *us* a lot."

Neema's smile widened. Her cheeks warmed and her heart skipped two beats. She suddenly leaned forward and pressed her closed lips to his. The gesture surprised them both, Neema being forward in a way that was unexpected. Davis kissed her back, his mouth like plush pillows against hers. It was a moment of exploration, an exciting sensual journey that started slow and quickly rose in intensity.

Davis teased her lips with his tongue, a gentle prodding until she welcomed his ministrations and he danced between her parted lips. They both gasped as he pulled her closer, one hand clutching the back of her head, the other dancing a slow drag up the length of her back. His fingertips teased the round of her buttocks and she jumped. The sensations sweeping through her had her disconcerted and woozy. Both were breathless when he finally let her go and she pulled herself out of his arms.

"Wow!" Neema murmured.

"Wow!" Davis echoed.

"You do that really well."

He chuckled softly. "I told you I had finesse."

Neema laughed. "I still had to kiss you first."

"I have no problems with that," Davis said as he kissed her again, the intensity as magnanimous as the first time.

Neema leaned against him, her knees like jelly, her whole body quivering with pleasure.

The moment was surreal, spinning in slow motion as they traded gentle caresses. In that moment the dynamics of their relationship shifted, both recognizing that their friendship was so much more. More beginning to feel a lot like love.

Hours later, when Davis opened his eyes after a much needed nap, Neema was gone. He found himself thinking about her and the step they had taken in their relationship. He enjoyed her company and was excited at the prospect of their relationship moving forward and their connection becoming deeper. Just thinking about her made him smile.

What he hadn't expected was the redhead sitting in the chair by his bedside watching him intently. She sat with her hands clasped together in her lap and her legs crossed. She was dressed all in black and her expression was slightly sinister.

He jumped at the sight of her and there was no keeping the surprise from his voice. "Ginger! What are you doing here?"

Ginger smiled but said nothing, tossing the length of her hair over her shoulder instead. She pointed to the other side of the room and the man sitting in the shadowed corner. Davis turned, following the line of her index finger, his gaze meeting Alexander Balducci's. Davis's heart began to race and the air caught deep in his lungs.

Davis gave the man a nod as he stood and stepped closer to the bed. His hands were pushed into the pockets of his wool overcoat. The classic line of the garment complemented by the plaid scarf around his neck. "Mr. Balducci!"

"What happened to Gaia?"

Davis shook his head. "I don't know," he answered honestly.

The man stared at him, his eyes searing. Davis couldn't help but think that he'd be dead twice over if looks were capable of murder. His eyes shifted back to Ginger, who suddenly rose from her seat to stand on four-inch stilettos. As she pulled her black bomber jacket closed, Davis took note of the gun tucked into the waistband of her knit slacks.

"I want answers," Balducci snapped.

Davis snapped back. "So do I! She was my friend."

The tension in the room was stifling, the energy thick with anger and fear. Davis was suddenly grateful when the room door swung open, his parents passing through the entrance. The moment was even more awkward as they all stood there looking at each other.

Judith moved first. "Alexander, we weren't expecting to see you here," she said as she wrapped her arms around his shoulders and hugged him.

Alexander hugged her back. "I just wanted to check on Davis. To make sure he was well."

"We appreciate that. His doctor says they should be releasing him soon."

"That's a good thing," Alexander noted.

Judith moved to Davis's side, leaning to kiss her son's cheek. "You okay?" she questioned, her eyes seeming to say more.

He nodded. "I'm fine. Mr. Balducci and his friend were just leaving." He turned to look at the man. "I appreciate you stopping by, sir."

Balducci shook his head, attitude washing over his expression. "I came for answers, son, and I'm not leaving until I get them," he said, shaking his head from side to side. "I'm sure you can appreciate the importance of that."

"I do, sir," Davis answered. "But I can't help you. I honestly don't know anything."

Jerome shook his head. Rage seeped from his eyes, his ire rising with a vengeance. "You're out of line, Alexander," he growled, fighting to keep his tone low and even.

Balducci snarled. "I'm out of line? I'm out of line? I want answers. My daughter is dead! My sources in the police department say your son had something to do with it and you're trying to cover it up."

"Your sources don't know what the hell they're talking about and the FBI investigation will prove that."

The two men stood toe-to-toe, looking like two bulls ready to lock horns. It was a side of his father Davis didn't ever remember seeing.

"Enough!" Judith snapped. "You're not each other's enemy. You have the same goal. You want to get to the truth. You'd be better served working with each other than against each other. Now enough. This is not the time or the place."

There was a moment of pause as the two men continued to appraise each other. It was only when Alexander took a step back that Jerome visibly released the weight holding him hostage where he stood. He rolled his shoulders forward and then back, leaning his head from one side to the other. He moved to Judith's side, easing an arm around his wife's waist. "We appreciate your concern for our son, but you need to stay away. When I know something concrete, I'll let you know," he said sternly.

Balducci narrowed his gaze on the man. His jaw was tight, his lips pursed. He looked older than he had the last time he and Davis had been in a room together. Davis could see the hurt in his eyes and suddenly realized the pain Balducci had to be feeling was probably greater than his own. He had lost his daughter before the two could have forged a relationship with one another. Davis couldn't begin to fathom the guilt he had to be feeling.

Davis inhaled, a deep gust of air lining his lungs. "How's Emilio?" he asked, changing the subject.

Alexander finally shifted his gaze from Jerome to

Davis. "My grandson will be fine. He'll want for nothing. Ginger has been taking good care of him."

Davis shot Ginger another look. She had eased closer to the door. He instinctively knew that had anything jumped off between his father and her employer, she would have been in the wind, out the door before anyone could have blinked. He sensed that, despite her loyalty to her employer, she wasn't willing to make all Balducci's battles hers.

"You know we're here if you need us," Judith said softly.

Balducci nodded. "There will be a memorial service for Gaia on Monday. I'll have Ginger send you the details," he concluded. As he moved toward the door, Davis called his name.

"Yes?"

"I didn't kill Gaia. And I swear, I don't know who did or why. I just know it wasn't me. She was my friend and I loved her."

There was a moment of pause as Balducci stood reflecting on his comment. Then, with one last nod, he was out the door.

Davis closed his eyes in a moment of brief respite, still feeling little was well in his small world.

Sticky notes covered the one bare wall in Neema's bedroom. She had tried to make sense of her scribblings most of the night, hoping to piece together who might have killed Gaia and how Davis figured into her murder. Deciphering what little he had told her and what her source at the police department had shared, she had a sizeable puzzle with a lot of missing pieces. Knowing the FBI had stepped in to head the investigation meant her window of discovery had narrowed substantially.

What she did know was that Davis was their prime suspect and the Feds' efforts to talk with him had been thwarted by his attorney brother. His family was running serious interference and she knew the FBI had yet to formally interrogate him. She also knew a witness claimed to have heard the gunshots *after* Davis had arrived on site and entered the building. That witness was Neema's first stop of the day. She hoped a casual conversation with the woman would shed some light on what had happened, and perhaps point Neema in the right direction.

Neema was determined to help clear Davis's name. She knew he was innocent and she was determined to get to the truth and clear him as a suspect before things really got out of hand and he was charged.

Thirty minutes later, Neema was searching out a parking space on the street across from Davis's office. The witness, a young woman named Eloise Harper, lived four doors down. Ms. Harper was fairly new to the Chicago area, having moved from Miami the previous year. Ms. Harper had an arrest record; she'd been charged twice with solicitation. She was currently employed as a dancer in a local strip joint called The Gentlemen's Club. If nothing else, Neema figured a conversation with the woman would be colorful.

She had just parallel parked and was gathering a notebook, pen and her purse from the passenger seat when she saw them. The woman she'd identified as Eloise was in deep conversation with Alexander Balducci's assistant, Ginger. The young woman's flaming red hair was like a neon light cascading down her back. Her expensive designer attire and stiletto heels also made her stand out in the working-class neighborhood.

Neema reached for the digital camera she always

kept close, aiming it toward Eloise's front door. When the two women were in frame and focused, Neema snapped the shot. Once, twice, and a third time, taking photos until both women had gone their separate ways. There had been an exchange of cash and then Eloise had climbed into a yellow taxicab, carrying enough luggage for someone to assume that she was moving. The conversation Neema had hoped to have with Eloise suddenly became more critical. Clearly, there was more to the story than Neema could begin to imagine.

As she sat weighing her options, deciding where to turn next, there was a knock on her front passenger window. As she turned to see who it was, Mingus Black peered through the window, gesturing for her to unlock the door. Neema's stomach was suddenly in her throat and she began to shake. He knocked a second time and, bracing herself, Neema disengaged the lock.

Sliding into the passenger seat, Davis's brother tossed her a look. "Hey."

"Hi," she responded, her voice squeaking awkwardly.

"What are you doing here?"

"I could ask you the same thing."

"You could, but my brother knows I'm here and why. Can you say the same for yourself?"

Neema sighed.

"What's your end game, Neema?"

"It's not what you think."

"Then what is it? Because I'll be damned if you're going to hurt my brother."

"I would never purposely hurt Davis. I care about him."

"He would care about you, too, if he knew the truth. But since he doesn't, we don't truly know how he feels, do we?"

Neema shot him a look but didn't bother to answer the question. She suddenly felt as if her worst nightmare had come to fruition.

Mingus continued. "I have to assume you're working him, hoping to get a story for your newspaper. I'm told you're one of their star reporters."

"That's not…it isn't… I wasn't…." she stammered, suddenly ashamed and embarrassed. Hearing him call her out felt like a bomb dropping, but there was no hole for her to fall into and hide. She took another breath to collect her thoughts, then made an earnest effort to explain herself.

"I'm not writing a story on Davis. The day he met Mr. Balducci at my father's restaurant, I saw them exchange cash and I thought he might be a dirty politician. That was a story I thought I could get behind—our beloved alderman on the take. But as I got to know your brother, and the more time I spent with him, I realized there was no possible no way he could be involved in any criminal enterprise. He has too much integrity to put himself in that kind of position."

"And you're here now because…?"

"Because I want to help. I want to help clear his name. I know he wouldn't hurt Gaia and I want to help prove that."

Mingus sat staring at her, his countenance making her nervous. She kept talking. "Davis has become very important to me. I believe he and I could have something very special together. I plan to tell him the truth. I never intended to keep my secret for as long as I have. I just never seem to be able find the right time."

He gave her a look, dismissing her comment with the blink of his eye. His expression spoke volumes, shouting loudly through the space.

"That's the excuse I've been using," she concluded. "The truth is I'm a coward and I've just been too scared. I didn't want your brother to break up with me when we really just found our rhythm."

Mingus gave her a nod. "Tell him. Or I will."

"I promise. I'll tell him before the week is out."

"You might not have until the end of the week. Don't take too much time."

Neema closed her eyes, opening then again as she breathed a sigh of relief. "Thank you, Mingus."

"Don't thank me. I'm not doing this for you. Davis trusts you. I don't. I'm just giving you the benefit of the doubt."

Neema nodded her understanding, nothing else left for her to say.

Mingus looked at his watch but made no effort to move. They both sat and watched as two meticulously dressed investigators exited a black SUV and made their way to the front door of the alderman's office. A uniformed police officer stood waiting to let them inside.

"You need to do a better job of being inconspicuous," Mingus said matter-of-factly. "I saw you a mile away."

"You only saw me because you were looking."

"That, too," he said, chuckling. There was another moment of pause before he spoke again. "My kid brother is a good man. He likes you. He likes you a lot. He's not going to take this lightly, so you need to be prepared. But understand, if you're lying to me and you hurt him, I'm going to be the least of your problems. Vaughan and Simone will destroy you."

"I appreciate the warning, but I'm not going to do anything to jeopardize my relationship with your brother. He means too much to me," Neema said.

Mingus nodded, reaching for the door handle.

"Before you go, I have something I think you should see," she said. She passed him her camera.

Mingus gave her a dismissive shake of his head. "I saw. I saw when she arrived."

"Why is Ginger paying off the witness? Why do you think she's here? What do you know about her?" Neema was suddenly firing off questions, her mind racing as she added yet another piece to the puzzle that didn't make any sense.

"Just keep those photos safe," Mingus answered, "they may come in handy. And if you find out anything else, you bring it to me first. No one else, and definitely not Davis! You don't tell him anything that might put him at risk. Is that understood?"

Neema nodded as Mingus handed her a business card with his personal cell phone number printed on the back. With that, he eased out of the vehicle and headed back to his car.

Not needing to wait around, Neema started her engine and pulled onto the main thoroughfare. Something told her Eloise Harper was headed to the bus station and if she had any chance of catching up with her, she needed to hurry.

Chapter 11

Neema prayed until she pulled into the Greyhound bus station. If she got this wrong, she would miss her window of opportunity to ask the eyewitness a few questions. A quick call to a friend at Yellow Cab Chicago had pointed her to the terminal on Harrison Street. She knew she was taking a risk hoping that she was headed to the right place at the right time and that she'd be able to find the woman she was looking for. She prayed that everything would align in her favor, feeling like she was asking for the moon and the stars.

The rank scent of musty bodies, stale smoke and marijuana greeted her at the terminal door. She had to navigate her way past a gathering of homeless men and two prostitutes peddling their wares. Although the bus terminal was considered a boon for the city, its less than stellar atmosphere made for traveling hell. The floors were nasty, the bathrooms were filthy, there wasn't enough seating and staff was sometimes less than helpful, bitter about having to work the job at all.

Neema could feel the frustration as an announcement came over the intercom system that the next bus to Miami would be delayed. Fatigue, weariness and ire danced in the raised voices and loud chatter. That's when Neema saw her.

Eloise Harper was anorexic thin. She was leathered skin over thick bones, no ounce of tissue between the two. Her blond hair had been overbleached, the coloration and texture like dried straw. Her facial features were nondescript and she wore far too much makeup; the baby-blue eyeshadow, mauve blush and vibrant red lipstick garish. She was sitting near the USB charging station, her new iPhone juicing through a thin white cable.

Neema eased over and took the seat beside her. "Eloise, hello! I don't mean to interrupt," she said, "but I'm a reporter with the *Chicago Tribune*. Do you mind if I ask you a few questions?"

"A reporter?"

Neema nodded. "Yes, with the *Chicago Tribune*," she repeated, passing the woman a business card. "My name's Neema. Neema Kamau."

"How'd you find me?" Eloise gave Neema a narrowed gaze, looking like she might bolt if pushed too hard.

"It's what I do," Neema said, giving her a smile. "I know you reported the shooting at Alderman Davis's office. I'd like to know what you saw."

"I didn't see anything."

"Is that what Ginger told you to say?"

Eloise bristled, shifting nervously against the wooden bench. "You know Ginger?"

"We're acquainted."

"You work for her, too?"

Neema shook her head. "Not like that. Is that how you two know each other? You used to work together?"

"Something like that. I was living on the streets and she helped me get out of my situation. She got me some work, found me a bed and four walls, and made sure I ate. She's good people."

"You told the police that you heard gunshots after the alderman arrived. Where were you?"

"Headed to work. I dance. I was walking down to the bus stop."

"And you saw the alderman go into the building?"

"Yeah. Something like that."

"Something like that?"

"That's what I said."

"Then you heard gunshots."

"Yeah."

"How many?"

Eloise shrugged. "Two, maybe three. I'm not sure."

"You're not sure?"

"Okay, two."

"You didn't hear the gunshots, did you, Eloise?"

"I said what I said." Her tone was laced with attitude.

They suddenly announced the arrival of the next bus to Miami. Eloise stood, reaching for a carry-on and her purse.

"Are you going on vacation?"

"Something like that," Eloise repeated as she turned toward the exit door.

"Can I have your cell phone number to call you?" Neema asked.

Eloise shook her head. "I have nothing else to say."

"You're not coming back, are you?"

"Look." She tossed Neema one last glance. "I can't help you. If you want answers, go talk to Ginger. This was her gig. I was just helping out an old friend." And with that, Eloise Harper was gone.

Davis stood in the doorway of his mother's office; he knew his hangdog expression had moved Judith to laugh. He'd been released from the hospital the day before and was going stir crazy trying to get the rest the doctors had said he needed.

"What did you do?" she questioned. "Because you look guilty of something."

"I ate the last slice of chocolate cake."

She laughed again. "You know your father had laid claim to that cake. He's not going to be happy."

"I thought maybe I could charm you into making another one," he said as he moved into the room and dropped down onto an upholstered chair.

His mother leaned back in her seat. "I might be able to do that. But just for you."

"I knew I was your favorite."

"Mothers don't have favorites."

"And that would be a lie."

"Perhaps, but not one I'll ever admit to."

The smirk on his mother's face made Davis smile. "I appreciate you and Dad wanting me to stay here, but I'm ready to go back to my own place."

"I know, but you heard your father. He doesn't think that's a good idea until this is all resolved. And I have to agree with him."

"I feel like I'm twelve, Mom. I need to get back on schedule and get back to work. I have a life."

"No one's disputing that, but right now, someone's trying to destroy that life and we're not going to let that happen. There's nothing you need to do at your place that you can't do right here. You can even work."

"Oh, there are some things I can't do!" Davis said facetiously.

His mother shook her head. "I'm sure you and your brothers have even done that under my roof thinking you were getting away with something."

"Not me! Maybe Armstrong and Ellington. Definitely Mingus. And you might want to question both your daughters."

Judith laughed. "Since we're on the subject, when do I get to meet this young lady? Your father says she seems very nice."

"I don't think that's the subject we were on."

"Are you sure about that?"

Amusement danced in Davis's eyes. "Do you believe in love at first sight, Mom?"

"I believe attraction can shift so quickly that we think it's love at first sight." She sat forward in her chair. "Why? Do you think you love this young woman?"

Davis shrugged, drifting into thought for a moment. He lifted his eyes to find his mother staring at him intently. "I think that what she and I have could be pretty special," he concluded. "Obviously, we're still getting to know each other. Right now, I think it's an intense adoration with a robust degree of lust."

His mother nodded. "I appreciate that you're not rushing into anything. That never serves you well."

"You and Dad rushed into your relationship."

"Your father and I were great friends prior to becoming romantic with each other. We had no reason to wait, but I wouldn't necessarily say we rushed into anything."

"Do you still love him?"

"Why would you ask me that? Of course, I still love your father!"

Davis shrugged his broad shoulders a second time. "Lately, you two seem to always be at odds with each other. We've all noticed, and we're worried."

"Well, don't. Your father and I are fine. We go through things like all married couples, but we go through them together. And it's our love for each other that helps us get through. I love your father even more now than when we were first married. You never have to worry about that."

Davis stood. "I need to go change. I'm meeting Neema for coffee, then I have to meet Ellington down at his office. We have an appointment with the FBI investigators."

"Please, listen to your brother's advice. He won't steer you wrong."

"I will. It'll be fine." Davis moved around the over-size desk and kissed his mother's cheek. "Don't forget the chocolate cake," he said with a wide smile.

Judith chuckled. "I'll tell you what. Invite your friend to Sunday dinner and I'll make chocolate cake."

Davis grimaced. "You really want to subject her to Simone and Vaughan? That kind of scrutiny might kill my relationship."

"Your sisters have your best interest at heart."

"My sisters get great joy in making my life miserable."

"That's called love, son."

Davis exited the room, calling back over his shoulder, "If that's love, I'd hate to see what they'd do if they didn't like me!"

* * *

"So, how's your day going?" Neema asked as she slid in opposite him in the booth.

She'd been looking forward to seeing Davis since he'd invited her to join him for coffee at Bang Bang Pie & Biscuits. Two cups of freshly brewed coffee with two slices of buttermilk pie with cranberries, whipped cream and a graham cracker crust rested on the tabletop.

Davis leaned across the table to kiss her lips, his hand gently cupping the side of her face. He kissed her until they were both breathless. He sat back in his seat, grinning like he'd won the biggest prize at the state fair. "Better now. How about yours?"

"My day has improved substantially now that I've seen you. I'm happy to see you're feeling better."

"I do feel better. My mother's been spoiling me with home-cooked meals and I've gotten plenty of rest. Now I need to get back to work."

"Please, don't rush. If you need more time, take it."

"You sound like my mother."

"Your mother is a very wise woman."

"She would like you to join us for dinner on Sunday. My family has been telling her about you. I would love to have you there if you don't have other plans."

Neema's eyes widened. She hesitated, pondering the invitation. "With your whole family?"

"It's what we do. If you don't want to, I understand. I know it can be overwhelming."

"No, actually, I would like that."

His exuberance was palpable. "Excellent! My mother is going to love you, so I don't want you to worry."

Neema reached for his hand, giving his fingers a quick squeeze. "So, what's going on with the case? Do they have any leads on Gaia's killer?"

Davis shrugged, pausing as he took a bite of his pie. He closed his eyes briefly as he savored the taste against his tongue. When he opened them, Neema had taken a bite of her own pie and was smiling warmly. He held up his index finger as he chewed and swallowed, then took a second bite before answering.

"I don't think they're any closer to finding her killer. I don't doubt they're still looking at me for the crime. She and I had history. She'd called me upset about something. I was there. And she was shot with my gun. To everyone else, that makes me guilty."

Neema shook her head. "But we know you didn't do it."

"We still have to prove it. Who accessed my office and how did they get it? Who knew I kept a weapon in my desk drawer? Who benefits from Gaia's death, or from me being charged for the crime? There are still more questions than answers."

"May I ask a question?"

"Of course! Anything. You know that."

Neema nodded. "The night we were at the gallery, that woman Ginger said something that upset you. Could she be involved?"

"I don't know. She was actually there to warn me about my business arrangement with her employer. She said I shouldn't trust him."

"Did she say why?"

Davis shrugged. "No. I don't have a clue."

"What kind of business dealings do you and Mr. Balducci have together?"

Davis paused. "I'm sorry," she said. "I was just being nosey. I understand if you don't want to discuss it with me."

"It's fine. He asked me to facilitate a sale between him and Gaia."

"That's why you purchased those four paintings!"

Davis nodded. "I'm sorry. I wish there was more I could tell you, but…"

"Don't apologize. You don't owe me any explanation. I appreciate you sharing that."

"It's important to me that we be open and honest with each other."

Neema's stomach did a quick flip, her anxiety level rising. She sat with her hands in her lap, twisting her fingers together. "Since we're sharing," she said, "there's something…"

Davis's cell phone suddenly chimed loudly. He stole a quick glance at the incoming number and cursed under his breath. "I'm sorry. I have to take this," he said, rising from the booth. "I'll be right back." He answered the call, moving toward the restaurant's door as he started the conversation.

Neema exhaled, a heavy gust that felt like weight pressing on her chest. She mumbled a low whisper, talking to the air around her. "Tell him! Just say it. Davis, I'm a reporter!" She repeated herself a second, and then a third time, tossing a look to see if anyone was staring at her.

A good few minutes passed before Davis returned. Neema had finished her pie and was finishing the last few sips of her coffee. Suddenly her phone rang, her father's image filling the screen.

"Hello, Baba!"

"Where are you, Neema?"

"Having coffee with Alderman Black."

"You are having coffee with the alderman?" He repeated her comment as if he wasn't sure he'd heard her correctly.

"Yes, sir."

"Well, I am sorry to interrupt, but I need you here at the restaurant. Your mother isn't feeling well, and I am taking her to the doctor's office."

"What's wrong? Do you need me to come with you?"

"I need you to help out at the restaurant while we are gone. I don't know that I can trust the new hire just yet. He is still learning, and Tobias can be lazy when we are not there. Your mother will be fine. She doesn't even want to go, but the doctor has an opening, so I am making her."

"Are you sure it's not serious?"

"She has been complaining about the pain in her knees. I imagine it's just old age catching up with her like it has caught up with me!"

Neema chuckled. "Okay, Baba. I'm on my way, but call and let me know what the doctor says, please."

"You're a good daughter, Neema. Please, give the alderman my regards."

"I will, Baba. Love you!"

As she disconnected the call Davis was moving back in her direction. He looked quite dashing in his navy blue suit, pink dress shirt and paisley tie. Neema eyed him with appreciation, noticing that hers were not the only eyes paying him attention.

"I hate to do this, but I've got to run," Davis said as he dropped cash onto the table to cover the tip. "Are you working tonight?"

"I have to head to the restaurant now, actually. My father needs me to cover for him and my mother while they run to a doctor's appointment."

"Is everything okay?"

"Mom's having some problems with her knees."

"I hope she's feeling better. Please, give them both my regards."

"I will. And thank you for the pie. It was very good. In fact, I think I'm going to order one to take home for my parents. I think my mother would love the chocolate pecan."

"That's one of my favorites, too!" Davis bent to kiss her mouth, his lips dancing sweetly against hers. He tasted like ginger and orange with a hint of caramel. Neema pressed her palm to his chest, wanting to hold on for just a moment longer. When he finally pulled away, taking a step back, they were both breathing heavily.

"Call me," he said, giving her one final peck on the lips. "Or I'll call you!"

The FBI interrogation ended as quickly as it started. The two men dressed in black suits had little interest in Davis. Forensics had concluded there was no possible way that he had pulled the trigger. But they still didn't know who had murdered Gaia and why.

"Did you know your friend had a substantial life insurance policy?" The man asking the question was short and squat with a thinning head of blond hair combed over from one ear to the other.

Davis shook his head. "No. It wasn't something we ever discussed."

The investigator nodded. "Her son stands to receive ten million dollars after her cause of death is made official."

Davis blinked, digesting the information slowly. "That doesn't make any sense," he said. "Gaia didn't have that kind of income to afford that kind of policy. Nor did she have assets that needed to be conserved like that. I know Gaia would have wanted to ensure Emilio was protected, but ten million dollars...?" His voice trailed, his eyes darting back and forth as he considered the ramifications.

"Her father purchased the policy, from what we understand," the other investigator said. He was taller than his partner with more hair and leaner facial features.

"Her father?" Ellington looked confused, tossing Davis a look.

"And the son is listed as the only beneficiary, correct?" Davis questioned.

"Yes, that's correct," the second agent answered. "In fact, it goes into a trust until his twenty-fourth birthday."

Ellington gave them a nod. "I would think that might rule out money as the motivating factor for her murder, do you agree?"

The two men suddenly rose, neither responding. The short investigator extended his hand. "We appreciate you taking time to speak with us. Our office will issue a formal statement clearing you of any wrongdoing, Alderman Black."

"Thank you," Davis said. "I appreciate that."

"Have a good day, sir."

The two brothers watched as they exited the room. When they were out of earshot, Ellington turned to his brother. "Do you know who her father is?"

Davis nodded. "Yeah, but I'm not at liberty to say. I was sworn to secrecy."

"Does this have something to do with Dad insisting you meet with Alexander Balducci?"

Davis's eyebrow hitched upward, the answer to the question on his face. But he said nothing out loud.

"Gotcha!" Ellington quipped. "I swear, if it's not one

thing, it's another. Do you think her *father* had something to do with this?"

"I don't know, but I plan to find out."

Davis arrived at the Balducci home unannounced.
He came bearing gifts for Emilio and four paintings of
the boy for his grandfather. The housekeeper granted
him admittance and as he stood in the foyer waiting
for Balducci he couldn't help but wonder if he'd made
a mistake. No one knew he was there and he imagined
his parents would probably have insisted Mingus tag
along if they had supported him going at all. But he had
questions and he knew that Balducci was the only one
who could answer them for him.

The man was clearly not happy to see him. Davis got
the distinct impression he had interrupted something
important and he was prepared to be turned away. Instead, Balducci gestured for him to follow as he led the
way to the back of the home and into his private office.

"I appreciate you seeing me, sir," Davis said. "I
wanted to deliver the paintings you purchased. I was
also hoping that I might be able to see Emilio and give
him my condolences."

"I'm surprised your father allowed you to come,"
the man said.

It was his first full sentence that wasn't a grunt,
Davis thought. He shrugged. "I didn't ask for his permission."

Balducci shot him a look. "You surprise me. I
wouldn't have thought you had it in you."

"Why is that, sir?"

"Your father has always described you as his obe-
dient son."

"I have my moments."

Balducci gave a slight chuckle. "Well, thank you for dropping by. But I need to get back to work."

"I would like to see Emilio. I'm sure a familiar face would be a comfort to him."

Balducci hesitated, seeming to consider Davis's request. He finally nodded. "You'll find him in the basement with his cousin Pauly. Pauly is my late son Leonard's child. He came to live with me after his father's death, so the two have much in common."

There was an awkward pause as Davis reflected on his comment. "Thank you," he finally said.

"After you say hello, let yourself out. And in the future, don't come back, unless I extend an invitation."

"I meant no disrespect, Mr. Balducci. Gaia was a good friend and I know she'd appreciate me staying in touch with her son."

"I'm sure that's true. But our two families have a complicated history that makes our relationship very tenuous. It's better that we maintain some distance."

"Better for whom? I thought you and my father were friends?"

There was another moment of hesitation before the man spoke. "As I said, it's complicated."

"I'd like to understand…" Davis started before his comment was cut short.

Balducci help up a hand. "Ginger will show you to the basement," he said.

Davis turned, suddenly realizing the woman stood in the doorway. She met his stare, the faintest of smiles pulling at her thin lips.

"Show Alderman Black to the basement. Then show him to the door," Balducci commanded as he settled in the leather executive chair behind his desk.

Davis turned, understanding that he had been summarily dismissed, the older man having nothing else to say to him.

He followed Ginger down the length of hallway and through the kitchen. A set of stairs led them to the basement of the home, the entire space a family playroom. Much thought had gone into the décor, the room designed to entertain and delight. There were old-school pinball machines, an oversize flat-screen television with a surround sound system, a pool table, bean bag chairs and a wall of bookcases that highlighted a collection of video games, movie DVDs and a few books.

Emilio and his cousin were playing Fortnite, the online video game filling the television screen. Both were lost in play, oblivious to his arrival.

Davis stood watching, thinking that Emilio had grown some since he'd last seen him. Ginger stood by his side and he shot her a look as she stared where he stared.

"Why are you here?"

"I wanted to check on Emilio."

"He's doing well," she said softly. "His grandfather is good with him. He misses his mom, though."

"I also wanted to ask you a few questions. When you came to the gallery, you said Balducci was setting me and Gaia up. That I shouldn't trust him. What did you mean?" Davis questioned, cutting another eye in her direction.

"It was nothing," she answered.

"No, it was something. You purposely came to warn me. What did you want me to know?"

"Give them enough time and people will always show you who they are."

"Did he have something to do with Gaia's death?"

Before she could answer, Emilio suddenly jumped

from his seat. He rounded the sofa and raced toward him, throwing himself against Davis's chest.

"Uncle Davis!"

"Hey, bud! You okay?"

"Yeah. I have a grandfather. And this is my cousin. His name's Paul Balducci but everyone calls him Pie." Emilio giggled. "Except my grandfather. He calls him Pauly."

"It's nice to meet you," Davis said, throwing the man a wave of his hand.

The man they called Paul, Pauly or Pie barely looked up from his game. He gave Davis one quick stare, his eyes narrowed into thin slits, his jaw tight. Turning back to his game, he continued to ignore Davis, seeming uninterested in him being there.

Davis shifted his attention to the little boy standing before him. "I came to check on you, bud. I wanted to make sure you were doing okay."

Emilio shrugged. "I'm good."

"He's doing very well," Ginger said. She had moved to stand behind the boy, her hands pressing against his narrow shoulders. "Emilio is very resilient. He's been having a good time getting to know his new family."

"Is that true?" Davis asked.

Emilio shrugged. "I guess," he muttered.

"Do you mind giving us a minute?" Davis said, directing his question at Ginger.

She smiled. "Of course not." She stepped away, moving to go sit on the couch with Pauly, or Pie, or whatever the man called himself.

Davis dropped down on one knee. "I just want to tell you how sorry I am about your mom. She was a good friend and I'm going to miss her."

Emilio nodded. "My grandfather said someone hurt

her. He said he's going to make them pay for what they did to her."

"We all want to find who did it. We want justice for your mother."

"No," Emilio said, shaking his head. "Grandfather says we want revenge."

Davis inhaled swiftly, holding his breath for a moment as he thought about how best to respond. Before he could find the words, Emilio gave him a fist bump and returned to his seat in front of the game.

Davis suddenly felt like he'd been dismissed a second time.

Ginger returned to his side. "He'll be fine," she said.

"I'm not so sure about that. Those values are nothing his mother would have wanted for him."

"Maybe not, but now he'll learn how to survive and to excel. He'll succeed where Alexander's other sons failed. He's been given the keys to the kingdom and he'll reign. Alexander will make sure of it. And I'll be here to help in any way that I can."

Davis studied her expression, something like awe and wonder lighting her eyes. "I'm sure you will," he responded.

"You should go now," she said, pointing him in the direction from where he'd come.

With a nod of his head, Davis turned, heading back up the stairs. As he maneuvered the steps, he noticed the family photos lining the length of the wall. One, in particular, captured his attention.

Oddly familiar, it was a formal portrait of two small boys standing on either side of an elderly man. Both wore identical outfits, miniature replicas of the older man's tuxedo. One child was fair with blond hair that had a cowlick in the center of his head. The other's complexion was significantly darker, his jet-black hair swirled in silky, close-cropped curls. The family resemblance was in the eyes, but Davis needed to stare hard to see it. Until he did, and then there was no denying the connection. For a few brief moments, Davis stood staring, trying to remember where he'd seen the image before. Suddenly, Balducci's words felt like a harsh slap. *Our two families have a complicated history that makes our relationship very tenuous.*

In that moment, Davis realized things were more complicated than he could have ever imagined, and he needed to speak with his father. And he needed to talk with him right now.

Chapter 12

When his parents entered the family home, Davis had been sitting in his father's office for some time, his head between his hands, his shoulders rolled forward, dejection wrapped around him like a wool blanket. The room looked like a hurricane had blown threw it. Papers were strewed across the floor, books pulled from the shelves, and there was a large hole in the drywall. He looked up as Jerome and Judith both gasped, trying to comprehend what had happened.

"What the hell…!" Jerome shouted.

"Davis, what happened?" his mother questioned. "Are you hurt?"

He held a photograph in his hand, the edges yellowed and frayed with age. He held it out to his father, the two men locking gazes.

"What's going on? What is that?" Judith asked.

"I saw this photo today on Alexander Balducci's wall

and, for the life of me, I couldn't remember where I had seen it before. Then I remembered.

"Simone and I found this copy in some old pictures Dad kept in a box. We'd been snooping around and when you caught us, you yelled at us for going through his things. I think Simone even got a spanking because of it since she was the ringleader."

He turned to stare at his father. "This is you and Alexander Balducci, isn't it?"

Jerome visibly paled. He reached for the photo, pulling it from his son's hands. He stood staring, a flood of memories seeming to possess his spirit. A tear rolled down the curve of his cheek. He wiped at his eye with the back of his hand and dropped the photo to the floor. He turned and, as he passed his wife, took her hand, holding it briefly.

"It's time," Judith said softly. "It's time we told them all the truth. They're not children anymore. Besides, our secrets keep coming back to bite us and that's not good."

Jerome nodded in agreement, squeezed her hand one more time, and then left the room, having nothing more that he was ready to share.

"So, that's it. He's just going to walk out?" Davis said as he got to his feet.

"Watch your tone," Judith snapped. "He's still your father and you're in his house. You will not be disrespectful—and what you just did was as disrespectful as can be."

"He's been lying to us! Both of you have!"

"Enough! Not everything is about you or your brothers or sisters. Some things weren't meant for you to know for a reason, and you don't get to judge us for making the decisions we made. You don't have a heaven or a hell to put either one of us in, and we don't have to justify our actions to you. When we feel it's appropriate to share something or to explain our decisions to you, then we will. But you certainly don't get to point fingers and make us feel bad because you don't like how we chose to do things."

Davis bristled, the scolding pushing every one of his buttons. He was squarely in his feelings and not in the mood for more emotional overload. Because he wasn't twelve anymore and he was tired of being admonished for feeling the way he felt. But she was also his mother and she would neither tolerate his reproach nor give him a pass if he came at her out of turn. He bit his tongue, knowing that if he said what was in his heart to say, he would live to regret it. "I'm going back to my home," he finally said instead.

Judith nodded. "I think that's a very good idea. Before you go, though, you need to clean up this mess you made. Put your father's office back the way you found it, and don't you ever violate his privacy again. Is that understood?"

"Yes, ma'am," Davis said, his sardonic tone moving his mother to eye him with a narrowed gaze.

She held up her index finger, the warning obvious. There wasn't much more attitude she planned to take from him. She spoke, the command final. "Let everyone know there's an important family meeting this Sunday. Your father will answer your questions when everyone is here."

"I'm still bringing Neema," Davis said, an edge of defiance in his voice.

His mother stared at him for a moment and Davis sensed she was weighing whether to make it an argument. "That's your choice. If you consider her family, then she's more than welcome." Judith turned on her high heels and made her exit.

Air blew past his lips like helium out of a popped balloon. He bent to pick the photograph up off the floor, staring again at the image of Jerome Black and Alexander Balducci and the patriarch clearly related to them both.

The man who opened the door to greet him did so cheerily, his disposition slightly disconcerting for the late hour. Davis appreciated his efforts, but he was not in the mood to be as jovial back. "Thank you for seeing me," Davis said, his somber tone forecasting his mood.

"I try to avail myself to patients when they need me, no matter what the hour," Dr. Wayne Jacobs responded.

"You're an anomaly. Not everyone is as accommodating."

"So, what brings you here this evening?" Dr. Jacobs asked. He led the way to his home office, pointing Davis to the leather couch as he took a seat in an upholstered chair. "You were agitated when you called."

"I feel like everything I've ever believed about my life, my family, everything, has been a lie and the lies have begun to unravel. Now I don't know what's true and what isn't. I feel lost."

Dr. Jacobs nodded. "Why don't you tell me what happened that has you feeling this way?"

For a moment, Davis wasn't even sure where to begin. He felt conflicted but that was more about him finding it difficult to process what he'd recently learned. Feeling like he needed to make sense out of it all.

"A woman died in my office recently. She was a good friend and, for a minute, the police thought I might have been responsible for her death."

The doctor frowned, his brow furrowing as he processed the news. "I'm so sorry for your loss. How are you holding up?"

Davis shrugged. "I haven't taken the time to mourn her the way I probably should. There's just been a lot going on."

"Have you considered that maybe you're having such a hard time because you are mourning the loss of your friend? There's no set method to mourning, and we each do it in our own way. Yours may be manifesting in your frustration with everything else that's going on in your life right now."

A pregnant pause blossomed full and thick between them as Davis pondered his comment. After a moment of contemplation, he sighed, then continued. "I found out that my parents have both been keeping secrets from us."

"And that's upset you?"

"It's pissed me off! Why didn't they think my siblings and I deserved to know the truth about their lives?"

"Why do you feel they have a responsibility to share everything about themselves with you? We're all allowed to withhold information from friends and family if it doesn't directly impact them. Or do you share everything?"

"Well, no, but they're my parents and…" Davis hesitated. "They set that standard."

"Did they? Or did you just project your personal opinion upon them?"

"I…well…it's…" Davis stammered, searching his thoughts for the words to explain himself. "They lied."

"Did they lie outright?"

"No, they lied by omission. They just didn't tell us. And they should have told us."

Davis spent the next thirty minutes detailing the ill will he'd been harboring in resentment against his parents. Ten minutes in, he felt foolish for complaining, the wealth of his criticisms feeling nonsensical. Twenty minutes in, he felt vindicated, that his rational made all kinds of sense for anyone willing to examine the evidence. By the end of the half hour, he didn't know how he felt or even why, just that trying to put all the pieces together had him feeling out of sorts.

"You are entitled to feel the way you do. And your parents were entitled to those feelings that made them do what they did. I think for you to better process why you feel the way you do, you need to better understand their motives. Have you talked to them?" Dr. Jacobs asked.

"We're having a family meeting on Sunday."

"That meeting may give you more clarity and understanding. But if it doesn't, you need to consider how you move forward. Will you be able to forgive them? Will you let this change your relationship with them? How does it impact your future? You'll have to ask yourself some hard questions."

Davis nodded as he considered the doctor's comment. He suddenly changed the subject. "I've met someone. A woman I really like. I worry that my family's dysfunction may impact how this relationship develops."

"Is your family truly dysfunctional?"

"We have our moments."

"Like most families. But from what I know about you and your family, you are truly a tight unit and very supportive of each other. Why not focus on what's positive about your family and allow your new friend to get to know that?"

"That's sometimes hard to do."

"How have you been handling your anxiety?"

"I have good days and then I have bad days."

"Perhaps we need to consider medication. I'd like to prescribe you something that might help take the edge off and allow you to ease into situations that elevate your stress."

Davis shook his head. "I don't know. I'm very anti-pharmaceutical."

"Give it some consideration. Talk to your primary care physician and get his input. Then let's revisit the idea again when I see you next week."

The text message Davis sent to his siblings an hour later was short and sweet.

I need help. Can you all meet me?

Armstrong responded first.

Peace Row. One hour.

Five more responses followed, everyone agreeing to meet up at the private nightclub. Peace Row was a membership-only establishment for law enforcement officers. The brainchild of his brother Armstrong, it was owned by him, specifically for cops who needed a private space to unwind. It was also their go-to spot when Davis and his siblings needed to gather in solidarity.

Davis was actually the last of his family to arrive, parking his car behind Simone's. He maneuvered through the door of the old brick building on what appeared to be a deserted street. He made his way down a flight of newly carpeted stairs to a second door that had been freshly painted a vibrant shade of glossy red. He lifted a heavy gold knocker to announce himself, waiting for someone on the other side to allow him inside.

The elderly man who answered the door gave Davis a nod. Davis recognized him from his days on the force with his father. The octogenarian had retired many years ago.

"Hey, Mr. Henry. This is a nice surprise!" Davis exhorted. "I didn't know you were working here."

The old man nodded. "Your brother's been good to me. Keeps me busy so these old bones don't go cold too soon." He chuckled, the toothless laugh making his lean body shake.

"Well, it's good to see you, sir."

"It's good to see you, too, son. Nice to see all you young folks." The old man pushed past him. "Your brother said to lock the door behind me. Your kin are here already, waiting on you. I need to get on home to my wife."

"Well, you be safe out there, Mr. Henry."

Mr. Henry tapped the holstered weapon hidden under his wool blazer. "I'm gonna be just fine," he said with another laugh.

Davis followed the old man as he made his way down the length of hallway and disappeared out the front door. He turned the door lock, securing the entrance, and retraced his steps toward the inner sanctum.

On the other side of the red door it was like being transported to another time and place. The walls were oak-paneled, polished to a high shine and looking like an expensive old library. Round tables were neatly arranged around a dance floor and full bar. Except for his family, who were seated around a table in the center of the room, the space was empty.

Most of the staff had retired for the night. Only one waitress dressed in black slacks and a black turtleneck had stayed and she was circling the table taking drink orders. The bartender and the cook stood shoulder to shoulder, arms crossed, waiting to see how their services would be needed.

"You hungry?" Armstrong questioned, tossing Davis a look.

Davis nodded, realizing that it had been some time since he'd enjoyed coffee and pie with Neema. His stomach did a flip, affirming his need for something to eat. "Yeah. That would be good," he said as he took the empty chair between Mingus and Vaughan. Vaughan rubbed a warm palm against his back and the gesture was instantly soothing.

Minutes later, after ordering food for the table, the family sat chatting amongst themselves. They waited just under a half hour for the cook, a robust Jamaican woman with waist-length dreads, to personally delivered platters of stewed oxtail, peas and rice, fried plantains and potato pudding. The conversation was casual as they each ate heartily, savoring every forkful until they were stuffed and ready to be rolled home.

After helping to clear away the dirty dishes, Armstrong followed the last of his staff out the door, locking it tightly behind them. When he returned, he shut down the sound system and turned up the lights. He pulled his chair up to the table and in near perfect synchronization, they all turned to stare in Davis's direction.

"What did you do?" Simone said, her hand gliding over the protrusion of tummy beneath her formfitting blouse.

"What your sister meant to ask," Parker interjected, "is what's wrong and how can we help?"

"Does this have anything to do with Daddy?" Vaughan asked. "Because I was at the house earlier and asked about your case and he damn near took my head off!"

Davis dropped his head into his hands, his elbows propped on the table. "I ransacked his office earlier. He's probably still pissed."

Armstrong sat forward in his seat. "You went through the old man's office? Were you looking to get yourself killed?"

"What were you looking for?" Mingus queried.

Davis reached into the pocket of his overcoat and pulled out the photo he'd swiped. He dropped it in the center of the table then pushed it toward his brother. "This."

Mingus and Simone both reached for it at the same time, elbowing each other to get the first look. Mingus deferred to his sister and her mood swings that could prove to be problematic given the late-night hour.

"Who are these people?" Simone asked.

"It's a photo of dad and Alexander Balducci when they were children. I think that man is their father. I saw a copy of it on the wall at Balducci's home this afternoon and I remembered seeing it in Dad's office years ago."

Mingus snatched the photo from Simone and seconds later Parker snatched it from him. Davis said nothing as it passed from one sibling to the other, each of them studying it intently.

"What do you guys know about our family tree?" Davis finally questioned.

"Do we have a family tree?" Ellington responded. "Personally, I always thought we were it."

"The old people never talked much about our family," Parker interjected. "All the grandparents were dead before any of us were born. They were both only children, so we didn't have any aunts and uncles."

"Or so we thought," Davis interjected. "Because it seems Balducci is our uncle Alexander."

"And Dad told you this?" Simone asked, looking skeptical.

"Dad hasn't said much at all," Davis answered. "Your parents just declared a family meeting on Sunday to tell us all the family secrets they've been hiding."

"Ain't that some shiggity!" Mingus muttered under his breath.

"I definitely don't feel bad now," Armstrong said. "If Mingus didn't know, then surely none of us would have known."

"That's true," Vaughan concurred. "Because Mingus knows everything about everybody."

"Well, I didn't know that," their brother responded.

Davis shook his head. "First, Mom has a secret son and now Dad has a secret brother. It's some bull—"

"Watch your language!" Vaughan admonished. "I have delicate ears."

Simone rolled her eyes. "I am so confused," she said. "So, you're saying our grandfather is the white guy in this picture, but he's related to Daddy and not to Mommy?"

"Keep up, Simone," Parker teased.

"I thought I was. But Daddy's the parent who looks the least interracial. And we've seen pictures of his mother. She was definitely a Black woman. I just assumed his father was, too."

Parker leaned back in his seat, his arms folded over his broad chest. "Did you pay attention in science class, Simone, when they discussed genetics? If I remember correctly, there was a whole segment on recessive genes and dominant genes. Did you really never give our assorted eye colors any consideration? Blue eyes are recessive, but you must get the gene for blue eyes from *both* of your parents."

"Did I really care?" Simone snapped.

"Personally, I did always wonder why you all were as pale as you are," Vaughan quipped.

"Our mother is white," Simone said flippantly. "Not sure that one was hard to figure out. Science class or no science class."

Ellington held up a hand. "It's late and some of you are getting punchy, so let's cut to the chase. The parents plan on giving us a history lesson this Sunday. But since we're all together right now, I might as well update you all. I know Mom plans to have a conversation with each of you individually, but…" His voice trailed off momentarily before he took a breath and continued. "The FBI arrested the man who was trying to shake down Mom and Dad. He's no one any of us knows."

"How did he find out about Mom's secret?" Davis asked.

"From what Mingus was able to discover, he worked for the adoption agency. He happened to see a news article on Mom being a federal court judge, remembered what happened when, and thought he could make a quick buck."

"I hope they put him under the jail," Simone sniped. "Because that was shady as hell!"

"He'll likely get a few years," Ellington said, "and no possibility of parole."

"What about her firstborn son?" Davis asked. "Will we ever meet our older brother? Sorry, Parker," he said, shooting his brother a look.

Parker shrugged. "No need to apologize. He is the oldest. He's got me by a couple of years."

Ellington and Mingus exchanged a look.

"He's not listed with the adoption registry as wanting to be reunited with his birth family," Mingus said. "So, Mom has decided not to pursue it. She did register herself in case he ever comes looking, but she's decided not to open that door until he wants to do so."

They sat in silence for a few minutes taking it all in.

"So that's it," Davis said finally. "Her secret goes back to being a secret?"

"We need to respect her decision," Parker admonished. "I think she's right. If he doesn't want to be found, then we should leave him alone."

"It wouldn't be fair to disrupt his life if that's not what he wants," Armstrong intoned.

"Aren't you the least bit curious about him?" Simone questioned.

"Not really," Parker said. "And it doesn't look like he's much interested in us."

Mingus shrugged. "He was raised by a good family. He's very close to his adoptive parents. That may have something to do with why he's never been interested in finding Mom. Who knows? But he seems to have a great life and that's why Mom wants to let it go. So, let it go."

"I agree," Vaughan interjected. "Since we found out, we've all been off our game worrying about how it was going to affect us."

"Speak for yourself." Simone chimed in, rolling her eyes once again. "I wasn't that bothered."

Vaughan gave her a look. "My point being, our family dynamics don't change. We go on as usual and worry about it another day."

Armstrong nodded. "It wasn't like we were all going to have some kumbaya moment and suddenly be the best of friends," he said. "In fact, we don't know what was going to happen or if anything was going to come of it at all."

"And you don't think we should at least try?" Davis questioned.

"Let it go," Mingus repeated. "We've got more than enough going on right now to worry about. Just let it go."

Ellington looked at each of them. "Let Mom bring it up. Talk to her when she's ready. *Listen* to her and stop judging her choices. And try to understand why she's made this decision. Because this isn't about any of us. It's only about Mom and her son Fabian."

The silence billowed around the space a second time as they mulled over the comments.

Ellington broke through the quiet, changing the subject. "What do you need from us tonight, Davis?"

Davis shook his head slowly. "Help me figure out what's going on. I seem to have lost control and I'm having a hard time making all the pieces fit."

"Well, I want answers, too," Simone interjected. "You still dating that woman?"

Davis cut his eyes in her direction. "Neema doesn't have anything to do with any of this, Simone, so why are you asking about her?"

"Because something about her feels off and I want to make sure she's not playing my little brother, that's why!"

The brothers all laughed.

Armstrong shook his head. "He's not yours anymore, Simone."

Parker said, "She's still as bad as she was when Davis was born. Simone declared he was *her* baby and she wouldn't let any of us near him!"

"He's still mine," Simone said, feigning a pout. "He will always be mine."

"I'll be glad when you have that baby, Simone, so you can shift your focus," Davis said.

Simone laughed. "Like that's going to change anything!" She stood and moved behind his chair to give him a hug, then moved to sit back down.

"Why don't we just talk it through and see if that helps," Armstrong suggested.

Davis agreed, giving them all a nod. "So, nothing was out of order, no problems I was aware of, and then Dad commanded me to help Balducci."

"Help him do what?"

"Slip money into Gaia's pocket without her knowing where it came from."

"What are we missing?" Vaughan asked. "Who was Gaia to Mr. Balducci?"

Davis and Mingus exchanged a look. Mingus shrugged.

"Gaia was Balducci's daughter," Davis answered. He paused for moment, dropping into reflection before saying, "That would have made her our first cousin."

An exchange of looks swept around the table, none of them bothering to comment.

"Keep going," Armstrong prompted.

"Then someone shot up my house."

"Where are we with that investigation?" Mingus asked.

Armstrong shook his head. "Dead end."

"Actually, not quite," Parker interjected. "Ballistics came back tonight on the bullets you pulled out of Davis's wall. They are identical to the bullets pulled from a body last year in that trafficking case you and your wife investigated. The case that took down Balducci's son."

Armstrong suddenly pushed up from the table. The color had drained from his face and he looked like he'd been slammed in the chest. Reality swept through them all as they suddenly considered the familial connection.

Vaughan gasped. Loudly. Pulling a closed fist to her chest, she batted away the tears that misted her eyes. Rising from her seat, she moved to her brother's side and wrapped her arms tightly around him.

Davis dropped his eyes to the floor, empathy flooding the room.

Years previous, Armstrong had pulled the fatal shot that had taken the life of Balducci's eldest son. Last year, his investigation had put Balducci's other son behind bars, multiple life sentences guaranteeing he would never again see the light of day. Now, suddenly, they and Alexander's children were all family. Cousins. And that realization was like a punch to the gut that none of them could have ever expected.

Vaughan pulled Armstrong back to the table, the two sitting beside each other. She looped her arm through his and held on to him.

Davis gave his sister the slightest smile, nodding his approval.

Mingus took up the mantle. "So, whoever pulled the trigger on that body, also pulled the trigger on Davis."

Parker nodded. "Actually, there are three bodies on that gun. Gaia wasn't killed with Davis's gun. The shots from his gun were fired after the fact. And now we need to figure out how Balducci is tied into it all."

"Or a Balducci employee, maybe?" Mingus said, tossing Davis a look.

"What are you thinking?" Armstrong questioned.

"What do you know about Ginger? The redhead who works for him?"

"Danni knows her better than I do. They became close when she was undercover. She was a big help when we needed her."

"She's tied to this," Davis muttered. "I'm not sure how, but something about her doesn't feel right to me."

"I agree," Mingus said. "She's been on my list."

Armstrong nodded. "I'll talk to Danni. See what she thinks and go from there."

"The FBI cleared you, Davis, but we're still digging under rocks to see what we can find. I've already gone through ten hours of videotape from cameras in a twenty-mile radius of your office and I have another ten to go through," Parker advised.

Davis nodded. "She knew," he said softly, thinking back to his last conversation with Gaia. "She knew that we were family."

"You don't know that," Simone said softly.

"Yes. I do. She knew and she thought I knew. She was furious on the phone and she was ranting. She asked me how I could keep something like that from her when I knew how important family was to her. She questioned why I didn't think I could trust her with something so important. Neema was there and I was trying to get Gaia off the phone. I just told her we needed to talk in person, and she insisted I come down to my office to face her. Thinking about it now, I'm sure it wasn't just about Balducci being her father or the money. I think she may have known it all and I think her knowing is what got her killed."

"But why?" Simone questioned. "It doesn't make sense. Who would benefit from that news staying secret and what would they get?"

"Good question," Davis stated. "Now we need to figure out the answer."

For another hour, the siblings sat together trying to make sense out of what felt like nonsense. All the pieces spun in a near perfect circle, but still didn't fit together in a way that helped propel the case forward to give them the answers they so desperately wanted.

"Thank you," Davis said as they wound down for the night, ready to head to their respective homes. "I appreciate each of you."

"It's what we do," Parker said.

"Amen to that," Simone concluded.

Davis echoed his sister, his voice barely a whisper. "Amen to that!"

Chapter 13

Sneaking out of her parents' home came with challenges Neema hadn't anticipated. First, her mother standing in the center of the kitchen prepping vegetables for a pot of soup she was planning for the next day's meal. Spying Neema, the woman who rarely had much to say, suddenly had a lengthy list of questions she insisted be answered. What was Neema doing up? Why did she have her coat on? Where did she think she was going?

Second, her father calling down to ask who had triggered the motion sensor that turned on all the outside lights shining into his bedroom. Then came his list of questions, which were essentially a repeat of what her mother had just asked. With each question, Neema had to admit that she was really bad about sneaking around in her parents' home.

With both interrogations Neema told a series of little

white lies. She felt bad about doing so, but there was no way she could tell her parents she was headed to Davis's house because he had called and had begged her to come. That would have been a whole other lecture, so it was easier for them to think she had been called into work to cover for a reporter who had phoned in sick.

There had been something in Davis's voice that tugged at her heartstrings. Something that whispered her name and his, spinning seductively as it pulled them toward each other. Something that spoke of need and want and hope and understanding. Something that made a little white lie well worth the risk of her parents' wrath.

Davis and Titus were standing in his front yard when she pulled her car into a parking space. The Rottweiler didn't immediately recognize her and visibly bristled as she approached, his posture suddenly protective. Neema came to an abrupt halt as the dog suddenly rushed in her direction, his exuberance leading the way. As Davis called his name, Titus barreled into her, knocking her to the ground. Neema landed with a resounding thud as the dog licked her face and yipped in greeting, his docked tail wagging eagerly.

Davis hurried to her side. "I am so sorry. Bad dog, Titus!"

Titus licked her one last time and sat, a paw resting against her leg.

"Are you okay?"

Neema was wide-eyed and looked slightly frazzled. "I think I'll live," she said and then began to giggle. Her giggles were soon a full-fledged, gut-deep laugh.

"Are you sure you're okay?"

She shook her head. "Not really."

"Did you hurt something?" Davis questioned, worry crossing his face.

"I think I landed in dog poo," she said, wrinkling her nose. "And I think it's in my hair!"

Davis sniffed, a squirrelly expression pulling at the muscles in his face. She saw him try to maintain a straight face and not laugh, but he failed miserably. Soon the two of them were laughing hysterically together.

"So, I can offer you a hot shower while I throw your clothes into the washing machine," Davis finally said.

Neema chuckled as she slowly straightened. "If siccing your dog on a woman is how you get her out of her clothes, you might want to rethink your game plan."

Davis extended his hand to help her to her feet. "Not sure how I missed that pile," he said.

"I'm not sure how Titus and I *didn't* miss that pile," she said sarcastically.

"You really do stink," Davis said as he guided her by the arm to the house.

"You think?"

Minutes later, Neema was standing under a hot shower rinsing shampoo out of her hair.

The damage had been as bad as she'd anticipated, remnants smeared down the back of her wool blazer and the collar of her white blouse. She'd insisted that Davis toss the blazer into the trash, the well-worn garment having outlived its usefulness. Sending it to the dry cleaner wasn't worth what it would have cost her. Davis had insisted on buying her a new one, wanting to replace it to apologize for his dog's transgression. Her blouse, jeans and undergarments were in his washing machine, Davis personally overseeing their washing.

It took three shampoos before Neema began to feel

clean again. A fourth sudsing for good measure and two douses of conditioner left her feeling considerably better. The stench of excrement no longer lingered in her nostrils, replaced by the fresh scent of lemon and lavender soap. Despite the hilarity of what had happened, it wasn't how she'd imagined the night going.

She stood beneath the hot spray for another ten minutes contemplating the situation and trying to decide what to do next. There had been no expectations on either's part, just a desire to be near each other and allowing that to evolve organically. Neema fantasized about his touch, his hands dancing in places that were most private. Places that water now trickled over. A current of electricity vibrated through her feminine spirit and she found herself clenching the muscles below her waist to stall the rising sensations flooding her most private place.

When she finally shut off the water, stepping out into the cool air, she snatched up the plush white towel Davis had left on the counter and wrapped it around her body. He'd graciously afforded her privacy in the home's guest bedroom. The tranquil space had been painted a robin's-egg blue accented with lemon-yellow pillows and sheer white fabrics. With the minimalistic décor, the room was very pretty, his sisters' feminine touches obvious.

Moving from the adjoining bathroom into the bedroom, Neema found an oversize sweat top and pair of gray sweatpants resting on the bed. A second choice lay beside it; a pair of track shorts and a T-shirt. A long-stemmed rose pulled from one of the arrangements he'd received in the hospital rested between both. Lifting it to her nose, she took a deep inhale of the fragrant aroma, allowing it to soothe her anxiety. Excitement fueled her nervousness and had her knees shaking just enough to fear falling flat on her backside. Again.

After slipping into the sweat top, which landed just at her knees, she opted to forgo the sweatpants. They made her look like she was swimming in cotton fabric and there wasn't enough elastic to keep them on her slim waist. She chose the shorts instead, the look more like a dress with panties beneath it. Granny panties, but at least her bottom was covered so that she didn't feel so exposed. She checked her reflection in the mirror one last time and took a deep breath. Then she opened the bedroom door.

Titus lay on the floor outside the door, the dog sitting up as she leaned to give him a scratch behind his ears. He licked her palm then lay down again, barely giving her a glance as she headed for the living room.

Davis had been kicking himself for the disastrous turn the night had taken. He'd been excited when Neema had agreed to come over. And grateful that she hadn't thought he'd been looking for a late-night booty call. Explaining that he just needed a friend and the company of someone he could talk to easily had sounded cheesy at best, but his pleas hadn't been met with cynicism. Neema hadn't thought him crazy and, if she had, she'd spared him the embarrassment of saying so out loud.

He imagined the mishap with Titus would be fodder for many a joke and much laughter at some point in their relationship, but he wasn't sure now was that time. Despite her good nature, he imagined the moment was not one she wanted either of them to dwell on. So, after taking care of her clothes and providing her with a temporary wardrobe until the buzzer sounded on his dryer, he figured a large bowl of his Rocky Road popcorn and a bottle of Moscato would turn the tide of his intentions back in his favor.

He drizzled hot popcorn with butter, vanilla extract and kosher salt. Just as he was tossing the popcorn mix with mini marshmallows, chocolate chips and toasted pecans, spreading them on a baking sheet to go into the oven, Neema sauntered into the room. Her smile was sweet and consoling, and instantly eased the tension he'd been feeling.

"Something smells really good," she said as she eased over to the counter and one of the stools.

"I made my special popcorn for you. And I opened a bottle of wine," he said as he reached for the bottle and poured her a glass.

Neema laughed. "Wine and popcorn. You know how to make a woman very happy!"

"I try," he said, his smile pulled full across his face. "Seriously, though, are you okay? I was really worried that you might have hurt yourself."

Neema smiled back. "My pride was bruised more than anything else. Here I was trying to look cute when I got here and I literally stepped in it!"

Davis laughed. "Actually, you kind of slid and landed in it."

Neema laughed with him. "Don't remind me. I think I'm sending this night to the top of my Most Embarrassing Moment list."

"You have a list?"

"Don't you?"

Davis grinned and shrugged. "Now that I think about it, I guess I do."

He slid the pan into the oven, peeking through the door just before moving back to lean across the counter. "Thank you," he said as he reached for her hand, gently kissing the backs of her fingers.

"For what?"

"For coming to my rescue."

"You hardly look like you need saving, Davis." And he didn't, Neema thought to herself. He looked slightly smug, shouldering an air of confidence that she found quite sexy. He also wore a T-shirt and gray sweats identical to the pair he'd left for her to wear, and he filled them nicely. She found herself wondering how often he worked out to keep himself so fit and then felt bad for being so superficial. Most especially because he was being so open. She shook the reverie away, refocusing on what he was saying.

"You'd be surprised. It's been a rough few weeks."

"I hate that you're going through a hard time," she said.

"I feel challenged. So much has happened that I'm not sure if I'm coming or going. That's what's most frustrating. I hate having questions that I can't easily find the answers to."

"Did something else happen?" Neema asked, concern flooding her face.

Davis shrugged. "Just one more thing added to my list," he said and then told her about his discovery and what he thought it might mean for his family. He pushed the family photo across the counter for her to see.

"This doesn't have to be a bad thing," Neema said as she stared at the image of the old man and the two young boys who looked like bookends beside him.

"No, it doesn't. But when you consider the history between our two families, it's hard to imagine anything good coming from this. I don't see us ever breaking bread together over a Thanksgiving table."

Neema gave a slight shrug. "And maybe nothing at all will come of it. Things might stay just as they are now. No more, no less."

"You make it sound so easy," Davis said, turning from the counter to the stove.

Neema watched him remove the oversize baking sheet from the oven. The sugary sweetness scented the air as he transferred the popcorn into a large bowl.

"Something tells me that popcorn will make all of our problems go away," Neema said with a soft chuckle.

"It will definitely make us forget about them for a minute or two." He checked that the oven was off then added, "Why don't we take this into the living room and get comfortable?"

Neema grabbed their two glasses and the wine bottle and led the way.

Davis followed, the bowl of goodies and a stack of paper napkins in hand. He found himself staring as she walked away. Her feet were bare, the oversize sweatshirt exposing her lean legs. She'd rolled up the arms of the top past her elbows. She was just a wisp of a woman and he found himself imagining her cradled in his arms, lying tight against his chest.

Her stride was easy, each of her steps led by the gentle sway of her hips. Her walk was sexy as hell and he felt heat surge below his waist, muscles rumbling as blood pulsed into his appendages. He took a deep breath and then another to stall the rise of energy that threatened to make the moment awkward.

When they'd settled comfortably on the couch, Neema sitting cross-legged and the bowl of popcorn between them, Davis reached for the remote to turn on the stereo and turn down the lights. Lauryn Hill's "The Sweetest Thing" filled the room, followed by

"Ex-Factor," then Jill Scott's "He Loves Me." The two settled into the ambience, relaxing with the music and the subtle exhalations of each other's breathing.

Davis shifted the popcorn bowl to the table and wrapped his arms around Neema's shoulders. As she allowed herself to settle against him, he pressed a damp kiss to her forehead.

"You smell good," he said softly.

She giggled. "Soap and water can be your friend, too!"

Davis laughed with her and hugged her closer. "I think about us a lot, Neema. About where this relationship could go if we let it. Every time we're together, I don't want to think about when we have to part. I really care about you and I hate that our getting to know each other has been mingled with so much drama."

Neema pressed her hand to his chest, her fingers teasing the flesh beneath his T-shirt. "The drama doesn't bother me, Davis. Because I like you, too, and I like that we're growing closer. I know that if we focus on supporting each other, we'll get through the drama."

Davis nodded as he pressed his lips gently to hers. The kiss was tender, until it wasn't, every ounce of emotion the two were feeling for each other exploding between them. Leaning back against the cushions, he pulled Neema down with him. As she fell against the expanse of his chest, his hands danced along the length of her arms and across her back. The tips of his fingers rested against the curve of her buttocks, heat burning beneath the tips. Her arms snaked around his shoulders and back, her hands clinging to him hungrily as her mouth twisted and turned with his. The kiss had become frenetic, both anxious for each other's touch.

When he shifted his body beneath hers, Neema straddling his legs, there was no hiding the rise of nature that pressed against the front of his sweats for attention. His excitement was on full display as he pressed himself against her.

Neema suddenly sat upright, pulling a closed fist to her mouth. "I'm sorry. There's something we need to talk about first…" she started to say. "There's something important I need to tell you."

Davis straightened, dropping his palm to his crotch to hide the very visible erection. "I'm sorry. I was moving too fast. I didn't mean—"

"No, that's not—"

Titus suddenly barked, standing at the front door, the fur around his neck standing on end. He growled, a low, deep, brusque snarl that vibrated loudly through the room. Davis stood abruptly, moving to peer out the front window. Titus barked again and Davis moved to the front door, stopping first to grab his gun.

Neema paused the sound system, the room going quiet save Titus's barking. She backed her way into the corner, her eyes wide. She stood perfectly still, listening to see if she could hear what Titus heard as she watched Davis move from one window to another, peering out to the street to see what he could see.

"Go sit," Davis said to the dog, finally breaking through the quiet. "It's just a raccoon." He heaved a sigh of relief as he turned back to Neema. "Sorry about that. I'm a little on edge. Since that drive-by, every strange noise makes me nervous."

"Better safe than sorry," she muttered.

Davis moved to her side and kissed her, wrapping his arms tightly around her torso. "If I made you uncomfortable before, I apologize. I would never—"

"You didn't," Neema said, interrupting him. "It was fine. It was…good…and I was enjoying myself. I just… well…" She was suddenly stammering, trying to find the words to explain herself. Because she needed to come clean about everything before they took things any further. Davis needed to know the truth.

"Let's sit," Davis said softly, guiding her back to the sofa. "I want you to feel comfortable and I don't want to rush you into anything that you're not ready for."

"And I appreciate that. I'm here because…well, I want to be here with you. But I want to be honest with you about everything and I need…"

The low jingle of his cell phone interrupted the moment. Davis held up his hand, stalling her words. "I'm sorry. I need to grab that. I've been expecting a call from my brother. I'll make it quick," he said as he hurried into the kitchen.

Neema grabbed the remote and turned the sound system back on. Alicia Keys was singing "You Don't Know My Name." As if sensing her anxiety, Titus jumped up beside her on the furniture, nuzzling the side of her face before dropping his head into her lap. She hugged the dog warmly, leaning her face into his.

Minutes later, when Davis returned, Neema and his dog were both sound asleep.

When Neema woke, it was dark in the room, a single light shining from the kitchen. Something had startled her out of her sleep and, for a quick minute, she wasn't sure where she was. She sat upright, a blanket tangled around her bare feet, and then she remembered.

On the floor below her, Titus slept soundly. Davis sat in the leather recliner beneath his own blanket. His head had rolled to the side and he snored softly. She had no memory of falling asleep or of stretching her body out against the sofa cushions. She knew Davis had draped the blanket over her and she imagined he had shooed Titus to the floor. Checking the time, she saw that it was almost five o'clock in the morning.

She sat watching Davis for a good few minutes, briefly debating waking him from his sleep, but deciding to let him rest. He appeared to be dreaming, the slightest smile on his face. He needed the rest and, since he appeared to be comfortable, she decided to let him be. It was too late for conversation and the moment for their romantic interlude had passed.

Stepping over Titus, she tiptoed through the kitchen to the laundry room and her clothes that sat on the counter. Davis had folded everything neatly, laying her silk panties and lace bra on top.

She slipped into her clothes, tossing his sweat top and shorts into the hamper. Tiptoeing back to the living room, she claimed her shoes and purse. Titus suddenly moved to her side and sat. His head was cocked to the side as he watched her.

"Don't look at me like that," Neema whispered.

The dog tilted his head to the other side, panting softly.

"You're really starting to make me feel bad, Titus, but this is for the best. You need to trust me on that."

The dog snorted, still eyeing her intently.

Across the way, Davis shifted in his seat. Neema froze and waited to see if he opened his eyes. When he didn't, she sighed in relief, feeling like she'd come too far to want to explain herself. Feeling like it would be best if she were gone when he woke.

As if he'd actually read her mind, Titus snorted at her a second time.

"Okay! I'll leave a note," she muttered as she reached into her purse for her notepad and pen.

Three quick lines later, Neema gave Titus one last rub. She snuggled his muzzle against her cheek and then she snuck out the door. The note for Davis rested on the kitchen counter.

Chapter 14

She'd left. Neema had risen early and was gone. Davis had been startled out of a sound sleep when Titus scratched at his knee, whining to be let out. Rising, he'd called her name. When he hadn't gotten a response, he'd gone in search of her. The note on the kitchen counter had been short and sweet.

You make my heart sing, Davis Black! Thank you for a wonderful time. Call me when you can.

The note made him smile, but a wave of sadness settled around his shoulders. He had wanted to wake up to her by his side. To start his day with her bright smile as he held her in his arms. He missed her. And in that moment, Davis realized that Neema Kamau had dominion over a large part of his heart. He felt a gasp catch in his throat as the reality of that swept over him.

He was falling in love. Hard. And despite his excitement, he wasn't quite sure what it should look like or if he should even try to label it.

Davis shook away the emotion that had risen full and abundant and in want of attention. He slipped his large feet into a pair of Nike sneakers and pulled a toboggan down low over his ears. Titus pawed at him and ran to the front door. Davis slipped a leash onto the Rottweiler, and the two took off for a morning run.

The air outside was crisp but the sun was bright, beginning to rise comfortably in a cloud-filled sky. The weatherman was predicting the first snow of the season and it felt like Mother Nature was prepping for the possibility. Five blocks from his front door, Davis stopped running, slowing to a walk. His breathing was labored, and his head had begun to pound. Maybe a run hadn't been a good idea, he thought as he pulled Titus to heel. Davis was feeling out of sorts and grossly out of shape. Although he knew some of it had to do with his head injury, it had also been a long minute since he'd last been in a gym or worked out.

Davis and Titus were only a block from his home when he spied the silver Mercedes. It pulled abruptly out of a parking space, the driver accelerating into the intersection. He and Titus had just stepped into the walkway when the vehicle purposely sped toward them, narrowly miss hitting them as it blew through the stop sign. Davis jumped back, landing harshly against the hood of another parked car and rolling to the sidewalk. He pulled Titus abruptly, the dog yelping as Davis snatched him to his side.

Davis cussed as he jumped back to his feet, following the car with his eyes as it disappeared around the next corner.

"Are you okay?" an elderly woman called out from the other side of the road.

"That car looked like it was trying to hit you on purpose!" her companion interjected.

"Some people don't need no driver's license," the old woman added.

"I'm good. Thank you for asking," Davis said as he leaned to check that Titus was okay, as well. The dog was licking his paw, pandering to his front leg as if it hurt.

"Damn fool could have killed someone," the old man muttered as the couple waved goodbye and continued their walk.

Davis pulled his cell phone out of his pocket and dialed his brother. Mingus answered on the second ring. "Someone just tried to run me down," he said, not bothering to say hello.

"You okay?"

"I'm good. I got the license plate."

Neema's father found her in the event room. She sat alone, staring out into space. She'd called in sick to her day job, not wanting anything to do with the newspaper. Instead, she'd chosen to open the restaurant to help her parents prepare for the day.

Leaving Davis the way she had felt like a gut punch. It had knocked the wind out of her, and she was finding it difficult to catch her breath.

She hadn't wanted to leave. Nor had she wanted to sneak out with only a note to remind him that she had been there. Doing so had only reinforced that she needed to step back and figure out what the hell she was doing. Because what she had already done had her feeling a lot foolish. And it was well past noon and Davis hadn't called. Wondering if he might be upset with her only added to her anxiety.

Neema had known that the longer it took to tell Davis the truth, the harder it would be when she finally did. Now it felt almost impossible to have that conversation. But before they could even begin to think about a future together, he needed to know what she did for a living and what her initial intentions had been when they'd first met. She needed to apologize, and she had to let him decide if he truly wanted to move forward with her. She had no doubts that he would see her actions as a betrayal, and she would have to regain his trust if such a thing were at all possible.

Her father stood staring at her and Neema girded herself for an interrogation. Her father's radar rarely faltered when it came to her mood swings and she could tell he wasn't going to let her be until he was satisfied with her answers.

"What is wrong with you today, daughter? Something seems to have upset you."

Neema shook her head. "I'm sorry, Baba. I just needed a moment to myself to think."

"You did not go to work today. Did you get time off for working so late last night? Is there something wrong with your job? Because responsible people show up to work, every day and on time. Unless, of course, they are sick. Are you sick, Neema?"

Neema shook her head. "No, Baba. I am not sick. I'm just tired."

"You need to keep more respectable hours. You would not be tired."

A low gust of air flew past her lips in a soft sigh. "Baba, have you ever kept something important from your wife?"

"Why would I do that? Your mother and I are one. We function as a single unit. I would never keep something important from her. She must be able to trust me, and I must trust her. It's why we do not keep secrets from each other. It would also be disrespectful, and your mother would never disrespect me, nor I her."

Neema nodded, her head bobbing up and down slowly. "How did you know Mommy was the one?"

"What one?"

"How did you know she was the woman you wanted to spend your life with?"

"Ahh! That one!" He dropped into the seat beside hers. "I have loved your mother since we were children playing together in our village. I was blessed that she loved me back. There were several men who were vying for your mother's hand in marriage. She came with a sizeable dowry."

Neema laughed. "Really? A dowry?"

"Dowries were very important back in the day. Of course, girls from wealthy families fared much better with finding partners because they could afford larger dowries. Your grandfather owned a whole heard of cattle. My family was very impressed."

"I'm sure they were," she said wittily.

"I had hoped by now that a good man would want to negotiate your bride price, Neema."

"And I'm glad we don't do that anymore."

"There's much to be said for the old ways, daughter."

"Them being old says more than enough," she responded with another giggle.

"So, who is this man who has you asking these questions? He must be very important to you." There was a twinkle in his eye, his paternal radar signaling loudly.

Neema dropped her eyes to the floor, her hands

twisting together in her lap. "He has become very important to me, but I've not been honest with him."

"Neema!" Her father fanned his hands at her. "Why would you not be honest with this man? What would you want to tell lies about?"

"He doesn't know I'm a journalist. If he did, he might not want to know me."

"Who is this man, Neema?"

Neema hesitated, meeting the stern look her father had given her. His tone had changed, an edge of admonishment clinging to his words. She took a deep breath and then spoke. "Alderman Black. He and I have been seeing each other, and he thinks I only work here at the restaurant. I never corrected that assumption."

"Why would you not do that? Alderman Black is a fine man. An honest, honorable man! He would want a woman who was equally as honest."

"Because the night he was here…well… I thought there might have been a story there. A story I could use to boost my career and—"

Her father sprung from the chair as he tossed up his hands in frustration. "Where is your respect for me and my business? We are not here to spy on our customers! You do not invite people into your home to use them for your own selfish gain. How could you do this, Neema?"

"I meant no disrespect, Baba. It just happened, and I haven't been able to walk it back and make it right."

"You make it right by telling the truth. No more, no less. You must tell the truth."

"I know, Baba. And I will." A tear rolled down Neema's cheek.

Her father reached a large hand out to wipe the line of saline from her face. "If the alderman knows your heart, then you two will be able to work it out. If your heart is pure, Neema. A man must trust that you have his best interests at heart. Because his best interests will also be yours if you are meant to be together."

At that moment, her mother stuck her head into the room, calling Neema's name. "You promised to help me with the chapati," the older woman said as she eyed the two of them curiously.

"Coming, Mama!"

Neema rose from her seat, drawing a deep inhale of air into her lungs to calm her frazzled nerves. She leaned forward to give her father a hug, allowing herself to settle into his warmth for just a moment. "Thank you, Baba."

Adamu gave his daughter a nod then gently patted her back. "Talk to your mother more, Neema. She will teach you to be a good wife and a good wife does not keep secrets from her husband," he said as he turned, pausing a moment to kiss his wife's cheek before making his exit.

The two women exchanged a look. Neema reached for her mother's hand and gave her fingers a squeeze.

The matriarch smiled, her voice dropping a few octaves to a loud whisper. "Pay no attention to your father, Neema. A good wife keeps the secrets she needs to keep," her mother said. "She just makes sure her husband never finds out!"

"And if he does?"

"Then she makes sure she can explain it in her favor, of course!" she said as she looped her arm through Neema's and kissed her daughter's cheek.

They played phone tag for most of the day. Neema missed Davis's call first and when she called him back, he had gone into a meeting. Before she knew it, they had two more missed calls each and the day was over. When her phone rang for the last time, she was in her bed. The television was on and someone's housewife was screaming about how her reality didn't mesh with how the show was portraying her.

"Hey!" she said as she turned down the volume on the TV set. "We finally caught up with each other."

"Finally. How's your day been?"

"It just got substantially better. How about yours?"

"I'd say the same thing. I've missed you. I've also been feeling someway about you leaving this morning. Loved the note, by the way, but I would have preferred your beautiful smile."

"Sorry about that, but I needed to get home. I didn't mean to fall asleep. I didn't realize just how tired I was."

"I'm glad you were able to rest. That says you were comfortable."

"I was."

"There was something you wanted to talk about. Is this a good time?"

Neema paused for a moment before responding. "I'd rather wait until I see you next. It's a conversation I'd like to have in person."

"Do you want to come over now?"

She laughed. "You're trying to get me killed. I still live with my very conservative parents, remember?"

"You didn't get in trouble this morning, did you?"

"No. I was able to sneak in without them knowing."

"That's good. I don't want your father to think I'm trying to take advantage of you. Although I might have been, a little. You have the softest lips! I didn't want to stop kissing you."

Her warm laughter rippled through the telephone line. "You tell him that and you might have to negotiate my bride price," she said. "As far as my parents are concerned, I should only be kissing my future husband."

"Bride price?" he questioned, amusement in his voice.

"It's what a man pays his future wife's family for her hand in marriage. In Kenya, cattle is a hot commodity to secure a wife."

Davis laughed. "And do I get a dowry once it's official? Because I'll need to recoup some of my investment."

"Touché!" Neema laughed with him. "But yes, you can negotiate a dowry. I'm sure my father would love to have that conversation with you."

"Seriously, though, I want to make sure we're good with each other. It got heated there for a moment last night and I don't want you to think I was purposely being aggressive. Especially since we hadn't really talked about sex. But I was excited, and I thought you were, too."

Neema felt herself blush. Heat warmed her cheeks. "I was very excited. And we were both consenting adults for what didn't happen, even if we thought about it. I'm not sure a conversation was needed. I don't think either of us initiated anything the other didn't want."

"Do you like sex?"

She giggled. "I haven't been with a lot of men, but yes, I do. With the right person, of course."

"Any idiosyncrasies I need to be aware of? Do you have a foot fetish or maybe an affinity for chandeliers?"

"Chandeliers?"

"To swing from."

"Cute, but no. What about you? What freaky things do you like to do?"

There was a moment of pause. "I have an oral fixation. I like to use my mouth and tongue," he finally said.

Neema's eyes widened and her mouth dropped open as she reflected on his comment. "Well," she replied, "I'd like to know more, but I think that, too, is a conversation I'd like to have in person."

"With examples and demonstrations, I hope?"

"Oh, most definitely with demonstrations!"

Laughter continued to lift the conversation. Before either realized it, a good two hours had passed. Neema, curious about the investigation into Gaia's death, questioned where everything stood. Davis updated her, doing his best to answer the few questions he could. He found it easy to confide in her, feeling confident about trusting her. There was an air of ease that settled between them; both instinctively knowing that their relationship had taken another deep turn toward forever.

"How did it get so late!" Neema exclaimed. "You need to get your rest."

"I need this time with you more," Davis said matter-of-factly. "Are you sure I can't convince you to come over?"

"You're trying to get me in trouble, because I'm sure you could convince me. But you have a meeting first thing in the morning, and I need to get up early, as well."

"I will see you Sunday, won't I? For dinner with my family?"

"Are you sure you still want me to come?"

"Only if you're sure you can handle the Black family brand of crazy. It's definitely not for the faint of heart."

"I like your family, and they've been very kind to

me. I don't think it will be a problem. But you and I still need to talk," Neema reiterated. "It's important."

"Then plan on coming back to my house after. I promise you'll have my undivided attention."

Chapter 15

When the idea came to her, Neema wasn't sure what she hoped to accomplish. All she was certain of was that she still had more questions than answers. Her concern for Davis motivated the inquiry and when the woman had agreed to meet with her, Neema knew she couldn't let the opportunity pass her by.

The coffee shop on California Avenue was quaint, catering to those who lived in the neighborhood. It was just early enough in the day to be slightly crowded, mostly college students, a couple or two out on a Saturday morning before shopping, and several singles with laptops and headphones browsing the internet.

Ginger was seated at a table by the window, positioned so that she could see anyone coming through the door or standing on the sidewalk outside. She sipped on a cup of hot tea and appeared to be lost in thought as she scrolled through her cell phone.

Neema stepped up to the counter to order a cup of coffee then headed to the table and introduced herself.

"Hello! Ginger Novak, I'm Neema Kamau. Thank you for agreeing to speak with me." She extended her hand to shake Ginger's and couldn't help but notice the massive diamond engagement ring and wedding band on the woman's ring finger.

Ginger appraised her before answering. "You said you're with the *Chicago Tribune*?"

"That's correct," Neema said as she took her seat across from the young woman. She slid her notepad, pen and a manila folder onto the table. "I'm doing a follow-up article to the trafficking scandal that was reported on last year. You were instrumental in bringing those involved to justice, and I wanted to see how you're doing now and maybe get a statement about the women you helped and how they might be faring."

Ginger gave her a nod and took a sip of her beverage. "I don't know that there's anything that I can really tell you."

Neema gestured at her ring finger. "Congratulations! I see that you got married. That's an exciting accomplishment. Who's the lucky man?"

Ginger folded her hands together and dropped them into her lap. "I'd prefer we keep my personal life personal."

"I understand completely."

"Thank you."

Neema changed the subject. "Do you know Eloise Harper?"

Ginger sat back, the shine in her eyes dimming substantially. "No," she said, the lie rolling easily off her tongue, adding, "not that I'm aware of. Why do you ask?"

"She's someone I interviewed for another story I'm doing, and she mentioned your name."

"She mentioned me?" Her eyes shifted from side to side and Neema imagined her brain had shifted into a third gear.

Neema continued. "Just saying that she admired what you were able to overcome and accomplish, and how she was working to do the same. You're very much a role model to some of these young girls who've gone through hard times."

Ginger stared at her but didn't bother to respond.

Neema pressed on. "Do you keep in touch with any of the girls who were rescued?"

She shrugged. "One or two."

"Have they returned home to their families?"

"No. I've tried to help them find work, shelter, whatever they might need. But once you get stuck on these streets, it's not easy to get off them."

"But you got off them, right?"

Ginger's gaze narrowed slightly. "I brought a unique set of management skills to my employer, so it's been easier for me."

"And you still work for Alexander Balducci, is that correct?"

Ginger sat upright, bristling with suspicion. She gave Neema a questioning look.

Neema tapped the folder she'd brought with her. "I read it in the transcripts from the trial. You said so under oath."

"Oh. Yeah," Ginger said as she sat back. She took another sip of her tea.

"What do you actually do for Mr. Balducci?"

"Whatever I'm asked to do."

"So, you're his assistant?"

"Something like that." The faintest smirk crossed her face, the look saying much more than her words.

"There were rumors that his illegitimate son took the fall for his father. Do you know anything about that?"

"About what?"

"About Mr. Balducci being the true ringleader of that trafficking ring."

"Alexander is a kind, decent man. His son was the criminal."

"But if you found out he was involved, would you testify against him, too?"

"Not something I'll ever have to consider."

"Are you sure about that?"

"Why wouldn't I be?"

"Mr. Balducci is fortunate to have your loyalty. Especially after everything you've been through. I imagine trust doesn't come easily to you."

"Alexander has been good to me. He has earned my trust. He's a pillar of this community and deserves to be respected. And if you're trying to make him look bad," she said as she leaned forward across the table, "don't!"

Ginger's voice had dropped an octave and her eyes narrowed into thin slits that expressed an air of hostility. She suddenly stood and gathered up the camel-colored cape resting on the back of her chair. As she wrapped it around her shoulders, she gave Neema one last look.

"Does Davis know you're a reporter?"

Neema's eyes widened. "Excuse me?"

"I was just curious if he knew. The Black family is very particular about who they let into their inner circle. I'm surprised he's allowed you to get so close, unless of course, he just doesn't know. Because you two seem very chummy with each other."

Neema masked her surprise as best she could. "I'm not sure what that has to do with anything."

Ginger shrugged her narrow shoulders. "You should be careful, Ms. Kamau. I imagine in your line of work pissing off the wrong people could prove to be hazardous."

"Is that a threat?"

Ginger chuckled but didn't respond to the question. Then she turned, her high heels clicking across the tiled floor. As Neema watched her walk away, she couldn't help but wonder how long the woman had been watching her and Davis, and why.

Neema left the coffee shop still feeling uneasy about her encounter with Ginger. She was almost certain the redhead hadn't seen her at the gallery and, for the life of her, couldn't think of any other place she and Davis had been where Ginger had been there to have seen them together. There was something unholy about the woman, a coldness in her eyes that Neema found disconcerting. Their meeting left her feeling like she was hanging precariously on the edge of a cliff with Ginger standing ready to give her a push off the side.

No, Davis didn't know she was a reporter, but Ginger couldn't know that, Neema thought. The woman had been reaching and, despite Neema's best efforts to maintain a poker face, she was fairly certain Ginger had seen it in the momentary surprise that had passed across her eyes. But why would she ask, or even care? She had a husband, whoever that was, didn't she?

Neema suddenly thought back to the exchange between Ginger and Davis at the art gallery. How blatantly familiar the redhead had been with Davis, the interaction seemingly too intimate. Was there something between them that Davis hadn't been whole-heartedly honest about? Or even aware of? Did Ginger have feelings for him that he had misread? Was there any chance Ginger might share her speculation with Davis, blowing Neema up? Was she going to drive herself crazy imagining the absolute worst-case scenario if Ginger did tell Davis before she could? Neema suddenly felt as if the weight of the world was on her shoulders and she was slowly sinking beneath the bulk of it. She felt sick, her stomach doing flips at warp speed.

She slid into the driver's seat of her car. For a moment, she thought about calling Davis and just telling him everything, letting the chips fall and settle, then dealing with the debris and dust after the fact. But that felt even more cowardly than being afraid to tell him. She might be a lot of things, she thought, but she wasn't cruel and that would have been plain mean for several reasons.

Neema groaned as she tried to fathom how things had gone left as quickly as they had and how easily she had lost control of a situation she'd been determined to manipulate. Minutes passed as she considered her circumstance and what she should do, feeling like her options were few and far between.

She reached into her handbag for her cell phone. Scrolling through her contacts, she found the number she needed and dialed. The call went directly to voice mail.

"Cheryl, this is Neema Kamau. I need a favor, please. Will you call me when you get this message? I need to get my hands on a marriage license. The bride's name is Ginger Novak. I don't have a date, but it would have been in the last year. Maybe in the last six months. I'll owe you one. Thanks."

Neema left her cell phone number before disconnecting the call. She whispered a quick prayer that her
friend might be in the office on Saturday so that she
didn't have to wait until Monday to get her answer.

She took another few minutes to decide her next
step. Digging back into her purse, she found the business card Davis's brother had left with her. She needed
Mingus's opinion and she also needed to tell him what
she knew. As she dialed, it began to snow, large white
flakes settling against the windows.

The home of Jerome and Judith Black was located
in the heart of Chicago's historic Gold Coast neighborhood. It was situated on a large corner lot, the stone-
and-brick architecture timeless. As she stood at the front
entrance, a solid wood-and-glass door with ornate iron-
work, Neema felt her knees shake, threatening to drop
her to the ground. She regretted telling Davis she would
meet him there, instead of taking up his offer to pick her
up so they could ride together. She'd been concerned
about not having her own transportation if things didn't
go well after they talked. The prospect of opening up
to Davis had her entire body in one tight knot, making
dinner with his family seem like a walk in the park.

As the front door swung open, a wealth of laughter
echoed through the interior, dropping into a moment
of silence as Davis greeted her.

"Hey, beautiful!" He pulled her into his arms and
hugged her tightly. His kiss was warm and welcoming,
and her lips trembled beneath his touch.

She hugged him back, not wanting to let him go.
"Hi," she murmured when they finally parted and he
stepped aside so that she could enter the home.

He reached for her hand, entwining her fingers with

his own. "Are you ready for this?" Davis asked. "You're actually shaking!" He hugged her again.

"I'm nervous," Neema admitted. "I want to make a good impression."

"You'll be fine. And right after we eat, you and I can slip away and head back to my house." He kissed her cheek.

Neema nodded, the quiver of a smile pulling at her lips.

"Everyone's in the family room," he said as he escorted her along the front foyer and past the formal living room. He took a moment to give her a mini tour, pointing out each room as they passed.

The interior space was stunning and Neema was awed by the home's beauty. The comfort and quiet of the family retreat contrasted starkly with the busy Chicago lifestyle on the other side of the front door. The décor imparted an Old World feel with walls papered in silk, sparkling chandeliers, ornate wood moldings and fireplaces painstakingly carved in stone. The windows were draped in sumptuous fabrics and every detail, from the coffered ceilings to the highly polished hardwood floors, had been meticulously selected.

Davis's mother met them as they reached the end of the hallway. She was a tall woman, nearly as tall as her son. She had picture-perfect features: high cheekbones, black eyes like dark ice and a buttermilk complexion that needed little if any makeup. She was elegantly dressed in white silk pants and a matching blouse that highlighted her fair skin. Lush, silver-gray hair fell in soft waves past her shoulders. A bright smile blessed her face.

"Neema, welcome to our home!" she said, giving Neema a warm hug. "I've heard so much about you."

Davis made the formal introduction. "Neema Kamau, I'd like you to meet my mother, the Honorable Judith Harmon Black. Judge Black, this is my friend Neema, the woman I've been telling you about."

Neema tried not to look surprised to discover he'd talked about her with his mother. She smiled brightly. "It's a pleasure to meet you, Judge Black."

"Please, call me Judith. We stand on little formality in this house. Come join us."

The matriarch looped her arm through Neema's and pulled her along. "I can't begin to tell you how excited I was when Davis told me he was bringing a friend for our family dinner. I actually think you're the first young woman he has ever brought home for us to meet, now that I think about it!" She tossed her son a look over her shoulder as he followed behind them.

As the trio moved into the living space, a hushed silence fell over the family, everyone turning to stare.

"I think you've met most of this crowd," Judith said, "but, just to be sure, let me introduce you."

Davis's father rose from the plush recliner he was sitting in. He extended his hand. "It's good to see you again, Neema. Welcome to our home."

"Thank you, sir. It's a pleasure to see you again, as well."

Judith began to point around the room. "That's Parker and Ellington. Mingus and his wife Joanna. That's Armstrong's wife Danni, and Armstrong, of course. And my daughter Vaughan."

Neema gave them all a slight wave.

"It's nice to meet you," Danni said as she moved to shake Neema's hand. "And you're even prettier than the guys said."

Neema smiled shyly, feeling her cheeks flushing with heat. She wasn't sure how to respond.

"It's okay," Joanna quipped. "Davis has been gushing every time he talks about you. Welcome to the family!"

"Thank you," Neema responded.

"Where are Simone and Paul?" Davis questioned.

"We're not sure they're going to make it. Morning sickness is getting the best of Simone," his mother answered. "Paul said if they do come, they'll be late. We'll catch her up when we do see her."

Davis nodded.

His mother gestured them to the sofa. "Make yourself comfortable, Neema. I want you to feel at home here," she said.

As Davis and Neema took a seat on the oversize sofa, an awkward silence flooded the room, the wealth of it vibrating off the four walls.

Judith moved to her husband's side, perching herself on the arm of the chair. She wrapped her arm around his shoulders. The gesture seemed protective, and the family that knew them best felt it, as well. Davis shot his siblings a look, each of them admittedly on edge and trying not to show it. As if she sensed the rise in his anxiety, Neema reached for his hand, holding tightly to his fingers between her palms.

"So, let me start," Judith said, "by apologizing to Neema for what may come. I'm sure this will not be what you expected when Davis invited you to join us. But for Davis to invite you means that you are very important to him, so we're all happy to have you with us." She gave Neema a slight smile then shifted her gaze over each of her children.

"With everything that's been going on lately, I appreciate that all of you have continued to lean on each other for support. I can't tell you how happy that makes your father and me. Don't ever take the bonds of your relationship for granted. Continue to love each other and, like we have always told you, that love will see you through anything."

Jerome pressed his hand to hers, tapping gently. "Your mother is getting all sentimental on us," he said with a chuckle. "You all know that, for me, it's about doing what's right and maintaining your integrity in whatever situation you find yourselves in."

"I want to apologize to you both," Davis said. He shifted forward in his seat. "I had no right to go through your things the way I did. And I never intended to put you on the spot or to back you into a corner. I just wanted to know the truth."

Their father nodded slowly, meeting his son's stare. "Don't ever do it again," he said firmly.

Mingus scoffed. "It would have been our asses if we'd done that. He always gets off light."

Armstrong nodded. "That baby child syndrome. He *always* got off easy."

"Because I'm special," Davis quipped.

They all laughed, the tension in the room diminishing substantially. Even their father chuckled with them.

Vaughan finally asked the question that was on all their minds. "Daddy, is Alexander Balducci your biological brother?"

Jerome took a deep breath and nodded. "He is. He is my half-brother. We share the same father."

"Why didn't you ever tell us?" Davis questioned. "We've always wondered about your friendship with him. It never crossed any of our minds that you two might be related."

Jerome leaned forward, his elbows resting on his

thighs, his hands clasped tightly together. Everyone in the room seemed to lean with him in anticipation. "It was complicated. Other people's decisions really didn't give us many other options."

Jerome stood, moving to the sliding-glass doors that looked out to the rear yard. Everyone's eyes followed him, staring intently. Neema found him to be stately, his presence almost majestic. When he spoke, she better understood the family dynamics, and why Davis and his siblings were in such awe of the man.

"Our father was a man named Salvatore Balducci. His family had immigrated here from Italy at the top of the century. My father's family made their money in the city's manufacturing sector. The steel industry, making war goods during World War II. Then he and his brothers started bootlegging whiskey. That began their foray into criminal enterprise. My mother's people came to Chicago during the Great Migration. Her father was a preacher and her mother was a domestic worker.

"My grandmother worked for the Balducci family. She was one of their housekeepers and she used to take my mother with her to work on occasion when she needed help. That's how Andrabelle and Salvatore first met. I was told that they were instantly smitten with each other. Your grandmother was stunningly beautiful, and they say he fell head-over-heels in love with her. But he was older and newly married with a pregnant wife."

Jerome took a deep breath, holding it briefly before letting it slowly back out. "I don't know the details of everything that happened, but I do know that the circumstances of my conception, and my birth, destroyed my mother. I was told that whatever occurred between her and Balducci broke her spirit. She wasn't ever able to come back from it and be a mother."

He took another deep breath before continuing. "I only knew my father briefly and only because my grandmother would take me to see him. His wife was not at all happy about my birth, most especially because I was half Black. But Alexander and I were able to play together occasionally.

"The picture was taken between our sixth birthdays. Alexander had already turned six and I was maybe a month from being six. It was the last time I saw our father alive. My grandmother passed away right after that and my grandfather's hatred for the Balducci family was such that he refused to have anything to do with them. Since my father made no effort to reach out to me, it was as if he never existed. He died when I was nineteen, and that's when Alexander and I reconnected. At his funeral. By then, Alexander was fully entrenched in the family business and I was headed to the police academy. We agreed to stay out of each other's way and neither of us ever spoke about our connection. Until now."

Armstrong stood, began to pace the floor. "When Leonard died, it surprised everyone that you two were able to continue your friendship. How did that not break the two of you?"

"It did to some degree. He was bitter about it for a while. But, bottom line, we were still brothers. He was the first to say that it wasn't my fault. It was the life Leonard had chosen to live and the risk he'd taken with his lifestyle. Given all that, though, because of who our parents were and the choices they made, Alexander and I have always held each other at arm's length. His mother hated me and my mother as much as my grandfather hated him and our father. All that hate wasn't good for any of us. Now, because of our shared history,

I don't see that things between us will ever change. It is what it is."

Neema brushed a tear from her eye. Vaughan was weeping openly, the story breaking all their hearts. They all watched as Jerome moved back to his wife's side to gently kiss her lips. Then he excused himself from the room, fighting to hide his own tears.

Watching the two, Neema was moved by the wealth of love that embraced them. She squeezed Davis's hand as she leaned against him, pressing her forehead to his cheek, one arm wrapped around his back as her palm gently caressed him.

"Wow," he muttered softly. "Wow."

Judith stood. "What your father didn't say is that his grandfather believed Salvatore Balducci raped his mother." An edge of anger tainted her harshly spat words. "She would have only been sixteen when it happened. She never recovered from that. Jerome was still a toddler when she took her own life."

Neema gasped, pulling her palm to her chest. "I'm so sorry," she muttered softly, more for Davis than for anyone else.

He shook his head, still trying to process it all, understanding more than he imagined. "Mom, can I ask you a question?"

Judith met his gaze. "Yes, Davis?"

"Is that why you made the decision you did? Were you assaulted, too?" he asked, something in her voice triggering the thought.

Mingus gave him a glaring look. "Davis! Let. It. Go."

"It's okay," Judith said, holding up her hand. "Nothing is off limits at a family meeting. You know that." She took a step toward her son. "I was seventeen and a college freshman. I'd been invited to a frat party and someone spiked my drink. I was intoxicated and I didn't realize what had happened until the next morning. I also didn't know who my rapist was and, when I found out I was pregnant, it felt like the end of the world.

"My parents were staunch Catholics, so an abortion was out of the question. So, I had my son and gave him up for adoption. I have never regretted my decision because I think both of our lives would have been very different if I had tried to keep him. Much like your father's mother, I don't know if I could have been the mom he deserved, and he's been blessed with a mother who has loved him unconditionally."

Davis stood, moving to give his mother a hug. "I'm so sorry," he said as she hugged him back.

There was a moment between them that all the family felt blessed to be privy to, sensing the embrace was for them all. Neema swiped a tear from her eye, thankful that Davis and his parents had allowed her to stay.

Jerome came back into the room. "You all need to wrap up this pity party," he said as he slid a box of tissues into Vaughan's hands and leaned over to kiss her cheek. "I don't know about anyone else, but I'm hungry. And your mother made chocolate cake for dessert. I'm ready to eat."

"Me, too!" Parker exclaimed. "Past ready."

"Then let me go serve the food," Judith said as she gave Davis one last squeeze and headed for the dining room. "You all come grab a seat."

A handful of questions kept everyone focused on their family lineage through the appetizer. Davis's parents answering them readily, their honesty and willingness to be vulnerable impressive.

By the time the entrée was served, the conversation

had shifted to Davis's case. Between the entrée and dessert, the family was sharing stories about the young alderman, laughter filling the home as they took Neema down memory lane. She enjoyed getting to know them and allowing them to know her. She instinctively knew she and Joanna could easily be friends and she had much respect for Danni and her career choices. They all welcomed her with open arms and in no time at all she felt like one of the family, which brought her and Davis both immense joy.

The ease with which the conversation shifted, and everyone's mood followed, was a model for what more families needed to practice. From where Neema sat, she felt like the Black family had mastered the art of self-irony, being able to laugh at themselves even when things seemed difficult. Their camaraderie and ability to engage with one another was inspiring. She better understood why Davis worried so incessantly about his parents and siblings, the depths of their love for each other undeniable.

She turned in her seat, staring as he wiped a cloth napkin across his full lips. Joy rained over him. There was an air of comfort that elevated the muscles in his face, his smile wide and full. Catching his eye, she gave him a bright smile and he bowed to give her a kiss on the cheek.

"You okay?" he whispered, his gaze shifting back and forth across her face.

Neema nodded. "I'm really good. I was just about to ask you the same thing."

"I'm good, too. And I'm glad you're here with me."

"Thank you for inviting me."

"My mother likes you, and it was important to me that you two get to know each other."

"I really like her. Your mother is very sweet, and I love your family."

Davis kissed her cheek a second time.

"You boys are on dish duty," Judith commanded from her seat at the end of the table.

Davis rose and began to help his brothers clear the table.

Judith gestured in Neema's direction. "Did you get enough to eat, Neema? There's plenty more if you want seconds."

"Thank you, Judith. But I couldn't eat another bite. If I did, you'd have to roll me out of here. But it was all delicious." And it had been, Neema thought. The matriarch had served them a pear and kale salad, roast pork with stewed apples, grilled asparagus, glazed carrots, garlic mashed potatoes and the most decadent chocolate cake with a raspberry filling, topped with a chocolate ganache. It had been so good that Neema had overeaten.

"We appreciate you supporting Davis the way you have, Neema. He speaks quite fondly of you," Judith said.

"He's become very important to me," Neema responded.

"And it seems that you're important to him," Vaughan interjected. "So, I know you can appreciate our concern about his privacy being protected. Most especially because of his political aspirations. You being invited to our family meeting makes him vulnerable if anything that was shared with you were to be made public."

"That would never happen," Neema said firmly. "I would never think to disrespect Davis, or any of you like that."

"So, you'd be willing to sign a nondisclosure agreement?"

"What are you all talking about?" Davis said, coming back into the room. "Please tell me you are not giving Neema a hard time, Vaughan."

Vaughan shot him an exasperated eye roll. "Neema is an intelligent adult and perfectly capable of holding her own with all of us in this room."

"I know that's right!" Joanna decreed as she gave Neema a wink.

"Are you about ready to head out?" Davis asked, turning his attention back to Neema.

"You aren't rushing off, are you?" his mother questioned.

"Neema and I were still talking," Vaughan persisted.

Before either could answer, Simone suddenly made an entrance, sweeping into the house like a storm wind. Her husband, Paul, followed on her heels, his expression telling as he gave them all a look.

Ignoring the family who greeted her, Simone moved straight to the empty seat directly across from Neema's. The expression on her face was venomous and Neema instinctively knew that what was coming would not be pretty.

Davis suddenly stepped up directly behind her, his hands pressing gently against her shoulders. His instincts had sent him into protective overdrive, the gesture shielding. Neema was grateful for his touch but knew it wouldn't last long.

"What's wrong, Simone?" Judith questioned.

"Neema is a reporter," Simone said loudly, her eyes locked on Neema's face. "Did you know your new girlfriend is a reporter for the *Chicago Tribune*, Davis? Because if you did, you should have told us."

"What are you talking about, Simone? Neema's not—" Davis started.

"Yes, she is," Simone said, cutting her brother off. "I told you I knew her from somewhere and then it came to me. That Women's Empowerment seminar I did last year? Neema was reporting on the event for the newspaper. A quick Google search confirmed that not only is she a reporter but, and I quote 'she's an award-winning journalist known to get stories others find problematic' unquote."

Neema dropped her eyes to the table unable to fathom how the tide had turned on her so quickly. The whole family had joined Simone in the dining room, and everyone was now staring at her. The once jovial mood had deflated, replaced by something dark and uncertain. If only they'd had thirty more minutes, then she and Davis would have been headed to his house to have this conversation in private. Thirty more minutes and she wouldn't have been under the scrutiny of his family, feeling like a pariah in their midst.

Davis took a step back as Neema turned, lifting her gaze to his. "I'm so sorry," she said. "I didn't want you to find out this way."

Davis blinked, shock blanketing his expression. "You're a reporter?"

"You didn't want him to find out at all, did you?" Simone snapped. "At least not until you got all the dirt you needed, right? Was that your plan from the start? Integrate yourself into my brother's life and try to take down our family from the inside?"

Neema shook her head. "No, it wasn't like… I… it's…" she stammered, searching for the words to explain herself.

"Why should anyone believe you? You've been lying since we met you." Simone's voice had risen a few octaves.

"Simone, that's enough," their mother admonished.

"You need to calm down, Simone," Jerome implored. "You getting your blood pressure up is not good for the baby."

The family patriarch stepped closer to Davis. "Did you know about this, son?" he asked.

Davis shook his head. The color had drained from his face and he looked like he'd been hit by a train. He had begun to perspire, sweat beading across his brow. Blindsided didn't begin to define how he suddenly felt. He didn't have the words to express the heartbreak. "No," he finally whispered. "I didn't."

Neema was still staring at him. "It's what I've been trying to tell you," she said. "What I had hoped to discuss with you later." She reached her hand out, pressing her fingers to his chest. Davis took another step back, bristling beneath her touch.

"Trying to tell him? Humph!" Simone scoffed. "That's rich!"

"Damn, Simone! Do you have to be so mean?" Parker snapped.

"I'm being honest," Simone barked. "Clearly, something our esteemed guest here knows nothing about."

"Shut up, Simone," Davis stormed.

"Everybody take a breath," Jerome said. "We need to give Davis and Neema some privacy."

"I haven't eaten," Simone muttered.

"Then head to the kitchen," her mother commanded. "But your brother doesn't need any more of your comments."

"He should be glad I'm looking out for him."

"Shut up, Simone," the siblings all ranted at the same time.

Neema and Davis watched as Simone rose from her

seat, tossing them both one last look. *I'm sorry*, she mouthed to her brother before glaring at Neema one last time.

Minutes later, the quiet in the room was suffocating. Davis was still trying to process the news, feeling like he was stuck between a rock and a hard place. Neema still hadn't said anything that made any sense to him, and he wasn't sure he even had the stomach to ask the hard questions he now needed answers to.

"You're really a reporter?" he finally said. "Was Simone telling the truth?"

Neema nodded. "I am. My degree was in investigative journalism and I've been with the *Chicago Tribune* for a few years now."

"Why would you not tell me something like that, Neema?"

"It's complicated, Davis. Then, when I did try to tell you, it was always the wrong time, the wrong mood, or I was just scared."

Davis shook his head. "That first time we went out, were you planning to write a story about me, or my family? Was that your intention?"

Neema took a breath, closing her eyes briefly before she met his gaze again. "I'd seen the envelope exchange between you and Balducci that night at the restaurant and I thought there might be a story there. That you might be on the take."

"So, this has never been about me. Or about us."

"That's not true. When I realized I was wrong, all I wanted was to get to know you better. I wasn't expecting our relationship to evolve the way it did. But as we grew closer, it's been all about us."

"I honestly don't know what to think," Davis said. "I trusted you."

"Please, let's just go to your place to talk about it. I want you to understand what happened and why. And it's important to me that you know just how much I care about you."

"Care about me? If you cared about me, you would have told me the truth."

"Do you think I haven't tried? That I knew we couldn't take things any further until you knew the truth? I've tried a few times to tell you."

"Obviously you didn't try hard enough." His words, wrapped in barbed wire, were bitter against his tongue. As he spat them out, Neema felt each like a targeted slap.

She gasped. Loudly. "I'm so sorry, Davis."

Davis heard the words but found himself questioning their truth. He was numb. His emotions having over-loaded and exploded, left him feeling broken. He was past ready for it to all be over, wanted to find a way to escape all that was happening. "I'm sorry, too, Neema. Right now, though, I think you need to leave."

"Please, I want you to understand—"

"Now!" he said, his voice rising. "You need to leave *now*. There's nothing else we need to say to each other. I want you out of my parents' home *now*."

A tear rolled down Neema's face, her eyes misting with regrettable sadness. She knew there was no advan-tage to arguing her point. Davis wasn't ready to hear her. Pushing to her feet, she gave him one last look and exited the room.

Judith Black stood in the foyer of her home, her arms crossed at her chest. Lost in thought, it wasn't until

Neema reached the woman's side that she realized she was not alone.

Neema forced the slightest smile to her face as she approached Davis's mother. "Thank you for dinner, Judge Black. And I am so sorry. I want to reassure you that anything shared with me about your family will never be shared with anyone else. I would never divulge what I heard or betray your family's privacy. Never!"

"I appreciate you saying that, Neema. But I wasn't concerned. Davis is a good judge of character. I'm sure, once he's past the shock of it all, he'll remember why he was drawn to you in the first place. Watching the two of you together, I can see that there's something pretty special between you."

"I feel horrible. I never meant for this to get out of hand or for Davis to be hurt by my actions." Her tears began to drop a second time.

Judith tugged Neema into a comforting hug. "Give him some time. I'm sure it'll all work out once you two are able to talk things through."

"I'm not so sure about that," Neema said softly. "He's really angry with me."

"He's disappointed right now. And he has every reason to be. But if you two are meant to be together, you'll get past this. It may just take some time." Judith reached to open the front door.

"Thank you," Neema said as she stepped over the threshold. "Thank you for your kindness."

"You take care of yourself, dear," Judith said and then she shut the door.

Chapter 16

Davis had paced the floor for a good ten minutes before dropping down into a dining room chair. His head hurt and, for a brief moment, he wanted to rage. He couldn't begin to understand what had just happened, but he felt like his entire life had blown up into flames.

For the life of him, he couldn't figure out how he'd been so wrong about Neema. Neema who made him laugh. Neema who listened to him. Neema who always knew what to say and when to say it. Neema who had stolen his heart and placed her claim on his soul. Now, she was Neema the reporter, who had only been working him for a story. How in hell had he missed that?

He was rewinding every conversation he and Neema had ever had. Trying to figure out when everything that had felt right had gone left. As he sat there, he felt lost, unable to comprehend how he had missed the clues, if there had even been clues. When his brothers entered the room, joining him at the table, he still had no tangible answers that made any sense.

"You okay?" Ellington asked, sliding a bottle of Budweiser toward his brother.

Davis shrugged. "She played me."

"That woman loves you," Mingus said. "And you love her."

"Love? I don't think so."

Armstrong laughed. "If it wasn't love, you wouldn't be feeling like you've been hit with a sledgehammer."

"Or looking like you just lost your favorite puppy!" Parker quipped.

"Y'all don't know what the hell you're talking about."

"You don't love her?" Mingus questioned.

"She played me!" Davis repeated emphatically.

"She was helping me with your case," Mingus said matter-of-factly. "She's got some serious contacts. Her informant list is almost as long as my own."

Davis's head snapped as he turned to stare at Mingus. "You knew?"

Mingus nodded. "Yeah, I knew."

"Why didn't you say something?" Armstrong asked.

"Because she said she was going to tell him and I believed her," Mingus said, answering the question. He turned back to Davis. "She didn't want there to be secrets between you."

"Leave it to Simone to spoil a surprise," Ellington said facetiously.

"I thought marriage and pregnancy would have reined her in. Instead it looks like it just ramped her up," Parker said.

"Your sister is psychotic," Davis gibed.

"Like she's not your sister. And you being her favorite brother, too!" Parker responded.

"You can always trust Simone to gaslight you at the most imperfect moment. She's actually made it an art form." Mingus chuckled.

"So, how long have you known?" Davis asked, shooting Mingus a look.

"Since that night you asked me what I thought about her."

"You ran a background check?"

"Better safe than sorry. Then I confronted her, and I liked her answers. More importantly, I believed her. I think Neema's good people. I also think this situation just got away from her. She was looking for the perfect time to tell you, and we all know there is never a perfect time."

"I can't trust her," Davis answered.

"Then trust your feelings," Armstrong said. "Your gut instincts are why your pursued her in the first place."

"And why you fell in love with her," Mingus added.

Davis shrugged again, adding their comments to the thoughts spinning through his head. *Who said anything about love?* he thought to himself.

"Mingus, you said she was helping with Davis's case," Parker noted. "Did she come up with anything?"

"Yeah, she did. You may want to bring Ginger in for questioning," Mingus said. He shared what Neema had learned about the so-called witness and her connection to the redhead.

"Hold on a sec," Armstrong said, rising from his seat. He went to the door and called for his wife.

A minute later, Danielle Winstead Black poked her head into the room. "You called?"

Armstrong gestured for her to join them. "We need your expertise." He gave her a wink of his eye.

Looking more like a kindergarten teacher than a dec-orated police officer, Danielle—affectionately known as Danni to family and friends—was a force to be reck-oned with. One of the best detectives on the Chicago force, her youthful appearance belied her experience and ability.

Her bright smile endearing, she gave Davis a com-forting look as she entered. "Everything okay in here? We were starting to worry."

Armstrong shrugged. "Davis's feeling are hurt, but it's all good."

Davis rolled his eyes as his brother continued.

"Mingus thinks your girl Ginger is somehow in-volved in Davis's case and Gaia's death. You know her well. Do you think she could have had anything to do with it?"

"Anything's possible with Ginger. She's all about self-preservation. I wouldn't put anything past her. But isn't she still working for Balducci? Because she was super-protective of Pie."

Davis looked confused, thinking back to the man who'd been playing video games with Gaia's son. "Pro-tective of him? Why?"

"He only has the mental and emotional capacity of a twelve-year-old. For the most part he's a big kid in an adult body. But he's easily frustrated and was prone to violence against women. Ginger is one of the few people he responds to. His grandfather keeps her on the payroll to keep a tight rein on him."

"Well, she's doing more than babysitting Pie for him," Mingus said. He reached for his cell phone and scrolled through his pictures. "I had to get an old friend of mine to open the records department this morning down at the county clerk's office to follow up on a lead Neema had. It seems that Ginger got married recently. Give you three guesses who the groom was—and the first two don't count." He passed his phone and an image of the marriage license to his sister-in-law.

Danni cringed. "Please tell me it's not so."

"Sorry," Mingus said with a shrug of his shoulders. "But your friend Ginger married her boss. Ginger Novak Balducci is our new auntie."

There was a collective gasp as they each let that information settle.

Parker leaned across the table, his voice dropping to a loud whisper. "Let's keep that little tidbit between us for the time being, please. No one outside of this room needs to know. At least not until we can figure out how she and Balducci both play into all of this."

Davis listened with half an ear as the family revisited the details they did know. Plans were made to question Ginger. He suddenly thought about the last time he had seen her.

"She carries a gun," he said. "Ginger does."

"And you know this how?" Ellington questioned.

"She had a gun on her when she and Balducci showed up at the hospital to see me. I saw it holstered under her jacket." As he thought about that moment, he couldn't help but remember Neema's visit and their first kiss, and his heart suddenly felt like it was going to stop beating from the hurt of it all.

As the family began to say their goodbyes and head to their respective homes, Mingus pulled Davis aside. "I try to stay out of other people's business," he said.

"I know, but you should have told me. I feel like Neema's made a fool out of me."

"I didn't tell you about Neema because it wasn't my

place to tell you. It was hers, and she swore to me that she would before the week was out. If she hadn't, then I would have told you. That was our agreement. And I think she had every intention of telling you if Simone hadn't beaten her to the punch."

"We were supposed to talk after dinner. She said she had something important to share with me."

"So now you need to decide what you plan to do about it."

"I don't plan to do anything. It's over," Davis said emphatically.

"You're just pissed that it was Simone who called her out. Had anyone else told you, you would have been more than ready to talk to Neema and make things right between you. Don't let Simone steal your joy. She would never have let any one of us come between her and Paul. So don't you sabotage what you and Neema could have with each other. You know you want that woman."

"Right now," Davis said, "all I want is to be left alone."

Mingus chuckled. "Good luck with that!"

They seemed to line up, everyone in the family wanting to leave him with a word or two of advice. Telling him not to make any rash decisions seemed to be the *ligne de jour*.

Simone threw her arms around his neck and hugged him tightly, contrition battling with her strong will. "I should have handled that differently," she muttered.

"You think?"

"I was just so mad! How dare she lead you on and try to take advantage of you!"

"Simone, I love you, but it's time you let go and stop trying to rule my life."

"That's not what I was trying to do."

"It's exactly what you were trying to do. I appreciate you wanting to protect me, but you need to turn all that energy toward your husband and my future nephew."

"I am not that bad."

"Yes, you are. Our mother isn't as overbearing as you are, Simone. You need to take some pointers."

Simone sighed. "Okay, so maybe I have moments."

Davis shook his head. "I know you were just looking out for me. But damn, Simone! Did you have to be so rough? You were like a pit bull the way you went after Neema."

Simone blew a soft sigh. "Truth?"

"Always."

"I may have been a little jealous. I may be having a hard time thinking of you loving someone more than you love me. Next to Mom, I was your favorite girl. I don't want you to have another favorite."

Davis laughed. "You may need professional help for that."

Simone hugged her brother a second time. "What are you going to do now?"

"I don't know. I just need to step away for a while to think."

"Well, don't think too hard. You might give her a second chance and that's not a woman you can trust."

"You don't know her, Simone."

"And I don't want to. Not yet, anyway."

"You really need to spend more time with Mom practicing patience and forgiveness and all those other traits you seem to be lacking. Preferably before the baby is born."

"Now who's being mean?"

Davis kissed her cheek. "I love you, Simone."

"I love you more, baby brother," she said as she

hugged him one last time, then followed her husband to the car.

Minutes later his parents stood together as Davis readied himself to go home. He hugged one and then the other.

"Are you going to be okay, son?" his father asked.

Davis nodded. "I'll be fine. I just need some time."

"Take a minute," his mother said, "then call Neema and talk to her. She owes you an explanation and you owe her the courtesy of listening. Nothing may come of it, but if you care about her the way I think you do, I believe you two can work it out."

"I need to make sure she isn't planning to write anything about what you both shared with us this evening. There'll be no working anything out if she does."

"I'm not worried about that," Judith said. "I don't think anything that was said here will be repeated. Her initial intentions may not have been above board, but I think once she fell in love with you, she was firmly committed to protecting your interests."

"Why does everyone keep talking about her being in love with me and me being in love with her?" He tossed up his hands in frustration.

Both his parents laughed heartily. "You still have a lot to learn, son," Jerome said. "A lot to learn! You and Neema care more for each other than either of you has been willing to admit. Everyone else can see it and you would, too, if you didn't spend so much time trying to fight it."

Davis shook his head. If he were honest, he hadn't been fighting it. He'd been concerned about labeling it and, with everything going on, he hadn't been able to give it his full and undivided attention.

Judith linked her arm through her son's. "Let me

share something with you. When your father and I met, I didn't tell him what had happened to me. When we married and I became pregnant with Parker, there were some complications. A doctor inadvertently told your father about my previous pregnancy. Needless to say, he was not happy with me."

Jerome nodded. "Actually, I was furious. I didn't think I could ever trust your mother again. I couldn't understand how she would keep something like that from me."

"We had to go through it to make it out the other side," Judith said. "And it was hard work on both our parts. That was an ugly time, and I'm grateful every day that we didn't give up on each other."

"If I had to, I'd do it all over again, too," Jerome said. He kissed his wife's mouth. "If you're blessed to find the love of your life, those battles are well worth what they may put you through."

"Thank you," Davis said. "I love you both more than I can ever express in words."

"We love you, too," Judith said.

"Call that young woman!" Jerome shouted as Davis made it to his car. "We like her!"

Neema sat in front of Davis's house for over an hour. For most of that time she cried, that really ugly cry that made her nose run and her eyes itch. She couldn't begin to express how much she hurt. Mingus had warned her that she might not have the time she thought to tell Davis the truth. Being a coward about it had probably lost her the love of her life.

Because she did love Davis. As he had stood staring at her, confusion, frustration and hurt blended across his face, she realized just how hard she had fallen for him. And now she was fearful she would never be able to tell him. That he would never be interested in hearing those words from her.

She'd thought about calling but knew that if he refused to speak with her, that would probably be the straw that broke her. She'd been able to walk out of his parents' home with a semblance of her dignity, despite the looks his family had given her.

His mother had been more than generous and even his sister Vaughan had been relatively kind. Davis had warned her about Simone, but even Neema knew there weren't enough pregnancy hormones in the world to explain away her bad behavior. Simone had been plain mean for no reason and, sadly, Neema had given her more than enough reason to be outright vicious. Neema imagined Simone would be the sister that gave in-laws a bad rap.

After an hour and a half, she was ready to pull her car out of the parking spot and head back across town. Hoping Davis would have been home by now had been wishful thinking on her part. She figured he'd stayed with his family to bemoan her actions. And although she understood it, she was slightly angry that he hadn't wanted to confront her about it instead.

For a moment, she thought about going to the office to put extra time on the clock, but she had no desire to be out pursuing other people's bad news. She had her own to deal with. And no idea how she was going to handle the fallout from the full disclosure that had devastated Davis and left her feeling like the most horrible person in the world.

She considered going to the restaurant but that would mean explaining to her parents why she was there and what had gone wrong. That was definitely not the lecture she needed. She opted to head to the house instead and hope her parents hadn't beaten her there so she could sneak into her room without anyone knowing she was home.

Just as she shifted her car into Drive, the lights in Davis's house came on, but Davis was nowhere to be seen. For a moment, she thought they might be on a timer, but a shadowy figure moving past the window gave Neema pause. If Davis was still with his family, who was sneaking around in his home? She reached for her phone.

"Nine-one-one. What's your emergency?"

"I need to report a burglary at the home of Alderman Davis Black. The intruder is currently on sight," Neema said.

The police presence in front of his home suddenly had Davis's heart racing, unable to imagine what had happened now. Then he remembered that he'd forgotten to set the new alarm system his brother had insisted on installing. Seeing Neema kneeling on the sidewalk, her arms around Titus's neck, sank his heart deep into the pit of his stomach imagining the worse.

Throwing his car into Park, he cut the engine and practically jumped from the vehicle. Mingus walking toward him stopped him from running foolishly forward. "What's going on?" he questioned as his brother met him in the driveway.

"You had a break-in. Neema was here waiting for you and called it in."

"Neema?"

"Yeah. And let me school you, little brother," he said. "When you're mad at your woman and she calls you—

you answer. A woman is not going to call if she knows you're pissed *unless* it's important."

Davis shook his head. Neema had called him twice and he'd ignored her both times, not ready to talk with her. He had cut his phone off instead. Now he was feeling bad about it and Mingus calling him out didn't help. "Is she okay?"

"Worried about you."

A uniformed police officer sauntered up to the two men. "That's some guard dog you have there, Alderman Black. He wouldn't let us in, or the perp out, until your wife called him off," he said, gesturing toward Neema and Titus with his head.

"She not my…" Davis started.

"It's a good thing she called before going into the house. She might have gotten hurt," the officer continued.

"Did you get the guy?" Davis asked instead.

"Handcuffed in the back of my patrol car. We're going to take him down to the station and book him. The house is clear, so you can go inside now to see if anything's missing."

Davis nodded. "Thank you."

Mingus gave him a look and he paused as the officer turned and walked away. "Dad's going to meet us down at the station," he said, his voice dropping a level.

"Why? What's up?"

Mingus pointed to the patrol car. Inside, Alexander Balducci's older grandson sat in the back seat. He was rocking back and forth, clearly agitated.

"Does everything have to be so damn complicated," Davis said, throwing his hands up in frustration.

"It gets better," Mingus said. "He was carrying and something tells me that gun is going to come back on those three bodies. From what we've been able to figure out, you were supposed to be the fourth."

"You're kidding me, right?"

"Little brother, I wish I was."

Neema watched the brothers as they stood in conversation. Davis's gaze kept skating in her direction and she could only begin to imagine what he had to be thinking about her being there.

She and Titus both stood as he walked toward them. Titus's tail wag evidenced his excitement. Neema was grateful hers didn't show, not wanting to embarrass herself. But she was excited, and hopeful.

"Hey," Davis said as he made it to her side. He reached his hand out to pat his dog's head. "Thank you."

"I didn't want anything to happen to Titus."

"I appreciate that."

There was an awkward pause as they stood staring at each other pretending to be focused on the dog.

"We need to go to the police station," Davis finally said.

"I gave them a statement," Neema responded. "Do they need something else from me?"

"I need you," he answered.

Nina's eyes widened and she simply nodded.

"Let me put Titus in the house and lock up. We can ride together in my car."

"Are you sure? I can follow you, if that will be easier?"

"Nothing about this is easy. And we need to talk. Please."

Neema watched Davis and Titus head through the front door. Moments later, he exited the home, locked the front door, and gestured for her to meet him at his car. Most of the patrol cars had already taken off, only one stayed behind to watch the home and street. Davis's brother had also disappeared.

As she slid into the front passenger seat, she wasn't quite sure what to say or if she should say anything at all. So she said nothing, deciding to let Davis take the lead. There was a moment of hesitation on his part as he sat in the driver's seat, not starting the car.

Without giving it a thought, Neema reached for his hand, gently caressing the back of his fingers. When he didn't pull away, she took it as a hopeful sign of what was yet to come.

Chapter 17

Davis knew he couldn't stay angry forever. He also knew his parents had been right about Neema needing to explain herself and him affording her the opportunity to do that. As the palm of her hand gently grazed the back of his, he shot her a look and the faintest of smiles.

He inhaled, drawing oxygen deep into his lungs. "Before we go, we need to talk," he said finally. "I need to understand why you didn't trust me."

Neema's dark eyes were wide, confusion washing over her expression. "But I did trust you! Why would you think I didn't trust you?"

"Because you wouldn't tell me the truth. If you trusted me, you could tell me anything."

Neema shook her head, dismay crossing her face. "It wasn't about trusting you. I regretted what I had done. Hated the choices I had made. I was afraid to confess because I didn't want you to hate me. And I knew you would hate me! I didn't want to lose you, but once you knew, I couldn't blame you if you never wanted to see me again."

"You should have told me, Neema!"

"I tried. Every time I thought I could get it out, something happened. Your phone rang and you had to take a call. We were distracted, or I simply chickened out! But I had every intention of coming clean because I did trust you. I trusted you because I love you and all I wanted was for you to love me back."

Davis shot her another look, held her gaze as she stared intently. There was something swimming in her tears that tugged at his heartstrings and made him want to forget every bad thing that had happened with them both in their lives. To bring them joy like never before. Something that made him want to protect her from harm by any means necessary.

"So, tell me now," he nodded. "Please."

And Neema did. She was brutally honest about her initial assumptions about him, and what she had accomplished. She detailed where she'd gone looking for information and who she'd talked to. Then she admitted that she had been wrong about everything, and how she had then tried to make it right. She expressed every fear and concern that she had battled, neither embellishing nor omitting anything. She told him every dirty detail and then she apologized one more time.

"I was wrong," she said softly. "You weren't the grimy politician I thought you would be. You turned out to be this incredibly sensitive, intuitive spirit, with one of the biggest hearts of anyone I've ever known."

Davis's smile lifted slightly. "I took it personally. It felt like a major deficiency on my part. That I had failed miserably in all my efforts to show you the man I was.

Because if you couldn't be honest with me or talk to me, then what had we been doing since we met? It hurt."

Neema expressed her regret one last time. "I can't apologize enough, and me saying it over and over again won't change what happened. I take full responsibility for not telling you the truth and for starting our relationship on a fallacy. I want us to move forward, but we can't do that if you can't forgive me. So the question now is, can you? Can you get past this?"

Davis started the car, shifting it into gear. Then he shrugged his shoulders as he gave her a quick look. "I don't know, Neema. I honestly don't know."

The ride to the West Harrison Street police station was quiet at best. Neither of them had much to say. Davis asked about the intruder and Neema told him what had happened after she called 9-1-1 and his cousin Pie was taken into custody. How multiple officers had surrounded the home only to find Pie curled up in a corner, Titus standing over him snarling. They both laughed at how readily Titus had gone to her when called, reminding them both that his dog's affection for her was very real.

Inside, a desk clerk had them take a seat to wait. They sat side-by-side, shoulders pressed tightly together. A man who was visibly intoxicated slumped on another bench, trying to convince everyone in the room there was nothing wrong with him. He was loud and cantankerous and only settled down when a uniformed officer threatened to throw him into a jail cell.

Minutes passed before an officer gestured for them to follow. He led them to Parker's office, where Davis's father and Mingus were waiting.

"Neema, it's good to see you," Jerome said politely. He stood, extending his hand in greeting.

"Hey, Neema," his brothers said casually.

She gave them a greeting back.

"What's going on?" Davis asked as they took a seat on the upholstered sofa in the room.

Mingus answered. "Armstrong is running the interrogation. Ellington is with Pie. He's representing him."

Surprise washed over Davis's face. "How did that happen?"

"It was obvious that he needed an advocate, and I wasn't able to reach his father," Jerome said. "Ellington was here, so it just made sense."

"Made sense to whom?" Davis said, his tone surly.

His father gave him a look. "We still do what's right, son."

"Do we know anything? Why he was at my house? Or what he was hoping to accomplish?"

They all shook their heads.

Parker stepped forward. "Neema, if I can steal you, please. I'd like to get a signed statement from you about what happened."

Neema nodded. "Whatever you need," she said as she got to her feet.

"I'll bring her back shortly," Parker said to Davis, giving his brother a nod.

As Neema stepped past Davis, he reached for her hand, stalling her steps. There was a split second of hesitation and then he kissed the backs of her fingers, his warm breath like a gentle breeze against her skin.

"I'll be here waiting for her," he said softly, the comment intended more for Neema than for anyone else."

When the door closed behind the two, his father

chuckled. "It's damn hard to stay mad at a woman you love hard."

"I know that's right," Mingus said agreeably. "You two good?"

Davis shrugged. "We'll get there," he said, believing it more as he thought about it. "We'll get there."

Two months later, Davis reread the article that carried Neema's byline. For many, the brief story said absolutely nothing. For his family, it spoke volumes. He read it for the umpteenth time.

A local man appearing before the magistrate this morning on felony breaking and entering charges no longer faces prosecution, the Cook County District Attorney's Office said today.

Paul Balducci, 21, the grandson of real estate mogul Alexander Balducci, was arrested for allegedly breaking into the home of Alderman Davis Black. Cook County Deputy Prosecutor Lynne Burgess filed a motion to dismiss on Wednesday, citing a "lack of sufficient evidence to prove the case beyond a reasonable doubt."

Balducci's defense attorney, Ellington Black, confirmed the charges were dismissed but declined further comment. Alderman Davis Black could not be reached for comment.

Few people would ever know the backdoor wheeling and dealing that had enabled the Balducci heir to be released into his grandfather's custody and to walk away scot-free. Under any other circumstance, Pie would have been charged with three murders, the attempted murder of Davis and a litany of other charges too numerous to detail. Instead, he was probably sitting in his grandfather's basement playing Minecraft or Grand Theft Auto. The reality of that still didn't sit well with Davis.

The night Pie had been arrested, he'd eagerly admitted to his role in Gaia's death. How he had bribed the cleaning person for the key to enter Davis's office. How he'd been following her for weeks. How he had confronted her, and then shot and killed her. His motive had been jealousy upon discovering that Gaia was the newest object of his grandfather's affection.

As Pie had begun to tattle on himself, owning up in detail to a host of crimes known and unknown, his grandfather and Ginger had arrived. Ginger had been like Svengali, mesmerizing Pie into silence. Only they and Ellington knew the full text of Pie's admissions and, when it came time for him make a statement to the detectives working the case, Pie regressed to his adolescent state and had nothing at all to say.

It had been Davis's father who'd asked Neema to help control the narrative. Every local news outlet was trying to get the story. Neema had been given a heads-up before Pie's appearance in front of the judge to be able to file her story first. It had been the last in a series of stories about persons living with mental disabilities. Her previous article had included an interview with Alexander Balducci about his experiences with his grandson and his late son Leonard. The question-and-answer session had been a real coup for her career.

That night Davis's father had asked him to lie outright. To say that Pie had not entered his home without permission and that he had no interest in pressing charges. Two minutes trying to have a conversation with Pie and Davis understood why. But that lie had left him ravaged with guilt thinking Gaia's killer might get away with her murder. Discovering Balducci and his father had agreed to handle the matter privately, out of the public eye, further plagued his spirit and left him bewildered. He found himself questioning his own sense of morality as he came to terms with his father's admonishments and insistence that Balducci would ensure justice would be served and Pie would be punished for his transgressions. Imagining what Balducci might do further complicated Davis's sense of right and wrong.

Parker and his team were still investigating the disappearance of the gun confiscated from Pie the night of his arrest. The chain of custody was being scrutinized and questions were being asked. Without that weapon, Forensics would never be able to tie the two to Gaia's body, or any other.

But for everything Pie had admitted doing, there was just as much that he claimed to know nothing about. Swearing he'd had nothing to do with assaulting Davis or shooting up his home, his proclamation had been believable, the man-child not wanting to be blamed for something he had not done. Figuring out the disconnect had been challenging at best.

Alexander Balducci called Davis directly to request a meeting. Davis had no idea what he wanted but was willing to meet with him to find out. He opened his front door and welcomed his father's brother inside.

"Thank you for agreeing to see me," Balducci said as he removed his wool fedora, holding the hat with both hands.

"I appreciate you meeting me here at my home," Davis said. "Can I offer you something to drink? Water? Coffee? A pop?"

"No, thank you. I'm not going to be here long. I'm headed to the airport."

Davis pointed the man toward a seat. "Going somewhere nice, I hope."

Balducci smiled. "Somewhere."

Davis sat in the wing chair facing his uncle. "So, what did you want to speak with me about?"

"You needed to know that my grandson had nothing to do with the attacks on you."

"So he said. I don't know that I believe him, though."

"My Pauly rarely lies. Unless he's being influenced by someone else. My grandson killed my daughter. We have no doubts about that, but I have had to ask myself why. Why would Pauly believe his place in the family would be threatened by her presence? Why is he accepting of Emilio, but not accepting of Emilio's mother? How was he able to plot and execute his plan so flawlessly? Pauly is barely able to tie his shoes by himself. Then I had to question who had the most influence over him."

Davis shifted forward in his seat, listening intently as Balducci continued.

"I often say that given enough time, people will show you who they are," he said, his expression reflective.

"I've heard that before," Davis said. "Ginger said it to me."

Balducci sneered. "I'm sure she did. Most recently, Ginger has clearly showed me exactly who she is. And that is why I am making this trip."

"I don't understand."

"There is little my Pauly has ever done that someone else didn't control or know about. Ginger has had her claws in Pauly for some time now. He will do her bidding without a second thought. It wasn't my Pauly who was jealous. It was Ginger. Afraid that her standing in my family would be usurped if another woman were welcomed into the fold. Pauly may have pulled the trigger, but Ginger put the gun in his hand and pointed it. Now they both must suffer the consequences of their actions."

"But you married her!"

"I did do that. A moment of whimsy, as my late mother would say. Ginger is quite a mesmerizing beauty. She has made playing on a man's weakness an art form. She will soon discover that I am anything but a weak man," he spat.

Davis shook his head. "What about Emilio? Will he be safe?"

"Emilio will be fine. Ginger's maternal instincts came out with Emilio. She was as protective of him as she was of Pauly."

"Was? You say that like she isn't any more."

Balducci's smile was disconcerting. "Ginger will be traveling abroad with me, but unfortunately she will not be returning. It has recently been brought to my attention that Ginger directed Pauly's steps. She followed him the night he shot Gaia. It was Ginger who hit you from behind. With a metal trophy, I'm told. It was also Ginger who shot up your home, hoping to make you the focus of any police investigation. Ginger is very good at what she does, but I am better. Her thinking that she can run my kingdom better than I can has become her downfall. Her using my grandson to execute her personal agenda has been a detriment to us all. Now she'll have to pay the price for her betrayal."

"The price?"

Balducci eyed him with a raised brow but didn't elaborate.

Davis shook his head. "What will happen to Pie?" he asked.

"I have found a wonderful facility in England that has accepted my Pauly as a patient. He will be well taken care of. He will be locked away and kept out of harm's way. You need not concern yourself with Pauly ever committing another crime. I love him dearly, but I will see him dead before that will ever happen again."

Davis's eyes widened at the comment. "Why not have Ginger arrested and let the law handle her and Pie? Under the circumstances I'm sure Ellington could get Pie a plea deal that would send him to a mental facility."

"Because when it comes to my family, I am the law! The Balduccis have never allowed others to resolve our problems. We take care of our own."

Davis blew a heavy sigh. "Who will be caring for Emilio?" he asked.

Balducci's expression brightened, a smile pulling across his face. "Emilio has a very bright future ahead of him. He will start boarding school in the fall. He has been accepted to the Milton Academy in Boston. And I hope that you will continue to stay in touch with him. It's important that he know his family."

Davis nodded. "Of course, sir."

Chapter 18

Neema and Balducci crossed paths as he made his exit. She carried two canvas totes filled with fresh produce from HarvesTime Foods. He tipped his hat at her, smiled and wished her a good afternoon.

"Thank you," she said, her expression incredulous. She tossed a look over her shoulder as he stepped into the limousine that had brought him there.

"What's going on?" she questioned as Davis closed and locked the door after the man.

"It was Ginger," he said. "It seems that she was behind all of it and he wanted me to know."

Neema's eyes widened. "Ginger? I don't understand."

Davis nodded, sharing with her what Balducci had just shared with him.

"So, what's going to happen now?" Neema asked.

"I honestly don't think either one of us really wants to know," he said, leaning in to kiss her cheek. He took both bags out of her hands and headed to the kitchen.

Things between them had been exceptional. Time
had given them both clarity and allowed them to revive
the bonds of their relationship. Healing had come after
hours of conversation. They were able to rebuild an exceptional friendship and being friends allowed them to
evolve into so much more.

Neema moved up against Davis's back, slipping her
arms around his waist. She pressed her cheek against
the soft cotton of his shirt, inhaling the fragrant scent
of his favorite cologne. Being near him always made
everything feel better, Neema thought.

"I love you, Davis Black. I hope that you never forget that," she said sweetly.

Turning, Davis pulled her into his arms and kissed
her mouth. She tasted like the lemon and turmeric candy
she loved so much. The hold he had around her waist
was gentle and protective and everything she needed
in that moment to remind her that she was loved and
wanted. "I love you, too, Neema Kamau. You have my
whole heart."

He dropped his mouth back to hers and the kiss in-
tensified, tongues dancing an erotic tango against each
other. It was the sweetest pleasure and, when Davis
lifted her to the counter, settling himself between her
legs, all thought of the groceries had been pushed aside.

He pressed himself against her pelvis, his body like
steel against hers. His hands lapped her body, fingertips trailing across her back, over her breasts, skating
against her belly, teasing her inner thighs. His touch
was heated and Neema felt like she might combust as
she held to him, her nails digging deliciously into his
arms and shoulders.

Titus suddenly barked, eyeing them both from the
floor.

Davis groaned. "Go away, dog! She's mine!"

Neema giggled softly. "I don't think that's the problem," she said. "I think he's trying to tell you that your brother is at the door."

She pointed to the front of the home. Mingus's face was pressed against the sidelight, looking in. Titus barked again.

"What the hell," Davis muttered as he adjusted himself in his slacks. He took a deep breath and helped her down from the counter.

Neema giggled again as she made her way to the front entrance and pulled open the door.

"Hi," she said.

"Sorry to interrupt," Mingus said, his expression smug as he stepped inside.

"No, you're not! What brings you here?"

Davis moved to Neema's side, wrapping his arms around her. "Yeah, what brings you here?" he questioned, his eyes wide.

Mingus smirked. "I was in the neighborhood…" he started.

The couple laughed with him, eyes rolling to the ceiling.

"Seriously, though," Mingus said, his mood shifting, "Dad has called a family meeting. He needs everyone there as soon as you can get to the house."

"What now?" Davis questioned.

Mingus shrugged, moving back to the front door. "I don't know. I'll find out when you do."

Davis nodded. "We have something we need to do first, but we're on our way."

Mingus waved a dismissive hand and closed the door after himself.

"What do we need to do?" Neema asked.

Davis pressed a damp kiss against her neck, his hands clutching her shoulders. "I have something I want to show you," he whispered.

She giggled. "And what's that?"

Davis laced his fingers with hers, gently pulling her toward the master bedroom. "It's personal," he quipped.

As the door closed, Titus stood in the hallway on the other side of it. He lowered his body against the door-sill, his massive head dropping against his front paws. Hearing the laughter coming from inside, he gave a hearty bark and then drifted off to sleep.

* * * * *

Don't miss the previous volumes in the
To Serve and Seduce miniseries:

Seduced by the Badge
Tempted by the Badge
Reunited by the Badge

Connie Shaw, VP of a security firm, is the only person able to identify a murderer. Luckily, she has access to protection in the form of her former one-night stand— now coworker—Trace Halstead. As the lines of their relationship blur, danger circles closer. Will Trace be able to keep Connie safe while they explore the connection between them?

Read on for a sneak preview of Sharon C. Cooper's debut Harlequin Romantic Suspense, His to Protect.

"I'm glad you're okay."

"I'm fine. I just don't know if I'll ever get that man's gray eyes out of my mind."

Trace turned to her. "Exactly what were you able to ID?"

"I saw his eyes and part of a tattoo on his neck."

"Did he see you?"

Connie swallowed hard and bit down on her bottom lip, something she did whenever she was uncomfortable. "We made eye contact, but only for a second or maybe two. Then just as quick, one of the other men pulled him out the door."

"Damn, Connie. That means he might be able to identify you, too."

"No." She shook her head vehemently. "I don't think so. It was just a split second. Trace, everything happened so fast. There's no way he could've gotten a good look at me. Besides, he doesn't know who I am," she said in a rush, sounding as if she was trying to convince herself. "He knows nothing about me, and the FBI agent assured me that what I shared with them and my identity will be kept confidential."

Worry wound through Trace as he watched her carefully, noticing how agitated she was getting. He reached over and massaged the back of her neck.

"If you believe that, then why are you trembling?"

"Maybe because you have the air conditioner on full blast," Connie said, trying to lighten the moment. Trace wasn't laughing, though.

"It's like you're trying to freeze me to death," she persisted, trying again to ease the tension in the car. "Of course, I'm—"

"Sweetheart, quit deflecting and talk to me."

Don't miss
His to Protect *by Sharon C. Cooper,*
available April 2021 wherever
Harlequin Romantic Suspense
books and ebooks are sold.

Harlequin.com